# Tales Of Aras:

# Becoming Fire and Lightning

Terrance Niedziela Jr.

Tales of Aras: Becoming Fire and Lightning, Terrance Niedziela Jr.
Issued in electronic and paperback formats.
Paperback ISBN: 978-1-970354-21-8
E-book ISBN: 978-1-970354-22-5
LCCN: 202-691-1783

First Edition

Publisher: Dressed in Love Press, LLC
www.drkatherinehayes.com

Cover Designer: Katherine Hutchinson-Hayes and Terrance Niedziela Jr.
Book Interior Designer: Jenifer Jennings

Printed in the United States of America

*To Ruth,*

*Sorry, this is 20 years overdue!*

Savelis' Prophecy

In Aras' darkest hour, Eimai will send Fire and Lightning.
Theirs is the crimson river.
Through them Eimai will restore what is in darkness.
Aras will unify to fight the last of all wars.
Darkness will be defeated forever,
and the prisoners set free.

Speaker Savelis' Prophecy of Restoration
Year 17,437 of the 4th Age of Aras

"It was not by their sword that they won the land,
nor did their arm bring them victory;
it was your right hand, your arm, and
the light of your face, for you loved them."
—Psalm 44:3 (NKJV)

# Table of Contents

ARAS
5TH AGE
OZIAS SEA
EFROSYNI
O'BRAL
ZENDIN
SIANA
PROVINCE
STYRKUR
TERYAL
SEA OF SIANA
MERERID
GYNIS
CERIDWYN
HANDITH
MA'LIS
JURGIS
JES RIVER
ULA
PROVINCE
KER'AN
SIGVARRD
UDRITH
ZEPHYRIN
GREAT
FOREST
CHY'KYN
SOUTHERN FOREST
KABAS
TIRTA RIVER
MIWA RIVER
VOILGA
ARRUS
UMLINDI
SHOICHI
EMER
PROVINCE
PERRIN
MELANIA DESERT
PHYX
SKEPNA PITS
SELUCIA
BRENUS RIVER
ARMORER'S
FOREST
XJIN
MUSHROOM
FOREST
CLUSTER
FALLS
RÙN
KRESO
CITALI
PROVINCE
ISSISS
THEITAI
KEY
TOWN
RITES
CITY
CAVE
RACIAL
CAPITAL
FLOATING
MOUNTAIN
EA'KH
OUTPOST
BRONZE
PORTAL
BA'KEL'S
PORTAL

# Chapter 1: Michael

*Minneapolis, Minnesota: June 4, 2004*

Dr. Michael Jenkins straightened his polo, fastened the top two buttons, and put on his tweed jacket. After glancing at his reflection in the two-way mirror at security, he'd noticed his exposed scars. The raised red burns on his upper chest contrasted sharply with his bronzed skin, as did the one on his left arm and the two on his right. Grateful to have the ability to cover his wounds, he sighed and brushed the front of his slacks while ensuring they sat evenly over his dress shoes.

*Seventeen hours on a plane and I look coherent, although I don't feel like it. Now, if I could get through this line without being searched, that would be a miracle.* He examined his Tissot and stifled a groan after observing the time.

Finally, the person in front of him approached the customs agent.

*Who's picking me up? Is it Mom?* He rubbed his temples, hoping his blurry mind would recall the details he needed. *I should check my phone to see if someone left me a message.*

He reached for his cell and looked up at the sign next to the customs agent.

NO PHONE USAGE WHILE STANDING IN LINE.

HAVE ALL DOCUMENTS READY.

He retracted his hand as his stomach rumbled. The meager airplane meal that morning had done little to curb his appetite. *If Mom is picking me up, there's no way she'll get fast food on the way home. She's probably made something for lunch. I can't wait to—*

"Next!"

*Father, please give me favor with this guy. In Jesus' name, Amen.*

The agent flipped through Michael's passport and paused when he saw the visas for Israel, Egypt, Lebanon, and Syria. "What were you doing in these countries?" he asked without looking up, his tone flat.

Michael cleared his dry throat. "Doctoral research while attending the University of Tel Aviv." *Is he going to ask about the scars? Maybe he saw them before I put on my jacket. Should I just tell him? Does he recognize me from the news? It was two years ago, but coverage went all over the world.* He kept his facial expression neutral and kept his eyes focused on the agent as his mind wandered. He'd seen the news reports and the video someone had taken on a phone of him running to pull victims from the burning bus station after a terrorist attack. They had also recorded him doused in burning fuel from a secondary explosion. The news reports heralding him a hero hadn't stopped the nightmares.

The agent returned the passport and waved to the family behind Michael. "Welcome back to the United States. Next!"

He hurried to the terminal to retrieve his luggage. "Thank you, Father," Michael whispered as he checked his phone for messages. He had several missed calls and messages from his mother indicating she was picking him up. Michael exhaled and smiled as he combed the crowd waiting near the baggage claim for his mother's familiar face.

Standing in front was Rosalind Jenkins, who looked like a soldier and a runway model at the same time. When his mother's mahogany gaze met Michael's gunmetal-gray eyes, her face blossomed into a wide smile. Waves of lush, honey-colored hair danced about her shoulders, and the flowing sleeves of her blouse fluttered as she waved.

*Fifty years old, and she still looks in her early thirties. I hope I look that good when I'm that age.*

His dark hair tangled with his mother's hair as her hug forced the air from his lungs. She smelled like florals and expensive spices. He stepped back and held her hands. Her strength had not diminished since she abandoned her life as one of France's premier chefs to marry an American plumber. Their Hallmark channel romance had caused quite a stir. The wealthy Louviere side of the family had encouraged her to find someone more worthy of her affections.

"Mon beau fils—*My handsome son*," she gushed in French, her usual greeting for him. "It's good to have you home. I've missed you."

"Moi aussi, tu m'as manqué—*I missed you too*," he responded.

"How were your flights?" she asked as he backed away and grabbed his luggage.

"Good. I'm glad to be home."

When they reached his mother's SUV in the parking garage, he shrugged off his jacket. His stomach rumbled, the sound echoing in the tight space.

His mother frowned as she started the vehicle. "Didn't they feed you on the plane? You look thinner. My darling boy, you haven't been eating. If you needed money, you should have told us."

He laughed. "Yes, they fed us, but it wasn't much. I had enough money for food."

She allowed the engine to idle and pulled a container from her purse. "I had a feeling you might be hungry, so I brought you this."

The aroma of freshly cooked dough wafted through the air when he lifted the lid. "Oh, Mom. Beignets. With powdered sugar. Mes préférés—*My favorite*." He took a bite and moaned, his eyes closing with delight.

She clapped him on the shoulder. "Je conduis, tu manges—*I drive, you eat*."

They were neck-deep in traffic when his mother tapped the steering wheel the way she did when she was nervous. "It's good to see your burns healed. You only have three scars? The burn center did a great job."

"I have one on my chest and two on my back. My legs don't have any. God was merciful." *As long as I don't go swimming, I won't have to explain the other scars.* "How's Cass doing?"

His mother stopped at a light and shot him an "I know you're trying to change the subject" look, but didn't press the issue. "Ta sœur va bien—*Your sister is doing fine*. She graduated this year instead of next and leaves for Princeton at the end of July. She's excited. But she doesn't seem to be looking forward to having you home."

"Is she still mad that I 'abandoned' her to go to Israel?"

"I think she's gotten over that. I believe it's living in your shadow that she struggles with."

"She needs to be her own person and stop comparing herself to me."

"I agree, and she's done that. But she's still trying to live up to the standard you set."

"What standard?"

His mother gasped. "You made all A's in school, graduated from high school at seventeen, earned your PhD at twenty-seven." She took a breath. "You earned second-degree black belts in taekwondo and jujitsu. You're an amazing cook. You play the guitar, dance, speak several languages, and you rushed into danger to rescue five people during a terrorist attack. Did I forget anything?"

He held up his hands and chuckled, feeling his face flush. "Okay. I see what you mean. But in my defense, I had the best cooking teacher in the world."

She shot him a sideways glance. "Not the best."

"You're just being modest. But as for Cass and me, I hope we can start healing our relationship this summer."

"You should have plenty of time for that. Have you found a job yet?"

He shook his head. "Not yet, but I'm hoping to find a teaching position at either the University of Minnesota or Chicago. That way I can stay close by."

"That would be nice," his mother said. "Besides job hunting, what else do you have planned?"

"Rest and reconnect with people. Professor Braga said I can help teach jujitsu classes, so I can work towards my next level. I'm glad I was able to find a school in Tel Aviv where I could continue to train. Otherwise, I'd be down five years of experience."

"Cass takes her blue belt test this Thursday. It will be a great birthday present for her. I have no doubt she will pass without a problem," she said as she parked in front of their single-story house.

He stared out the car's window at the river-stone walls and rough-hewn timbers. Varnished wood lined the windows and door frame. A thick oak door wrapped in wide cast-iron bands guarded the way inside. It always reminded him of a European castle, but without the turrets. When he got out of the car and retrieved his luggage, muffled high-pitched barking resounded from the house.

"Oreo's sounding the alarm."

His mother nodded. "She's going to be excited to see you. Welcome home."

The moment she opened the front door of the house, the black and white paraplegic pit charged Michael. Oreo's wheelchair rattled on the sidewalk as her front half scrambled to get to him. She almost knocked him over as she nuzzled his face. The dog's love broke

Michael, and he wept as he petted the dog. She woofed and licked his profusion of tears.

When he regained control, his mother pulled Oreo off him and handed him tissues.

He wiped his face. "Thanks. Oreo, you want a treat?"

The dog woofed and scurried into the house behind Rosalind, with the same urgency she had shown when exiting.

"Go unpack. I'll start dinner."

Michael chuckled. "Mom, I know you. You started dinner hours ago, and I can't wait to eat the feast you've prepared."

She gave him a wink and returned to her culinary domain.

Walking through the halls, Michael noticed the house hadn't changed in his absence. Sunlight streamed through the bay windows overlooking the backyard—delicious aromas wafted through the air. As he neared the back of the home, he took in the golden stained hardwood floors, a sharp contrast to the stone walls. Rough-cut beams braced the ceiling.

His room felt like a warm hug when he entered. A floor-to-ceiling bookcase packed with his favorite books covered one wall. The other side of the room consisted of a bed and a desk in front of the window.

He lifted the largest suitcase onto the bed and began unpacking when a sound caught his attention. Seeing nothing, he continued putting his clothes away.

"Michael," a voice called from the distance.

*Dad must be home. Funny, I didn't hear his truck pull in, and Oreo's not freaking out. I'd better see what's up.* He spun around and began heading to the door

A wall of glowing liquid appeared in his doorway. Before he could backpedal, tendrils of the liquid grabbed him and pulled him in. The liquid vanished as soon as it swallowed him.

# Chapter 2: Cassandra

*Minneapolis, Minnesota: June 4, 2004*

Cassandra flipped through the air, her back connecting with the thick blue mats with a loud thud. She pushed the damp wisps of dirty blond hair from her undone ponytail out of her face as Lucy pounced. Their middle-aged instructor, Ademir Braga, circled them and called out instructions.

From the way Lucy attacked, onlookers would have never guessed the two girls were best friends. In retaliation, Cassandra wrapped her legs around Lucy's torso and twisted her body to reverse their positions. *I should have beaten her by now. Come on, Cass. You're better than this.*

Cassandra succeeded in gaining the top position, but not for long. Back and forth they tussled until Lucy got her in a hold she couldn't break.

With a growl, she tapped out.

Lucy untangled herself and stood.

Cassandra followed, fighting tears of frustration.

They bowed to each other and their teacher before hurrying to the sidelines while two other students took their place.

*Way to go, Cass. Do that during the test, and you won't advance. That'll put you even further behind Mike.*

Professor Braga squatted in front of her. "You hurt?"

She wanted to avoid his eyes but didn't want to come across as disrespectful. "No, sir."

He studied her for a moment more. "Get some water. We will talk later."

*He doesn't look happy about how I did. I bet he tells me I should have done better.*

With a soft "thank you," she trudged to the benches against the far wall, plopped next to her duffel, and gulped from her water bottle. Lucy joined her and took a long drink from her own bottle.

Her friend glanced at her from behind her bottle. "You, okay?"

Cassandra forced a smile and took another drink, her eyes on the grapplers on the mats. "I'm fine. You did a great job kicking my butt."

"Well, you usually kick mine, so I'm glad I could get one in for a change."

Cassandra sighed.

Lucy slid closer and put an arm around her friend's shoulder. "Stop beating yourself up. You win some, you lose some. It doesn't mean you're a bad person or a horrible martial artist. Get up and try again. I'm sure you'll beat me next time."

Cassandra sighed louder this time.

The sparring match ended, and Professor Brags stepped onto the mats to correct one of the students' holds.

"Several people asked if I was going to be a hero like Jimmy."

Cassandra shot her a sideways glance.

"My brother gets the Medal of Honor, and suddenly everyone thinks I'm gonna be like him." Lucy shrugged. "As though I could be a six-foot, two-hundred-fifty-pound Navy SEAL."

The absurd mental image made Cassandra laugh. She stared at her petite friend, observing that Lucy didn't inherit her brother's genes.

Cassandra nodded. "I got a call from Grandma L today. She told me how proud she was of me graduating from high school early and getting into Princeton. She said I was proving to be, quote 'Exceptional despite the environment you are forced to live in,' end quote."

"You have an awesome family." Lucy's eyes flashed with anger. "How can she be so mean?"

Cassandra shook her head. "I suppose Grandma hates my dad for taking her daughter away from her career and family. She bashes my dad and brother every chance she gets."

"What about you?"

"She acts as if she loves me."

Lucy frowned. "I wonder why."

"I think it's because I look like Mom."

"I'm glad you don't live in France. You'd have to put up with that all the time."

"Yeah, that would suck." Cassandra crossed her arms. "And if I lived there, I wouldn't have you as a best friend."

Lucy moved closer to her friend and leaned forward. "Are you still having your birthday slash graduation party this weekend?"

"That's the plan. Mike's coming home today, so it's going to be a double graduation party."

"That's right. Your brother is a PhD now. I guess we'll have to call him Dr. Mike. Or, to be more professional, Dr. Michael Jenkins."

Their peals of laughter interrupted Professor Braga.

He shot them a firm look. "If you two are done with your break, you're free to return to the mat."

The girls' faces flushed.

"Yes, Sir," they said in unison.

They took one last drink and rejoined the class.

At the end of class, Professor Braga stood by the door and wished everyone a good night as they filed past. Cassandra stood at the end of the line and watched him. His stoic expression was difficult to read.

The professor stepped outside with Cassandra. "You allowed yourself to get frustrated and lose focus. Excellence is important. But competing against your brother is dangerous. It clouds your perspective and perception, making you vulnerable."

*How does he know I'm competing against Michael?*

"I'm not blind, Cassandra," he said as he stared at the parking lot. "I know you strive to match your brother in everything. But remember, just because he progressed faster than most students doesn't mean you have to."

"What do you mean?" Cassandra asked.

"Stop putting unnecessary pressure on yourself."

She hung her head.

"The adventure ahead will challenge you in every way. But don't lose heart when things get tough. Remember all you've learned, persevere, and follow the directions you're given. I will pray for you. When you return, you can take your belt test. The Lord bless you, keep you, make His face shine upon you, be gracious to you, lift His countenance upon you, and give you peace."

"What adventure?"

"I don't know. This is what I was told to tell you. I look forward to hearing about it when you return."

"Who told you?"

"God."

"God told you to tell me this?"

He nodded and patted her shoulder.

Cassandra opened her mouth to ask him another question, but he'd already gone inside and locked the door behind him.

The OPEN sign to the studio flipped to CLOSED, and the lights went out.

A horn honked, drawing her attention to the parking lot. A beat-up white Ford Tempo idled in front of the Braga Brazilian Jujitsu Academy with Lucy in the driver's seat and her dad in the passenger seat. He waved, his pale hair and eyes shining in the setting sun.

She plopped in the back seat and buckled in. "Hey, Uncle Xander."

He turned to her, a wide smile on his face, displaying the joy he felt when Cassandra called him uncle. Although they were not blood-related, the two families shared a deep bond. His seat creaked under his burly frame. "Hey, Cass. What's wrong?"

"It's been a rough day."

"What did Professor Braga say?" Lucy asked as she exited the parking lot.

"Weird stuff."

At the stoplight, Lucy's eyes met hers in the rear-view mirror. "Like what?"

"He said I shouldn't try to be like Michael. Then he said I'd be going on an adventure that would challenge me in every way. I needed to remember all I've learned, persevere, and follow the directions I'm given. Then he said I can take my belt test when I get back."

"Get back from where?"

Cassandra shrugged and stared at the cars whizzing by. "I don't know."

"That's weird," Lucy said.

"He told me God told him to tell me this."

"This isn't the first time you've been given a message through others," Uncle Xander said. "Remember not to despise prophecy but test it with the rest of scripture to see if it lines up with God's will for your life."

"Yeah, that's true. But I'd like to know where I'm going."

"You need to talk to your dad and see what he says."

"I will."

"On another note, have you started packing yet?" Uncle Xander asked.

She swallowed. "A little. I still have some time, though."

"Lucy's already packed. You'd think she was ready to get out. After all we've done for her, she's ready to abandon us."

"Dad," Lucy said, drawing out the word.

His belly laugh filled the car, bringing light to the darkness that threatened to swallow Cassandra.

"You two remember us, little people, when you become famous."

"I doubt that will happen," Cassandra said.

Lucy giggled. "Exactly."

The car stopped in front of Cassandra's house.

"I'll call you later," Lucy said as her friend climbed out of the car.

"Sounds good. Have a good night."

"Good night, Cass," Uncle Xander said. "Remember to talk to your dad."

She waved at them as the car drove away. When she got to the door, she took a deep whiff of the delicious aromas wafting through the air. *I bet Mom made a feast to celebrate Mike's coming home.*

"Cassandra," her father's voice boomed.

"Coming," she said, expecting to see her dad's face.

Instead, a shimmering veil of color, liquid light cascading like melted rainbows, enveloped her.

# Chapter 3: Michael

***Armorer's Forest, Citali Province, Aras: Spring, Day 11, Year 1, 5th Age***

A strong current shoved Michael in the back, launching him forward through an endless sea of light. He flailed with all his might for what he thought was the surface of the water. But he remained submerged. He tried to remember Jimmy's swimming lessons.

*I can't swim. I have to get out, have to get air.*

His lungs burned, needing air.

The silvery waves surged around him, filling his ears and mouth even though he tried to keep them out. Water gushed into his lungs. Instead of drowning him, he was energized. Something in his chest changed.

*My lungs are opening, like the damage from the fire is reversing. What's happening?*

"Greetings, Michael," a male voice said.

Michael tried without success to find where the voice came from. The water vibrated around him, making his skin tingle like it did when a limb fell asleep.

"I am Eímai, Lord of Light and Life. I am using my water to bring you to the land of Aras in the world of Parrésia. I have chosen you to be an El'esh, a knight who wields my power against Ba'rel's Legion."

*Is he saying I'll be a paladin—a holy knight?* Michael struggled to breathe properly and see at the same time. However, he was powerless. "I've got to be dreaming right now," he said aloud.

"You're not dreaming," Eímai said. "Your power will be directly proportional to how much of my power you take in."

"Is Ba'rel evil?"

"Yes. He is a dragon who served me until he grew important in his own eyes and tried to overthrow me. His insurrection ended the first age of Aras and brought corruption to the races of Parrésia. Now he strives to conquer Aras and take my throne."

Lightless and the vision before him was formless. A cloud of luminous light glowed, forcing him to shield his eyes from its power.

"Before you decide to be my El'esh, you must know the task I have chosen you for is fraught with peril."

"What do you mean?" Michael asked.

"You will enter the heart of darkness and face greater trials, danger, and evil than you've ever faced before. If you fall away and become Ba'rel's slave, you will never be able to come back to the light. You will not want to."

"How can I avoid this?"

The light grew brighter. "If you consume my water, fruit, and Writings, my power will flow through you, and the weapons created to destroy you will not harm you. I'll provide for every need. You only have to ask in accordance with my will, and I believe I have answered your request; I will give you what you ask for. Consider carefully before you choose. If you reject my call, I will return you to your bedroom, and you will have no memory of what has happened here."

Michael's stomach clenched. *I feel like I'm on a cliff preparing to jump. What do I do? All those years reading books and watching movies where heroes fought evil and wishing I could join them, and now here I am with an opportunity to do it for real.* The Bible verse he'd studied earlier that morning popped into his head. "Cast off the deeds of darkness and put on the armor of light."

He nodded and swallowed, wishing he could be certain whether he was awake or dreaming. Just then, a clear chalice filled with dancing fire materialized before him. It hovered within reach but never drew closer, despite the current increasing its speed.

"Take and drink," Eímai said, his voice bellowing.

Memories of fire swallowing him exploded in Michael's mind. He gasped, and more water slammed into his lungs. He tried to get away from the flowing cup, but the current resisted his meager efforts.

"Do not be afraid. Like the water, the fire will not harm you. It heals, cleanses, and empowers. You must have the fire to have access to my power. Take. Drink. Be bold and courageous, for I am with you. I will never leave or abandon you."

Michael's hands shook as he took the chalice in both hands. He squeezed his eyes shut, opened his mouth, and drank the contents of the chalice as fast as he could. Sweetness reminiscent of tea with too much sugar filled his mouth. He released the cup, and it floated away.

Slowly, he opened his eyes. Tiny tongues of blue and white fire danced over his skin.

*I'm burning but not burning. I wonder if this is what Moses saw with the burning bush. What now?*

"Step into Aras," Eímai commanded.

A doorway opened before him, and the current launched him into a forest of purple-trunked trees with pink diamond-shaped leaves.

His fiery feet burned tracks in the tufts of frost-glazed purple, blue, and orange moss growing between the roots of the trees as he fought not to fall.

Something yanked him upright, and his ears were filled with the sound of beating wings.

He turned and observed a giant set of fiery blue wings protruding from his back. Their tips brushed the trunks of the trees on his right and left.

"If I have wings, can I fly?" he said, attempting to make his new wings flap without success.

"Yes. I will teach you."

The fire dancing on Michael's skin flattened to form a suit of blue armor. White mail wrapped his neck, his arms between the pauldrons on his shoulders and the vambraces on his forearms, and his legs between the plates covering his thighs and knee-high boots. A rectangular scapula hung from the front of a wide belt with a round buckle. The five sections of his helmet folded forward from behind his head and closed in front of his face. His eyesight sharpened so much that he could see every individual strand of moss and the tiniest line in the bark of the trees.

Michael rapped his knuckles against his chest and heard the crackle of energy. A rectangular shield of blue fire unfolded from his left vambrace, its edges blazing white. His shield, breastplate, and buckle bore the same rotating crest as his vambrace.

A white rod materialized in midair before him. He grabbed it, and it morphed into the handle of a sword. The cross guard sprouted from the handle, one end curving toward the blade and the other toward his hand. He pulled the handle to the right, and a broadsword with a double-edged blade of blue fire appeared as if from an invisible scabbard. The blade flared twice near the hilt and featured a raised line running down the blade's center. He swung the sword, and the blade crackled like his armor.

"This is awesome. I've dreamed of wielding a sword as a knight, and now I get to. But I don't know how to use it."

"This is your first El'esh lesson. Trust me for everything. I will teach you how to use all that I have given you. I will also make words from my Writings appear before your eyes. They are life and wisdom to you. Internalize them and follow them. You will also receive a bound copy when you leave the Armorer's Forest."

"What is the Armorer's Forest?"

"Where you stand is the Armorer's Forest. The trees gave arms and armor to the races of Aras in their most dire need. You have a spear in your arsenal. It will appear when you hold out your empty hand."

Michael transferred the sword to his left hand and held out his right. Fire sprang from his hand and solidified into a spear with a triple-edged point. The shaft thrummed with power like his sword.

"The spear will fly farther than the javelin you threw in high school and will both pierce and burn the target," Eímai said. "Open your hand."

Michael obeyed, and the spear melted into churning flames, which poured into his palm and vanished.

"Now to learn to fly. Your wings will follow your will. With practice, you will fly without thinking."

His wings flapped, and in seconds, Michael hovered above the treetops. He let out a whoop.

"Since they are a manifestation of my fire, your wings do not need air to function. Lean your body forward, and you will fly forward. Lean back, and you will slow down and also fly backward. Angle your body vertically, and you will hover."

A blinking orange arrow pointing to his right appeared inside his helmet.

"Follow the arrow," Eímai said.

During his flying lessons, he crashed into several trees, sending a pack of green squirrels flying as they spun their tails like propellers. Eventually, he got the hang of flying.

"Where am I headed?" Michael asked.

"Matu are sacrificing Lady Jovena, the daughter of the Talah chieftain, to Ba'rel. You will rescue her. Drop behind them and cut them down quickly."

"What are Matu?"

"Ba'rel's sorcerers. They are formidable, but no match for my power within you. Remember to strike quickly."

The sacrificial site was a round patch of packed earth at least forty feet across, surrounded by a wall of orange vines. Green fire blazed in tall braziers around the perimeter. In the grove's center loomed a crude statue of a seven-headed dragon. A black-haired woman in a purple-and-red tartan dress lay chained to the altar before the dragon. Yellow blood flowed from slashes on her cheeks, stomach, and legs. It rose like paint from a sprayer into the three dragon heads looming over her. The other four heads belched a thick cloud of darkness into a ten-foot-tall, swirling disc at the far end of the grove.

"They are using her blood to open a portal to Kabas, Ba'rel's domain. This will allow the Legion to enter Aras," Eímai said.

Six cloaked figures shuffled around the altar, chanting in a language he did not understand. They made a half-circuit around the altar and raised their three-fingered hands. Long red claws, splattered with yellow blood, tipped each finger.

Michael dropped and landed behind the figures on the right side of the altar. The fiery blade of his sword bisected two of Matu, and their bodies dissolved into black smoke that floated into the sky. Michael overextended his arm as he lashed out at the next Matu.

The Matu dodged his attack, but Michael rotated his sword and split him apart with a backswing. The rest of the group stepped back, their hoods falling to their shoulders, revealing their elongated heads and two slits for noses. Their red, slitted yellow eyes narrowed with malice, and their forked tongues writhed before their pointed chins as they hissed at him.

"Strike now before they attack," Eímai commanded.

He killed two more, but the last two stepped out of reach.

They raised their hands, and purple tendrils flew from their hands.

Michael launched himself into the air, pulling back from the altar.

The Matu followed, continuing to shoot tendrils at him.

He blocked them with his shield.

"You are too late, El'esh," the sorcerers said in unison. "We have completed the corruption and opened the portal. The Legion is coming, and there is nothing you can do to stop us. Hide behind your shield all you want. Vold is coming, and he will devour you."

"Use your spear," Eímai said, ignoring the sorcerers.

Michael hurled the spear at the Matu on his left. Another spear appeared in his hand, and he launched it at the other as the first impaled the gloating sorcerer. The spears lifted them off their feet, and they flew backward toward the portal.

The sorcerers' bodies disintegrated into black smoke, filling the air with a putrid stench.

Michael staggered back, instinctively covering his mouth, although it was encased in his helmet. He took a deep breath and turned his attention to the altar. It was vacant. His heart raced as he frantically searched the surrounding area for Lady Jovena. But there was no sign of the woman he was supposed to rescue.

# Chapter 4: Cassandra

***Armorer's Forest, Citali Province, Aras: Spring, Day 11, Year 1, 5th Age***

White light blazed around her. She tried to fight the current driving her forward, but only exhausted herself. Her lungs burned and screamed for air. Darkness blurred the edges of her vision.

*I have to get out of here. I need air. God, please help me. Is this a dream? I was awake a second ago. There's got to be a way out.*

"Do not be afraid. The water will not harm you. Breathe it in and live," an authoritative male voice said.

*What? That's crazy. Breathe water? I'm not a mermaid.*

A brilliant form with orange fire for eyes appeared before her. It had the vague shape of a person, but five times Cassandra's size.

She screamed.

Water surged into her lungs. It tasted sweet and clean, free from the chemicals in city water. The pain in her lungs and her fatigue vanished. Her body vibrated with power.

The figure's form shrank, taking the shape of a tall man wearing a crown of seven stars. His muscles filled out his robe, and his smile accentuated his strong jawline.

Waves of love, stronger than what she felt when held by her parents, flowed from the man and annihilated her terror. Strength bolstered her.

*I feel like I can swim out of here now.*

"Hello, little daughter. I am Eímai, Lord of Light and Life. You cannot swim out of my water. It is taking you to the land of Aras in the world of Parrésia."

*Daughter? Another world? This is too much.*

"I know there is much to take in," Eímai said. "But know I wish only the best for you and have chosen you for a special mission."

"Why me?"

"Why *not* you? I have chosen you to be my Speaker of Reconciliation and reconcile the seven races of Aras to me and each other. Only by unifying will they stand against the dragon Ba'rel's invasion. I will make you a conduit of my power and speak through you."

"Are you going to take over my body?"

Eímai laughed. "No, daughter. I will give you the words, and you will speak them."

"Why do you call me daughter?"

"That is what you are."

*Is that it? Isn't he going to explain?*

Eímai looked at her in silence.

"Won't the invasion automatically get everyone working together?"

"No. They have spent so much time considering themselves independent that they have forgotten how much they are dependent on one another."

"Sir, with all due respect, thank you for considering me. But I'm not even a little qualified for this. A couple of years in the Youth United Nations and a handful of political science classes aren't enough education or experience for a job this big."

Eímai shook his head. "Your lack of education and experience means nothing. It is by my power that you will fulfill my call."

The image of a dragon with purple scales and silver horns, back spikes, talons, belly, and a tail tip materialized before her. The dragon seemed to look at her with amber eyes split by vertical black pupils. Ice crystals danced between the dragon's large teeth.

"This is Lady Achima. I have sent her to teach you how to be a Speaker. You will also have my Writings to guide you. Do not be afraid. I will never leave you nor forsake you. If you need anything, ask me for it. If you ask in line with what I want for you and believe I have given you what you asked for, you will receive your request."

*I'm going to be taught by a dragon. That's awesome.*

"Be warned. You are not to meddle with the internal affairs of Aras. You are not to take sides in any conflict or fight against any Arasian leaders. You are not to seek power or position beyond what I have given you. Many things are not as they should be in Aras. Some will attempt to persuade you to overthrow the current government in the name of unifying Aras. They are willing to use violence to sway you to their side."

Cassandra's hands balled into fists. "That's what they think. I'm capable of defending myself."

Eímai raised a finger like her father did when he reprimanded her. "Speakers do not seek fights. They are not aggressive or argumentative. They do not kill. If attacked, you are allowed to defend yourself and incapacitate your attacker. But that is all."

Her eyes lowered as the fight left her. "What if they have weapons? How will I defend?"

"I have provided all you need. I will never send you into a dangerous situation without a way out. Previous Speakers did not listen to my warnings and were destroyed."

Her heart jumped into her throat at the weight of his words.

*He killed them because they didn't do as he said.*

"No, I did not kill them. I allowed them to receive the consequences of their choices."

*This is too much. I don't know what to think about all this.*

Eímai gave her another broad smile. "I will not force you to accept. If you choose not to be Speaker, I will return you home, and you will remember none of this. What is your choice?"

*Is this the adventure Professor Braga was talking about? It sure fits what he said. Father, what do you want me to do?*

A Bible verse popped into her head. "Now all things are of God, who has reconciled us to Himself through Jesus Christ, and has given us the ministry of reconciliation."

*God, I'm so in over my head. Please help me to not mess this up.*

She drew a deep breath and nodded.

Her clothes transformed into a sea-green hooded jacket, a hip-length tunic, and knee-high boots, accented by white leggings, a belt, gloves, and a pouch hanging from the belt.

A book with a leather cover and green, purple, yellow, and white pages appeared and floated within arm's reach.

"These are my Writings. Eat it. It will taste sweet in your mouth."

She arched a brow and stepped back. "You want me to eat a book?"

"Yes."

She nibbled a corner of the leather cover.

*It tastes like baklava. I love baklava.*

She ate the whole book, and her stomach felt full like after Thanksgiving dinner at Grandma Sophie's house.

"When you need them, my Writings will rise from within you. These words will bring healing, reconciliation, and hope."

"So, they'll automatically come out of my mouth? Or pop into my head and then I say them?"

"Yes. It will be your choice to say them," said Eímai.

*I'm glad I have a choice, and he's not taking over my body.*

"I told you we were co-laborers, Speaker Cassandra. I will not force you to do anything. I have placed a chata staff in the clips running down the middle of your jacket. Chata is an invisible metal stronger than Earth steel. You can see it because it is your weapon. The clips will release when you grip the weapon. The best way to access it is to reach behind you at the small of your back."

Cassandra reached behind her and found a smooth rod covered in upraised ridges. She felt a series of taps run up her back as the clips opened. A two-foot-long rod sat comfortably in her hand.

"I expected it to be longer," she said, twirling the rod.

After two rotations, the rod grew three feet, five inches shorter than Cassandra.

*Nice. It's about the size of the bo staff I use back home.*

"To return the staff to its former size, twist the middle, so your left hand is turning away from you. Rest the rod against the middle of your back, and the clips will close around it. You are now ready. Welcome to Aras."

Before she could say she was far from ready, a doorway opened before her, revealing a dense forest of purple-trunked trees with pink, diamond-shaped leaves. Tufts of orange, purple, and blue moss clung to the upraised tree roots. In the night sky hung a planet like Jupiter, but it looked as if a toddler had colored it with purple and orange crayons.

She slid through the door and bent her legs as she landed. The lower half of her jacket parted to give her legs freedom of movement while five buttons held the upper half closed. When she straightened, the bottom overlapped to keep out the frigid wind whipping around her.

*It's like a medieval duster.*

She looked behind her, expecting the door to still be there. But she saw only the forest.

"Guess there's no going back until I do what Eímai wants."

Eímai's voice filled her mind. "Your first assignment is to rescue Lady Jovena. She is the daughter of the Talah chieftain and will become chieftain in one and a half days. If she dies, the Talah race will be destroyed."

"Where do I find her?"

Glowing wedge-shaped writing appeared on the trees to her left.

"Follow the inscriptions. Hurry. She is close to death."

"How can I run on this moss? The frost will make me fall."

"Your boots adapt to the terrain. They will keep you from falling."

She looked at the bottom of her boots and grinned, noticing they looked like cleats. "You've thought of everything."

"Remember that in the days to come," Eímai said in a serious tone.

She bolted down the path. Fallen trees, moss-covered boulders, and hills tried to slow her down. But three years of parkour training enabled her to use each obstacle to launch herself forward. Her boots adjusted to rough and smooth alike, and Cassandra did not fall.

*I wonder if I could run up trees like in those cheesy kung fu movies Mike and Dad like to watch. I'll have to try it later.*

The path led to a wall of orange-leafed vines. A flickering green glow shone through tiny gaps in the leaves.

*Sounds like someone's fighting.*

"My El'esh is dealing with the sorcerers," Eímai said. "Cut through the wall and free Lady Jovena while they are distracted."

"How?"

"Shrink the staff and twist it so your right hand is facing away from you."

The rod split, and a curved blade slid out of the top end of each of the smaller rods.

"Kama," exclaimed Cassandra. "I know how to use these."

"I know. Hurry."

The kama slit the intertwined vines with the ease of cutting paper. She gasped when she saw the bleeding woman chained to the altar in front of a dragon statue. Almost imperceptible movement indicated Lady Jovena still breathed as the dragon idol's heads sucked yellow liquid from the slashes on her body.

Cassandra ran to the altar and touched Lady Jovena's neck. The faintest pulse tickled her fingertips. The woman's skin had taken on a waxy appearance. "Eímai save me. In you I rest," Lady Jovena said in a thick accent.

Cassandra laid her weapons on the altar and put her hand on Lady Jovena's bleeding shoulder. "Eímai, what do I do?"

"Command her wounds to heal in the name of Eímai," said Eímai.

"In the name of Eímai, be healed."

Energy flowed through her arms, and golden lightning burst from her fingertips.

It wrapped the woman like an electric cocoon.

Tendrils of energy dove into the gaping slashes.

The wounds closed.

Lady Jovena's skin became a healthy olive complexion.

She arched her back, took a deep breath, and her eyes popped open as she bolted upright.

Cassandra held up her hands and gave what she hoped was a reassuring smile. "Lady Jovena, Eímai sent me to rescue you."

"Command the chains to open the way you commanded her wounds," said Eímai.

The chains obeyed her command. Lady Jovena jumped off the altar, knocking Cassandra's kama to the ground.

"What was that?" Lady Jovena asked, cowering beside the altar and looking around. Her accent made her w's sound like v's and her th's like d's.

"My kama," Cassandra said, retrieving her weapons.

"I do not see them," Lady Jovena said, rising.

"That's because they're chata."

Lady Jovena's eyes grew wide, and she retreated to the far end of the altar. "You are a Speaker. Another Savelis."

"I'm a Speaker. But I don't know who Savelis is."

"An El'esh," she said, her gaze focused on the battle. "Hopefully, he is on our side. I do not see the king's mark." She returned her gaze to Cassandra. "You are not Talah."

"No. I'm a human from the planet Earth. Eímai brought me here."

Lady Jovena nodded, but the look on her face made Cassandra think she had decided something. "What is your name?" the woman asked.

"Cassandra."

"Come, Speaker Cassandra. We must cover as much ground as possible before the Legion finds out I am gone."

Lady Jovena spun around and ran through the gap Cassandra had cut in the vines, with Cassandra right behind.

"I'm supposed to protect you," Cassandra explained as she tried to steady her breath. As she ran, she clapped the blunt ends together and twisted them. The blades slid back into the handles, and they became a single rod again. *It'll be easier to run with this than with two razor-sharp blades, especially if I have to do parkour.*

Lady Jovena glanced over her shoulder without slowing her pace. "The Legion is in the forest, and if they have abominations, not even your holy weapons will save us."

# Chapter 5: Michael

***Armorer's Forest, Citali Province, Aras: Spring, Day 11, Year 1, 5th Age***

"Where is she? Did she die? I should have moved faster."

Eímai's gentle voice pierced Michael's raging thoughts and emotions. "Calm down. She is safe. My Speaker freed her from the altar and took her into the forest. The Legion has entered the portal. You must act quickly, or they will pour into the forest. hold them off as much as possible so help can arrive to deal with those you do not destroy."

"Who is Vold, and why is he going to eat me?" Michael said as he stepped in front of the portal and flexed his hand around his sword handle.

"In the fourth age, he was Rasmus, one of my most devoted El'esh and Captain of Captains. But he allowed Ba'rel to corrupt him and became Umoni. Fallen. Destroy the statue, and the portal will close."

His shield vanished, and the handle of his sword grew longer. He grabbed it with both hands and used all his strength to slash off the lowest head. The hot blade slid through the neck, chest, and pedestal so fast he fell forward, head smashing into the side of the dragon. The pieces of stone fell away, the ends where he had cut molten.

*Good thing I have my helmet.*

A wing and three heads thudded to the ground, their superheated stumps burning holes in the packed earth. He rose in the air to decapitate the higher heads when the surface of the portal snapped like mosquitoes hitting a bug zapper.

The first to exit the portal had badger-like heads, red leathery skin stretched over emaciated bodies, and backward-bending legs ending in huge paws. They wore bits of armor and held notched swords. They stood as tall as Michael. They rushed forward, plowed through the wall of vines on the other side of the clearing, and disappeared into the forest. They took no notice of Michael.

"Akzari, the foot soldier of Ba'rel's Legion," Eímai said. "Keep cutting."

Two heads and the other wing joined their sizzling comrades on the ground.

The portal snapped again, and fifty Matu strutted out of the vortex. The majority took the same path as the Akzari. But seven stayed behind and turned their attention to the El'esh, dicing their statue.

Flaming arrows shot from their upraised palms. He reactivated his shield, and the arrows dissolved into black vapor upon impact. Three continued to fire arrows at him while the four pointed at the statue. They chanted, and pieces rose from the ground to return to their original places on the statue.

He launched a spear at a Matu fixing the statue. "Oh no, you don't."

The Matu pivoted to avoid the spear. More arrows filled the air, and Michael dropped behind the statue. The flaming projectiles punched into the stone dragon and cracks spider-webbed over it.

"Watch what you are doing!" several Matu shouted in unison.

"If you can do better, you deal with the El'esh," one of the offending sorcerers shot back.

Michael summoned a spear, popped out from behind the statue, and hurled it at a Matu who was moving into a better position to attack him. The Matu dropped to the ground, and the spear burned a hole through the Matu behind him. He shrieked and dissolved into black smoke. Michael skewered the rising Matu with a spear and leaped into the air. He dropped to earth, and his sword bisected the dragon's body and pedestal.

The Matu shouted in their guttural tongue, and the statue erupted in a blast of purple energy. The blast knocked Michael into the wall of vines. The wall held, and he fell forward onto his face. In seconds, the Matu gathered around him, swords with wavy blades in their hands. Michael rolled onto his back and activated his shield as the blades ignited with purple fire. The shield held as the sorcerers tried to do to him, what he had done to the statue.

Michael lashed out with sword and feet, aiming for anything he could reach. A few lost their legs to his sword, and others their kneecaps to his armored feet. His wings slapped the ground, launching him to his feet. He finished off the Matu and scattered the smoke with his wings. A warrior with armor and wings made of black fire stepped out of the portal seconds before it collapsed in on itself.

He stood eight feet tall with a barbed spike capping his lashing tail. He held a scimitar with a blade made of swirling black fire. The roaring dragon-shaped helmet split into six parts and slid back to reveal the horror underneath.

Puffy gray scar tissue covered the right side of the white tiger's head. Gaping holes remained where his right eye and ear had been. Purple fire burned in the empty socket. The pure black left eye narrowed, and the left ear twitched. The tiger roared, and terror, like what Michael had felt as he burned in Israel, engulfed him.

"Do not be afraid of him," Eímai said. "Fear has no place in you. My power in you is infinitely greater than his evil. Raise your shield and speak the words I give you."

Michael forced his shield up, and words appeared before his eyes. His voice shook as he forced them out. "Eímai's perfect love casts out all fear. He has armed me with strength for battle and made me bold and courageous. I am not frozen with fear or discouraged. I rest under his protection."

The terror ended as abruptly as it came on. His racing heartbeat slowed, just as he faced Vold.

"A little El'esh," he said in a Scandinavian-sounding accent. Vold licked his lips with a black tongue. "It has been a long time since I have feasted on one of your kind. I will devour your flesh and lap up what remains, so nothing remains of your pathetic existence."

*He sounds like Goliath cursing David. If he wants to be Goliath, I can be David.* "You come against me in Ba'rel's power, but I come against you in Eímai's power. You and your master are no match for him."

Vold laughed. "You think slaying a few Matu and destroying the master's totem makes you able to stand against me? In this corrupted place, we can open another portal at will. I have never seen you before. You do not bear the ancient order, so you must be one of the recently called. Oh, you foolish little man. You have no idea who you face. Were this a different time, I would invite you to join the master, for he has proved greater than the one you serve. But he wants only the destruction of all in Aras, so no prisoners and no more Umoni." His helmet snapped shut around his deformed head. He leaped forward with scimitar raised.

The blade swept down, almost splitting Michael like a piece of firewood. Michael launched himself sideways, and the sword carved a sizzling gash where Michael had been seconds before.

"Keep moving and use his strength against him," Eímai said.

*Like in the martial arts.*

"Exactly. Those twenty years of training prepared you for this moment. Angle your shield so his scimitar slides off. When you can, use your sword to chop at his unprotected body. He has a shield but prefers to batter his opponents to the ground with two-handed strikes."

As the fight continued across the grove, Michael prayed under his breath and struggled not to be split in half. He deflected a scimitar swipe with his shield, and the black blade buried itself in the ground. He slashed at Vold's head, but the tiger dropped his sword and stepped back. Michael slashed him across the chest. Vold roared as red smoke poured from the wound. His paw shot out so fast that Michael did not see it coming. He batted Michael across the grove. His sword flew from his hand as the world spun. He flew end over end, and his vision blurred.

His upside-down form was struck by a solidly built creature with tan arms and massive paws, which wrapped around his middle. Michael felt himself slowly being turned upright, and whoever had caught him set him on his feet.

"Step aside, El'esh," said a rumbling female voice in the same accent as Vold. "Leave the traitor to us. You have done well. Captain Ragnar will be pleased to hear of your success. He waits for you in Rün to begin your training. But it seems you have already learned your lessons well."

He turned and looked up into the noble face of a lioness dressed in mottled gray armor with a broken four-claw slash across the breastplate. She flashed a jagged-tooth smile, then stepped around him.

Michael followed her gaze. Lions wielding battle axes, tigers holding a scimitar in each paw, cheetahs armed with short swords and bandoleers of throwing knives, clouded leopards with spears, and lynxes wielding compound bows with two rectangular quivers filled with brown-fletched arrows on their backs poured into the grove. The lions and tigers stood eight feet tall, while the cheetahs and leopards were a foot shorter. Only the lynxes looked to be Michael's height. They formed a wall between Vold and Michael. He no longer saw the evil tiger. But he could hear his words. "Where is Fléau? Where is that coward of a grand-cub of mine?"

"Captain Ragnar is not here, traitor," the lioness said in a calm, confident voice. "Your plans have failed. We have cleansed the Armorer's Forest of your forces. You are defeated. Yield to us."

*Yeah right. There's no way he'll yield.*

"Who's Captain Ragnar?" Michael whispered to Eímai.

"A great immortal warrior and our leader," a lynx with a proud smile whispered back.

"He is not immortal," another lynx said.

"He is over two thousand years old and cannot be killed," the first lynx said. "That means he is immortal."

"Eímai resurrected him whenever he was struck down. That doesn't make him immortal," the second argued.

"Be silent, you two, and pay attention. You're supposed to be Elites. Stop acting like cubs," a female cheetah commanded.

The two muttered apologies and fitted arrows to their bowstrings.

*Should I get ready to help?*

"No," Eímai said. "You must make sure Lady Jovena and the Speaker get out of the Armorer's Forest and reach Rün tomorrow during Full-Light. Captain Saara does not know the Legion is scattered throughout the forest to protect this place from my servants. You must hurry."

The orange arrow reappeared, pointing east.

"What's Full-Light?"

"It will be explained later."

"What about my sword?" Michael asked just when the handle reappeared before him, and he reached for it.

"Leave it. It will be easier to fly without it."

Michael obeyed, spread his wings, and shot through an opening in the trees into the clear sky. His wings hummed as he hurried to catch up with the fleeing duo. "I'm guessing there are Akzari and Matu. What else? Any more Umoni?"

"Hold your right-hand palm up and say 'Map.'"

A holographic map of the forest appeared above his palm. Scattered over the forest were red, black, green, and purple dots. Tiny claw slashes like those on the Outcast Clan approached and snuffed out some of the dots. Two gold triangles headed toward a cluster of two red and three black dots, and a blue-and-white flame quickly approached from behind them.

"The black dots are Matu, purple are Akzari, red are Isoni, and green are Sundered. They were Arasian until Ba'rel corrupted them. Isoni are dressed in crimson armor and wield throwing weapons. The two gold triangles moving east are Lady Jovena and Speaker. The flame is you."

Michael's eyes locked onto the cluster of enemies heading toward the Lady Jovena and the Speaker. "They're heading into an ambush." His wings roared as he accelerated. "Will I get there in time?"

# Chapter 6: Cassandra

***Armorer's Forest, Citali Province, Aras: Spring, Day 11, Year 1, 5th Age***

Cassandra scanned the trees as she and Lady Jovena tried to cover as much ground as possible before the Legion found them. An enemy could pop out at any moment. Her racing mind and heartbeat returned to her unexpected display of power in the grove.

*How did lightning shoot from my body? I told her to be healed in Eímai's name. Would I say, "Be fried in Eímai's name?" That sounds dumb. Maybe I should flex my hands like the superheroes do.* Cassandra flexed her gloved hands.

Nothing.

"My power manifests at my will, not yours," Eímai said. "Get to know me more, and you will learn how to let my power flow through you."

"I wish I knew how much ground we have covered so far," said Lady Jovena.

*All this running, and she doesn't look or sound winded. She said she needed armor and weapons. I wonder if she's some type of warrior princess.*

Three Matu leaped from the tree in front of them. Swords with wavy blades appeared in their left hand. Tongues of purple fire ignited on the tips of the long claws on their right hand.

Two warriors in crimson armor landed behind them. Curved blades decorated their vambraces and greaves. They pulled two throwing weapons consisting of curved blades connected by a large handle.

"The armored ones are Isoni from the western island of Velox!" Lady Jovena shouted over her shoulder, picking up a stout branch from a fallen tree and breaking off its twigs. "They will try to separate us. We must stay together. Beware of their glaives. They can slice through anything and return to their wielder when thrown."

Cassandra twisted her staff, and it grew to full size.

"No one escapes the Legion," the Matu in front hissed. His forked tongue danced in front of his face as he strutted toward them, sword at his side. "You think that stick can defeat us? This cursed forest will not give you a weapon, Talah. You are on your own. You will die, and we will feast."

Cassandra stepped in front of Lady Jovena. "No one's getting eaten."

The Matu pointed flaming talons at Cassandra, and jets of fire leaped toward the pair.

A shroud of lightning materialized around Cassandra and Lady Jovena and absorbed the fire.

Sorcerers dropped their swords and pushed both hands out to expel a larger blast of fire.

The shroud glowed brighter, but did not buckle under the onslaught.

The Matu snatched up their swords, and the lightning shield went out.

"Seriously?" Cassandra exclaimed.

Lady Jovena moved to Cassandra's left and caught a slashing Matu blade in the middle of her branch. The sword bit into the wood, but did not split it. She cracked his right knee and shattered the branch across his head. He melted into smoke.

Cassandra blocked a Matu's attack. The sword rang off the staff and sent vibrations through her hands. She barely kept her grip on the staff. His eyes widened, and he shook the arm holding his sword.

"How are you fighting with nothing?" he asked.

"Don't respond," Eímai said.

Cassandra silently drove the end of her staff into his stomach.

When the Matu doubled over, she swung her staff like a baseball bat against his back.

He crumpled beneath the blow, flattened in the moss, and lay still.

She turned to see Lady Jovena held against a tree by the two Isoni. The last Matu stood before the Talah woman, sword raised.

"Yell at the top of your voice, 'Eímai commands the Armorer's Forest to wake and perform its duty,'" Eímai said.

Though the instructions made no sense to Cassandra, she followed them and watched as the group by the tree jumped while she screamed the words.

The Matu whirled.

A sharp whistle and a rod of swirling blue fire flew down from above to impale the Matu. Another pierced the chest of the Isoni, holding Lady Jovena's right arm. The two released an echoing shriek and melted into black smoke.

Lady Jovena took advantage and pulled her arm free of the last Isoni. She backed away from the tree as the El'esh from the glade dropped from the sky, a spear flying from his hand.

The Isoni danced behind the tree, and the spear missed him. He threw both glaives, and the El'esh deflected them with his shield. He drew an oddly shaped sword from out of thin air.

"How'd he do that?" Cassandra asked, trying to make sense of the strange new world.

Lady Jovena ignored her question and pulled on her arm. "Let's get out of here."

The Isoni caught his returning glaives and charged the El'esh. The winged knight slid into a stance Cassandra recognized.

*How does he know taekwondo?*

"Come on," Lady Jovena insisted.

The two sprinted away, the sounds of battle filling the forest behind them.

After running for what seemed like forever, Lady Jovena slowed to a walk.

"Where'd you learn to fight?" Cassandra asked through ragged gasps.

"I trained with the Hod'ji since I was little."

"Hod'ji?"

"Hod'ji are the knights of the Talah race. Eventually, I became Hod'ji."

"Cool. In that sacrifice place, you called me Savelis. Who's Savelis?"

"Savelis was Speaker before you. He encouraged the races to destroy the Dragon and Drás races in the Dragons/Drás War. When the Hikaru seized power at the end of the War, Savelis deceived my ancestor, the man Eímai had chosen as the next king of Aras, into trying to seize his throne by force. They failed. King's Scelto executed Savelis and his followers, including my ancestor. Thousands of years later, and the Hikaru kings are still paranoid about threats to their power. This is why anyone called to be Speaker disappears. We believe the King's Scelto are murdering them."

"Who are the King's Scelto?"

"The Scelto are Hikaru knights. King's Scelto zealots who follow the king's orders without regard for whether or not they break Eímai's Writings."

"This just keeps getting better and better," Cassandra whispered under her breath.

An emaciated black reptile with a broad head crowned by six horns stepped out from behind a tree on spindly legs ending in three-toed feet. It had four neon-green eyes with horizontal black slits, two on either side of an elongated snout, and its light cast an eerie glow on the reptile's rotting fangs. Spikes ran from the top of the head to the tip of a whip-like tail. It wore armor on its torso and a kilt made of leather.

"I'm really getting tired of people dropping from trees," Cassandra said.

"This Sundered Drás is called Lusare," Eímai said. "She was one of my Sages but became bitter after the murder of her family in the Dragon/Drás War."

In a blur of motion, Lusare grabbed Lady Jovena by the throat with a four-fingered hand, and the long talons clacked against each other. She slammed her against the tree.

"Hello, morsel," the reptile said, her voice deep but female. "You should be dead."

The trunk rippled and sucked Lady Jovena into itself. Lusare pulled her hand away before the tree took her too.

"No!" Cassandra yelled, tightening her grip on her staff.

Lusare pulled two cutlasses from behind her back. Yellow, orange, silver, and green splotches covered the blades.

"Speaker. I have killed many of your kind. I will enjoy torturing you before I devour you."

Words and confidence filled Cassandra's mind. "Eímai says, 'I am not responsible for the evil choices that left you wounded. Let go of your pride and come to my water as you used to. I will meet with you, and we will talk. Though your crimes are like the deepest stain, I will purify you and make you whiter than snow. You will dwell in my presence once again.'"

"Never!" Lusare screamed. She leaped forward and attacked with a flurry of slashes.

Her attacks came in slow motion. Cassandra dodged some and redirected others.

*Why is everything in slow-motion?*

"My power enhances speed and senses," Eímai said. "Remember, though she is trying to kill you, you must not kill her."

Cassandra knocked Lusare's cutlasses from her grasp, and they flew into the forest. "Yield, Lusare!" she instructed. In her peripheral vision, she saw a female form step out from behind a tree. Overlapping gold and silver leaves covered her from head to toe. Leaves on the front of her head slid away to reveal Lady Jovena's angry face. She held two gold-tonfa, with the long shafts of the nightstick-shaped weapons resting against her forearms.

"I'm glad you're alive," Cassandra said as she kept her adversary at bay.

Lady Jovena ignored the comment and pointed at Lusare. "Kill the abomination!"

Cassandra stepped back. "Eímai invited her to return to him."

Long blades extended out of the short ends of Lady Jovena's tonfa, and lines of bright green light traveled down the edges. She pointed a glowing blade at Lusare. "Return?" she snapped. "Eímai would never forgive one who purposely betrayed him and ate his children. She devoured my closet friends, Speaker Cassandra. Women who had children and husbands waiting for them. Would you deny them justice?"

Cassandra shook her head and looked between the two women. "If he would never forgive her, then why did he tell me he would forgive? Is Eímai a liar?"

Lady Jovena shook her head.

"Yes, he is," said Lusare.

"It is not my place to pass judgment," said Cassandra.

"You are correct. It is mine!" Lady Jovena lunged toward Lusare.

The spikes along Lusare's back erupted outward, punching into the trunks of the surrounding trees. Membranous wings unfolded from her back. She leaped into the air, out of Lady Jovena's reach. "Fools. You cannot kill me," she cackled as she held out her hands. Her swords flew into her waiting palms. "But I will kill you!"

Cassandra jumped back as Lusare streaked toward them, blades igniting with orange fire.

A host of roars, growls, chirps, and meows filled the air. They seemed to come from everywhere.

Her chest clenched, and she willed the lighting shield to reappear. Images of being eaten by tigers and lions passed through her mind. No lightning manifested.

Lusare shot straight into the air. "You escaped me this time!" she screamed as she flew away. "But I will follow you and destroy everything you try to build. After you are broken, I will feast."

The noise stopped, and a soft chuffing sound came from Cassandra's right. But she saw nothing there. *Sounds like the sound a tiger makes. But I don't see any tiger.* "What's going on?"

"Vidarr," Lady Jovena said, glowing blades retracting into her tonfa. She put them on each hip, and they stayed there when she removed her hands.

"Vidarr?"

"You are supposed to help Aras, not destroy it. No one will listen to you now that you sided with the enemy."

"I didn't side with the enemy." Cassandra shrank her staff and put it on her back. "I delivered Eímai's message. It's not my fault she refused it."

"Of course, she refused it. She is evil. Now she is going to destroy more lives."

"She seems to only want to destroy mine," Cassandra muttered. Then louder she said, "Let's get out of here before we get eaten by cats."

"The Vidarr do not eat the flesh of the races. At least those who are not Sundered. They are close by, so we are safe."

"Are the Vidarr cats?"

"Lions, tigers, cheetahs, clouded leopards, and lynxes. They must have come from Mushroom Forest. It is not too far from here."

"Mushroom Forest? As in giant mushrooms?"

"Yes."

"Very cool. I hope I get to see it."

"When we get out of here, you will be able to see it in the far distance. One of the great trees grows at its center."

***

For the next several hours, they traveled without incident. At last, the dense forest thinned and released them into a vast valley that stretched to the horizon. Rolling hills rippled across the land like frozen waves. Knee-high grass the color of salmon swayed in the steady wind, broken only by wide patches of lingering snow that glittered beneath the fading light.

The valley was alive.

Whistling birds zipped through the air in darting bursts of motion, their calls sharp and musical. They skimmed low over the grass, snapping up urchin-like insects that clung to the seed-heavy tips. The insects curled into tight spheres when threatened, but the birds were too fast. Too precise.

Cassandra slowed, unable to stop staring.

Then something larger swept overhead.

Otters. At least, they looked like otters at first glance. Clear, shimmering membranes stretched between their legs, catching the wind like sails. Fish-like fins ran from the tops of their heads to the tips of their tails, guiding their movement as they glided through the sky. They swam on the wind. Not falling. Not gliding. Swimming.

One twisted midair with playful grace, snapping its jaws around a struggling bird. Others darted after drifting shrimp and lobster-like creatures that floated along unseen air currents, their shells glinting in the strange light. Everywhere Cassandra looked, life surged and collided.

Birds of every imaginable size and color filled the sky. Some swooped after insects. Others chased the airborne otters. Still more plunged into the tall grass, emerging with wriggling prey clenched in their beaks.

One bird rose triumphantly with a pink, furry creature squirming in its talons. The creature had twelve tiny legs that kicked wildly before disappearing into the hunter's waiting beak.

Above it all, the fading forms of three moons lingered in the sky, pale and ghostlike against the growing daylight. The sight pressed the breath from Cassandra's lungs. She could think of only one word. "Awesome."

Lady Jovena tapped her shoulder.

Cassandra turned as the woman lifted one hand and pointed behind them.

"The El'esh approaches."

The air shifted. A distant roar split the sky, growing louder with terrifying speed. Cassandra spun just as a streak of fire tore downward from the heavens. The flaming knight struck the ground with explosive force, landing in a deep crouch that cracked the frozen earth beneath him. Heat rolled outward in a shimmering wave.

When he rose to his full height, he towered over both women by nearly a head. Fire clung to his armor like living cloth, twisting and curling with each movement. He twirled his sword once in a smooth, practiced motion. The blade hummed as he slid it horizontally into an invisible scabbard at his side. The moment his hand released the hilt, the handle vanished into empty air. His shield collapsed inward, folding into itself with mechanical precision before disappearing into the metal vambrace on his left arm. Then the flames changed.

They peeled away from his body like obedient servants, spiraling upward in glowing ribbons. One by one, the fiery strands winked out, leaving only faint trails of smoke drifting into the wind. Silence followed. Where the blazing warrior had stood moments before, a man now remained. He wore a white hooded jacket nearly identical to Cassandra's. Blue flames traced along the cuffs, climbed the edges of the hood, and ran in thin lines down the outer seams, flickering with quiet power.

Slowly, he lifted his hands. Blue gloves covered his fingers as he reached up and pushed back the hood. The motion revealed his face. A familiar face.

# Chapter 7: Michael

***Northwestern Plains, Citali Province, Aras: Spring, Day 11, Year 1, 5th Age***

"Mike!" Cassandra exclaimed, smashing her brother's ribs in a vice-like embrace.

He responded with an equally tight hug. "I'm so glad you're okay," he said and released her.

She stepped back and exhaled deeply as she met his gaze. "Thank God you're alive"

"Who is your friend?" he asked, his eyes drifting to the armored Talah woman.

"Lady Jovena, this is my brother Mike. I mean, he is El'esh Michael."

She curtsied despite her armor. "El'esh Michael, thank you for coming to my aid."

He bowed. "Thank Eímai, my lady. He put me in the right place at the right time and kept us from getting dead." He gestured at the snow. "May I offer my jacket?"

"Yes, please." She flashed a bright smile.

He returned the smile, removed his jacket, and draped it over her shoulders. Five inches of the jacket lay on the ground around her feet, and two inches of the sleeves hung past her hands. It shrank to her size and buttoned itself. She raised the hood as a strong east wind whipped around them.

*Self-sizing clothes. Now that's the kind of magic we could use back home.*

Fire ran from his wings across his chest to spin around him and coalesce into his armor. He drew his sword and spread his wings to block the wind. Waves of superheated air flowed toward the two women, and they lowered their hoods.

"Did you see any cats?" Cassandra asked, looking back towards the forest.

"I did." Michael frowned. "The Outcast Clan is fighting the Legion in there."

Lady Jovena's face paled. "Are you saying you've seen the Outcast Clan?"

He nodded. "They showed up when I was fighting Vold."

"If you fought Vold and survived, you must be exceptionally close to Eímai—like one of the El'esh of old." She turned to Cassandra. "To think, Eímai sent a master knight from another world to aid us in our darkest moment."

The compliment sent a tidal wave of shame over him. He gave a derisive snort.

*Some knight. I disobeyed orders, got myself roasted, endangered people's lives, and got my butt kicked by Vold. If it hadn't been for the Outcast Clan, he'd be picking his teeth with my bones.* "Not even close." He ignored his sister's questioning look and ran a hand through his hair. "We need to get out of here in case any Legion gets past the Clan. Let's be on our way," he said as he motioned for the women to follow him.

They walked at a brisk pace for a few minutes when Lady Jovena stopped abruptly. "I must contact my father. If only I had my talking disk—"

"Tell her to check the left jacket pocket," Eímai said.

"Eímai says check the left jacket pocket," Michael repeated.

She drew out a bronze chain from which hung what looked like a pocket watch. Cuneiform writing covered the front, with the rotating crest of Aras on the back. It did not match any of Earth's languages that used cuneiform writing.

Lady Jovena placed the device on her palm with the writing facing upward. She pressed a small button along the edge of the disk, and the top half flipped open with a soft click.

The etched writing lifted from the metal surface, rising into the air as shimmering lines of light. Within seconds, the glowing symbols reshaped themselves into a miniature holographic image of the man who had previously used the device.

In the projection, he held a disk identical to the one in Jovena's hand. He spoke a name, and a sphere of pale light formed between the open halves of his device. Inside the glowing sphere, a person's face slowly appeared, as if emerging from mist.

Though no sound came from the image, Michael could tell they were speaking to one another. Their expressions shifted, their lips moving in silent conversation.

After a moment, the man in the projection closed his disk. The sphere of light vanished instantly, and the holographic image dissolved into drifting strands of light. The glowing symbols settled back onto the metal surface, returning to their original etched form as the device fell silent once more.

Lady Jovena brought the open disk close to her face. "Ewan, chieftain of the Talah."

In seconds, a man with a bald head, bushy white beard, and similar facial features to Lady Jovena appeared before them.

Michael gasped. *That's definitely her dad.*

The man's face instantly brightened. "Jovena! Eímai be praised, you are alive. When we found the destroyed wagon and half-eaten bodies, we feared the worst."

Lady Jovena blinked away tears. "The Legion ambushed us and sacrificed the survivors in the Armorer's Forest. I was near death when Speaker Cassandra and El'esh Michael rescued me."

Chief Ewan's head turned towards Michael and Cassandra. "You saved my daughter, and I am eternally grateful. Reports have been pouring in all morning that the Legion has entered Aras through dark portals. We have mobilized and are fighting on multiple fronts. We have won battles and lost more. El'esh Michael, what can you report?"

"Activate your map," Eímai said.

The map above his gauntlet depicted a country bordered by mountains to the west and split into quarters by four rivers flowing from a central mountain. Two dragon statues appeared in each province, and what looked like darkness spread from each. The dragon in the Armorer's Forest vanished, and a white patch of white swallowed the darkness spreading through the trees. Patches of various colors scattered throughout the country clashed with the spreading darkness.

"The dragon statues are Ba'rel's portals," Michael explained. "The darkness is the Legion's progress. The colored patches are Arasian forces. These portals can be closed by destroying the statues at the portal."

"Are the white squares in the Armorer's Forest El'esh?"

"No. Outcast Clan."

"Good. Did you see Captain Ragnar and Lady Achima?"

Michael shook his head. "I am to meet the captain tomorrow in Rün during Full-Light."

"You will make good time as long as the Legion does not hinder you."

"Vold is in Aras. I fought him, and the Vidarr took over the fight so I could get away to guard my sister and your daughter."

All levity left the chief's face. "Did you injure him?"

"Uh, I don't remember. Everything happened so fast. Why?"

"Vold is as vindictive as he is evil. Any slight or perceived slight will be met with a single-minded fervor to avenge himself."

Michael rubbed his temples, remembering something Vold had said. "As I flew off, Vold shouted something about hunting me down and eating me and those I loved. But I figured that was his super-villain rant."

"Is he planning to eat me?" Cassandra asked, eyes wide.

Michael stared at his sister. "If he tries, zap him."

Chief Ewan frowned. "What do you mean by zap?"

"When Eímai lets it happen," Cassandra said. "Lightning erupts from me."

"How long have you been able to do this?" the Chief asked.

"Since I arrived here. We're from the planet Earth."

"Another planet has the gift of lightning. Could it be that after all these centuries it is coming true?"

"What is coming true?" Lady Jovena asked.

"Speaker Savelis' prophecy. Fire and Lightning come in Aras' darkest hour. But if Speaker Cassandra is Lightning, who is Fire?"

"Is it El'esh Michael?"

"But he said theirs would be the crimson river. There are no crimson rivers in Aras or anywhere else in Parrésia. This takes further investigation. Did you see any King's Scelto in the forest?"

"No. Who are King's Scelto?" Michael asked.

"The king's assassins," Cassandra said. "They're after me."

Michael's armor burned brighter, and his wings spread to their full span as if to block his sister from any attack. "Why?" he demanded.

"The king thinks I'm a threat because the last Speaker tried to get rid of him."

"The king Speaker Savelis tried to remove died thousands of years ago. It is highly unlikely that King Tarin knows you are in Aras, and the invasion will keep him preoccupied," Chief Ewan said. "I do not see any supplies or mounts. Are you equipped for your journey?"

"We weren't given anything," Michael said. "What sorts of resources are available this time of the year?"

"The Brenus River to the north and Cluster Falls between you and Rün are the only sources of water. There may still be some large pockets of snow that you might be able to melt and drink. But we had a warm winter and did not get as much snow as usual. No fruit is in season other than along Eímai's rivers and the pool at the base of the falls. You may be able to find some winter potatoes. It will take your flaming sword to dig them out of the frozen ground. There are plenty of sky shrimp if you can catch them. Herds of rugi and pugal have been seen in that region. Rugi are docile and make excellent mounts and food. But beware of the pugal. They are timid, but fierce as ozulves if provoked. Their teeth can sever bone as easily as flesh."

"Lovely," Michael said and bit his lip.

"I must go. Captain Cynyr is here with news on the war. I love you, Daughter. Eímai watch over you all. I will look for you at Debash's zenith."

"I love you too, Father. Eímai watch over you all, too. Give my love to Mother and the boys."

She closed the disk, ending the call. She picked up her pace, snow crunching under her boots. "I must speak with Todor. Would you give us privacy?"

"Of course," Cassandra said.

"Who's Todor?" Michael whispered when they were twenty yards from Lady Jovena.

"Her fiancé."

He flew high into the air and turned a slow circle to scout out their surroundings. To the distant east, he saw a mass of brown hills. It looked like the hills moved, but he figured what he saw was due to fatigue and hunger.

"Eímai, thank you for protecting us and getting us out of the woods alive," he said under his breath. "Thank you for giving us clothes that keep us warm. We need food, water, shelter, and transportation. Please provide these for us. Thank you for taking care of us."

He landed next to his sister, and his helmet parted to reveal his face.

"I see some brown hills over that way. I'm not sure how far they are. One of the advantages of being an El'esh is that I have enhanced sight."

"Do you have X-ray vision too?"

He shrugged. "I don't know, but there's…"

After several seconds of silence, he cleared his throat. "There's something I'd been wanting to explain."

"Go ahead," Cassandra said, her voice soft.

"I had every intention of spending as much time as I could with you doing fun stuff and trying to rebuild our relationship. Getting launched into a war on another planet was not in my plans."

"I don't think anyone wakes up and says, 'I don't have anything better to do today, so I'm going to go to another world and get involved in their war.'"

He nodded. "That's true, but regardless, I'm serious about protecting you."

"I'm not sure how that'll happen if I'm running around trying to get Aras' races to unify against Ba'rel, and you're off fighting monsters."

He shrugged. "I don't know either. I guess we'll just have to make the most of it. Too bad we don't have talking disks. We could keep in touch wherever we end up. I wonder why Eímai didn't give us some."

"Eímai said he gave me everything I needed. Maybe…" She unbuttoned her coat, and a talking disk hung around her neck. "I wonder why you don't have one," she said as she caressed the device.

"I don't know."

"Ask Eímai."

"Eímai, why don't I have a disk?"

"Yours are built into your vambraces. Say the name, and the person will appear in the same way as the map."

"Mine are in my vambraces," Michael explained to his sister. "I just realized, it'll be like I was in Israel again when we had to video chat."

His sister's mouth thinned to a line, a sign that she was unhappy with the idea.

Lady Jovena's voice rose, but distance and his helmet muffled her words.

"In a change of subject, congratulations on graduating early and getting accepted to Princeton. That's a big accomplishment. When do you leave for school?"

She brightened. "I leave at the end of August."

"And you have your belt test in a couple of days. That's exciting."

"Well, when I get back. Prof. Braga seemed to know I'd be coming here, and he said I could rest when I got back."

"He knew? How?"

"God told him."

"Hmmm. I wonder why He didn't tell me ahead of time."

Cassandra shrugged.

Lady Jovena rejoined them, hanging her talking disk around her neck and tucking it under the jacket. Her smile seemed forced.

Michael knew better than to pry into her personal affairs. He pointed east. "I saw some brown hills that way."

"Those are rugi," Lady Jovena said. "Did you see any gray shapes?"

"No. Should I have?"

"The gray shapes would have been pugal. Maybe they are hiding behind the rugi. The sooner we get there, the sooner we can move faster."

"I have a question. Well, actually, I have many. But the biggest one is—what exactly is Savelis' prophecy, and why did he set out to destroy the king?"

# Chapter 8: Cassandra

*Northwestern Plains, Citali Province, Aras: Spring, Day 11, Year 1, 5th Age*

Before his execution, Speaker Savelis said:

> In Aras' darkest hour, Eímai will send Fire and Lightning.
> Theirs is the crimson river.
> Through them Eímai will restore what is in darkness.
> Aras will unify to fight the last of all wars.
> Darkness will be defeated forever, and the prisoners set free.

*Is it a riddle? What does 'theirs in the crimson river' mean? There was no Crimson River on Mike's map. This is weird. The chief thinks I'm this Lightning person. But there must be other people who zap others. Or even shoot fire?*

"There are many interpretations," Lady Jovena continued. "Some believe he spoke a prophecy from Eímai. These two will annihilate Ba'rel and return Aras to its former glory. Others believe his words were nothing more than another attempt to undermine the Hikaru."

"What do *you* think it means?" asked Cassandra, apprehension filling her.

"He was a deceiver who got my ancestor killed, and the Talah persecuted. Unfortunately, there are still many who see him as a martyr and look for the day when his words are fulfilled. They will flock to you when they hear you wield lightning."

"And that will make the king nervous," Michael said, crossing his arms.

Lady Jovena nodded and folded her arms. "He will do whatever it takes to protect his position."

Cassandra's stomach churned. *Will she throw me under the bus to save her family?*

Lady Jovena stopped her mid-step with a hand on her shoulder and turned her toward her. "You have nothing to fear from me. I will not hand you over to the king's assassins."

"What if he threatens your family?" Cassandra said, her voice quaking despite her efforts to keep it emotionless.

"Killing my family and me would unleash a firestorm he would not be able to easily extinguish. We are too well connected among the races, and the king knows not to move against us when the Talah are needed to beat back the Legion. You saved my life, and that is a debt I take seriously. I will protect you and help you unify the races. But if you step out of your assigned station, I will break all ties with you and do all I can to bring you the same fate as Speaker Savelis."

Her words ignited conflicting emotions in Cassandra. At first, she felt relief for Lady Jovena's support. But Lady Jovena's threat made her apprehensive.

*What does she mean by "step out of your assigned station?"*

"What do you mean by assigned station?" Michael asked, an edge in his voice.

*And the knight comes to my rescue. When I was a kid, I enjoyed his rescuing me. But now, I don't know.*

Lady Jovena did not seem to notice his tone and began walking again. "The Speaker's role is to mediate in disputes between the races and bring reconciliation. Anything else is to step outside of the Speaker's station."

"If Eímai tells her to do something that doesn't fit the traditional role, she can't be blamed. She's being obedient."

"Speaker Savelis said the same and led the massacre of hundreds of thousands of Arasians."

"That doesn't mean Cassandra will do the same. She isn't Savelis."

"Your loyalty to your sister is admirable, El'esh Michael. But I know what it is like to have a beloved sibling betray you."

*What is she talking about? Who betrayed her?*

"What are you talking about?" Cassandra asked.

"Todor told me my brother Djavan betrayed me to the Legion so he could become chief."

"Seriously?" Cassandra exclaimed. *And I thought I had brother issues.*

"He's Sundered," Michael said.

"Todor does not know. The Hod'ji have not been able to locate him. Sources say he has joined the Savelins. They are the ones I told you about who want Speaker Savelis' words to be fulfilled. Their goal is to overthrow the Hikaru king and put a Talah on the throne."

A trumpet sounded above them, drawing their attention. A host of winged soldiers in blue and white armor flew west toward the

Armorer's Forest. In the distance beyond them, three dragons headed east. Despite the distance, the dragons still looked massive.

"Mike. Dragons," Cassandra shouted, pointing.

"It is not polite to point or shout, especially toward dragons," Lady Jovena said. "We also do not want to draw Hikaru's attention."

The reprimand caused Cassandra's cheeks to flush. "Sorry," she said. "Are those flying people Hikaru?"

"Yes. I do not see any dressed in the ornamented armor of the King's Scelto, so for now, we are safe. We must keep moving."

"We don't have dragons in our world," Michael said. "We also don't know the manners and customs of this world. Are you willing to teach us some while we walk?"

"I will do what I can. We will begin with greetings."

*I wish I had a notebook. I have a feeling I'm going to need to take notes.*

Four hours later, a headache danced in time with her heartbeat.

*Not quite a migraine, but it sure feels on the verge of one. Probably because I'm hungry.*

"Eímai, please bring us food," she pleaded under her breath.

"Wait a little longer, and you will be fed," Eímai said.

"How long is a little?"

"Trust me to take care of you and believe I have answered your request."

With a groan of pain, she said, "Thank you for providing food and everything else we need."

Heedless of Cassandra's suffering, Lady Jovena continued her lesson on racial etiquette. "Lastly, the Dragon/Drás Confederation. They consider anyone outside their group an outsider and a potential enemy. They do not trust easily. A standard greeting and introduction are the best you can do. Being Speaker puts you at a disadvantage because Speaker Savelis promoted the Dragon/Drás War. El'esh Michael, they will hate you because the El'esh fought in the War against their sires."

"So, these people weren't even there when the war took place?"

"The war lasted from 17,430 to 17,436 of the fourth age. Each age of Aras is 20,000 years. That would make it," she paused to calculate on her fingers, "about two and a half thousand years ago. There may still be a few Dragons left from that time. But I doubt it because they will have nothing to do with Eímai. His water and fruit extend life beyond the normal limits. Father has lived for over two thousand years because he serves Eímai faithfully and partakes of his water and fruit daily. Not so with the Confederation."

"They hate people they don't even know because of something that happened thousands of years ago." Michael shook his head. "And I thought Humans were the only ones who did that."

"What are Humans?"

"Our race back home."

"Hate is passed on no matter the race," Cassandra said, massaging her throbbing temples against the intensifying pain.

Michael frowned. "What's wrong?"

"Headache. It'll go away after I eat something.

An approaching thumping and creaking drew their attention south. Cassandra blinked. *It's got to be the headache making me see things.* She observed five wagons filled with boxes and reptilian creatures, each pulled by four puffin-like birds, each the size of a pony. Some of the birds had dark blue feathers on their bodies and salmon-colored feathers around their eyes, while others had the colors reversed, with salmon-colored feathers on their bodies and blue feathers around their eyes. All had long, thick legs and three-toed feet covered in iridescent amethyst-colored scales.

Above them flew a bright yellow dragon and a red dragon. Both had horns pointing back from their heads and white bellies.

"Drás ride in the wagons," Eímai said. "They are Confederation."

Two Drás rode in the front of each wagon while six to eight perched on each load. Breastplates, pauldrons, and helmets the color of dark chocolate sat on lean, muscular bodies. Each held a red kite shield with a silhouette of a Dragon facing the silhouette of a Drás. Some had three fingers and toes, and others had four or five.

The red Drás had heads like velociraptors, the green like triceratops, the blue chameleons with rotating eyes, the orange like dragons with four short horns protruding from either side of their head, and the purple had frills sticking out of their necks.

"No matter what is said or done, do not respond in any way," Eímai commanded. "Remain silent band still."

*Why?*

"There is much you must learn before you can effectively communicate with the Confederation. What is about to happen is necessary for what will happen in the future."

Suddenly, she wanted to run away. But the wagons were feet away. Some hissed, while others growled and bared long, sharp fangs. They all readied axes, swords, and spears.

Lady Jovena stepped forward and raised her hand. "Greetings. I am Lady Jovena, daughter of Chieftain Ewan and Ilka. Where do you go on this beautiful morning?"

The wagons rode past and circled, cutting off all chances of escape. Her breathing quickened, and she reached back to pull out her staff. But the clasps would not release it.

"Do you have food and water we might buy from you?" Lady Jovena said.

A red Drás driving the wagon in front of Lady Jovena hissed his s's and drew out the z sounds as he said, "If you are the chief's daughter, where are your guards and supplies? Why do you travel with a murderer?"

"The Legion is in Aras and would have killed me if not for El'esh Michael and this young woman. He is newly inducted into the order and has not sworn an oath to the king."

"Makes no difference. Guilt by association. Where are you going now?" asked a blue Drás, her eyes cold and observant.

"We return to Rün as quickly as we may. Ba'rel's sorcerers succeeded in opening portals throughout Aras and have invaded."

"We saw no Legion," the red Drás said.

"Those in the Armorer's Forest were destroyed by the Outcast Clan," Michael said.

"Fléau has returned? I wondered when that murderer would show his ugly face again." The purple Drás spat the name as though it were an insult.

"He wasn't there. Vold asked about him, too."

"Another murderer. Murder runs in their line from one generation to the next," an orange Drás said.

The entire entourage climbed down and stood inside their circle.

The red Drás approached Cassandra, golden eyes split by horizontal black irises.

Her heartbeat tripled.

He fingered a long dagger in his belt.

Cassandra kept her eyes on the Drás as he circled her. He pushed his way between Lady Jovena and Cassandra. Michael took a step forward, and ten Drás pounced, pressing swords and spears against his neck. The tips of their weapons grew bright orange as Michael's flaming armor superheated the metal.

"Who is this? She does not look Talah. She does not smell like a Talah. She smells like a Speaker." He gave her the same malevolent look Lusare had given her.

"She is Speaker Cassandra. She was chosen this morning," Lady Jovena said. "As I stated before, she saved my life. No harm will come to her."

Cassandra shifted into a ready stance, her hands rising as she prepared to defend herself.

"Be still," Eímai ordered with such force that Cassandra immediately obeyed.

The reptile drew close, and she smelled wine and roasted meat on his breath. It reminded her of the roasts her mother made. But it did not still her rising terror.

The Drás stepped behind her, and she heard metal leave leather.

*He's going to kill me. He's going to kill me, and I can't do anything about it. Eímai, you're not good. You're evil.*

"Calm down. He will not kill you," Eímai told her.

She did not believe him.

"Leave her alone," Michael shouted.

"You have your own problems, El'esh. We cannot move against the chief's daughter. But you are another matter entirely," said a green Drás, his triceratops head nearly blocking her view of her brother.

Lady Jovena stepped between the red Drás and Cassandra. "Violence against those who did you no wrong is not the Confederation way. A move against her is a move against the Talah and me."

"Your threats are empty. You are not chief yet," the red Drás said.

"What's your name?" Lady Jovena asked.

"Onesimus."

The ground shook. The earthquake sent everyone stumbling about. The red Drás attempted to reach around Lady Jovena to stab Cassandra. But a giant wolf with six legs and blue fur with salmon-colored highlights jumped over the wagons and landed behind the

Drás. He carried a saddle and many leather bags on his back. He grabbed the reptile in his jaws and tossed him out of the circle. The tumbling Drás screamed and disappeared out of sight.

"Neric," Lady Jovena cried, "what are you doing here?"

Another wolf jumped into the circle, this one with salmon fur and blue highlights. She knocked away those who surrounded Michael.

*How do I know which one is male and which is female?*

"Xesa," Lady Jovena said as she scratched the newcomer's head. The top of Lady Jovena's head stopped a few inches from Xesa's shoulder.

*That thing must be six feet tall. Is everyone in this world taller than me?*

The rest of the Drás scrambled onto their wagons and, with much shouting, broke the circle and rode away.

"So much for peaceful negotiations. You ride wolves? Awesome," Michael said, the front of his helmet pulling back to reveal his face.

"These are osulves. Normally, their kind keep away from the races. But Father rescued them from a pack of fenrir years ago, and they have let us ride them."

The osulves locked their green eyes on Cassandra and released a combination of growls and barks. But in her mind, she heard, "Greetings, Speaker. We bring you food as requested."

# Chapter 9: Michael

*Northwestern Plains, Citali Province, Aras: Spring, Day 11, Year 1, 5th Age*

After a meal of dried meat, purple cheese, fruit from Eímai's oasis, and Eímai's glowing water, Michael was no longer famished and exhausted. Power thrummed through him, and his mind returned to their encounter with the Drás. He played out all the ways he could have beaten their attackers down, especially the one who attacked his sister.

"Being thrown by Neric is punishment enough," Eímai said. "Beware of harboring bitterness in your heart. It defiles you and those around you. It also gives Ba'rel an opening to corrupt you and sever our connection. You must forgive Onesimus."

Michael chuckled at the Drás' name. "Is he going to become a champion of light like his human counterpart?"

"That depends on you."

"What do you mean?"

"You will see soon enough. It is time to continue your journey."

Lady Jovena and Cassandra petted the ozulves and held a four-way conversation. His sister spoke with growls and barks and translated for Lady Jovena.

*She's always had a connection with animals. Oreo took a liking to her immediately. Is being able to talk to animals part of being Speaker?*

"Yes. It is one of the many gifts I have given her."

He pushed himself up from the ground and stretched. Vertebrae popped, and he sighed at the release of pressure in his back.

"We about ready to head out?" he asked as he approached the group.

"Yes. Xesa and Neric were telling us about life in their osulf pack. Neric is their Sage and Xesa is the Battle Leader."

"Sage?" Michael said.

Neric barked and growled.

"Their priest and prophet. Eímai gives him messages for the pack," Cassandra said.

"And Battle Leader means…?"

"When they have to fight against fenrir or those who invade their territory, she leads them," Cassandra said after Xesa barked and growled.

"Fenrir are osulves Ba'rel corrupted and unleashed on Aras," Lady Jovena said. "Never did I think I would be having a conversation with an osulf. This day has been full of firsts. I will ride Xesa. You two can ride Neric."

Michael helped his sister into the saddle and climbed up behind her.

"You okay?" he asked her.

"Yes," she said.

She barked, and the ozulves bolted away. Michael grabbed the back of the saddle to keep from falling off. Neric's six legs sped over the landscape with more speed than a thoroughbred horse.

"This sure beats riding a horse," he yelled, his words vibrating with his body. "We'll cover a lot more ground this way."

"Neric says we wasted too much time sitting and eating," Cassandra called over the wind blowing around them. "They have to make up for lost time."

"Lady Jovena, how much time do we have before nightfall?"

"Full-Dark will come in about nineteen hours."

"Full-Dark?"

"We have two suns, Debash and Chalab. Debash rises first. That is First-Rise. When Debash reaches First-Zenith, when it is at its highest point in the sky, Chalab rises. The time between First-Rise and First-Zenith is called Half-Dark. Debash sets when Chalab reaches its highest point in the sky, Second-Zenith. The period from First-Zenith to Second-Zenith is called Full-Light because both suns are in the sky. Lastly, when Chalab sets, that is called Second-Set. It signals the beginning of Full-Dark."

"So Full-Dark is the time between Second-Set and First-Rise?" Cassandra asked.

"Very good," Lady Jovena said with a smile.

"How long is your day?" Michael asked.

"Thirty-two hours."

"Are each of the segments of time eight hours?"

"What do you mean?"

He raised a finger as he listed each time. "First-Rise to First-Zenith, First-Zenith to Second-Zenith, Second-Zenith to Second-Set, and lastly Second-Set to First Rise. Eight times four is thirty-two."

"I had not thought of it in that light. No pun intended. Yes, each last for eight hours."

"I'm going to have to get a clock when we get to Rün," Michael said.

"What is a clock?" Lady Jovena asked.

"A device used to tell time."

"We have no need for such a thing. Eímai gave us the ability to tell time. We can also use the position of the suns if our internal measure is confused."

"I wish I had that ability," Cassandra said. "I'd never be late again."

*Without a clock, how am I going to know how much time I have left to get to Ker'an?*

"You do have a clock," Eímai said. "Turn your left wrist toward you and say *time*."

An image of a half circle split into two sections appeared on his vambrace. The smaller section had three hash marks and the label *Half-Dark*. The larger section had eight hashes and the label *Full-Light*. The first hash in the Full-Light section was labeled *First-Zenith*. A gold needle hand pointed to the first hash mark in Half-Dark. Written under the needle were the words, *Spring, Day 11, Year 1.*

"Wow," he exclaimed. "Check this out."

He held up his vambrace.

"What are we looking at?" Cassandra asked.

"The clock and it even tells the season, day, and year," he said.

"I see nothing but your vambrace and the rotating crest of Aras," Lady Jovena said.

"Me too," Cassandra said.

"Unless I allow it, you are the only one who can see the clock, map, what appears inside your helmet, and other things I have yet to show you," Eímai said.

"I guess I'm the only one who can see it. Sorry," Michael said.

"El'esh Michael, you speak as a scholar," Lady Jovena said.

"I am. I recently received my doctorate. That's the highest level of education in my world."

"You are a master?"

"Basically."

"One of the most famous El'esh is Miklos, and he was a scholar before Eímai called him. Father knows him well. He says El'esh Miklos travels with the Outcast Clan."

"I'd love to meet him."

Lady Jovena took on a sad expression. "He disappeared centuries ago. The Clan hasn't been able to find him. Father thinks he was captured by Ba'rel and taken deep into Kabas. If that happened, he is either Umoni or dead."

"Cass said the King's Scelto were the king's assassins? What can you tell me about them?"

"They are a sect of the Hikaru knightly order of Scelto willing to do anything the king commands without question."

"Hikaru Knights? Does that mean the other races have knightly orders?"

"Yes. They enforce the will of their racial council of elders." She raised a finger as she listed each order. "Talah Hod'ji, Vidarr Ridarri, Drás Élu, Dragon Kerato, Ichtaca Icno, and Gwenfrewi Gwas."

The osulves stopped on the outskirts of at least a hundred creatures with tall, rounded bodies grazed among the pink grass. Their long brown hair reminded Michael of yaks. Termite mounds stood at intervals throughout the herd. The creatures raised scaly lizard heads to look their way.

"That is the weirdest lizard I've ever seen," Cassandra said.

"There are others that make the rugi look tame in comparison," Lady Jovena said with a laugh.

The rugi bellowed and stampeded away. Their hulking bodies plowed through tall mounds of dirt that reminded Michael of termite mounds. The towers exploded. Thousands of two-inch-long black beetles the size of Michael's hand poured out of the ground and swarmed over the retreating rugi. They had large scissor-like mandibles.

"Let's get out of here," he yelled, trying to get Neric to retreat. But the osulf resisted his kicks in his sides and pulled on the saddle.

"They will not hurt us. Those are clipper beetles." Lady Jovena said. "The worst they could do is shave us bald. Oh! I know why we are here."

"Why?" Cassandra asked, pulling her hair as far into her hood as she could. She cared about her hair more than the rest of her appearance.

"The only thing that destroys pemakin is greater clippers. Ancient legends say when a clipper eats an El'esh's hair, the power in the hair transforms them. The clipper's body grows to twice the size, their shell thickens to armor toughness, and they burn with Eímai's fire. Supposedly many of the ancient El'esh traveled with greater clippers riding on their shoulders."

"What are pemakin?"

"Clipper beetles corrupted by Ba'rel. They hunger for flesh instead of hair and fur."

"You want me to go into that mess and let them shave me?" Michael said with a laugh.

"Yes. Extinguish your armor and walk into the middle of the swarm," said Eímai.

"I don't have that much hair," he said as he dismounted. He strode toward the clicking insects, and his armor melted away. The temptation to refuse grew in him.

*What happens if I twitch or move while they're shaving me? I could lose an ear, nose, or eye. This is crazy.*

"Take three drinks of my water before entering the swarm. It will help calm you. But you will have to deal with the evil thoughts you are thinking. Do not give them a place. Trust me to protect you," Eímai said.

Michael drank the water and said as he walked toward the swarm, "Mind be still. Destructive thoughts, I command you to leave now. Eímai protects and cares for me."

His mind cleared as the hair on his head and face grew with super speed until it trailed after him on the ground. Each strand held the same swirling fire that burned under his skin.

"You look like a Bigfoot splattered with glow-in-the-dark paint," Cassandra called from her safe position on Neric's back.

"My eyebrows and beard are so long I could use them for jump ropes," he said as beetles attacked his trailing hair and scurried up his body.

Gorged clippers rolled to the ground. Blue fire danced along the grooves in their carapaces and along their mandibles. They doubled in size, and their carapaces changed, making them look as if they wore glowing blue armor. Blue fire surrounded stag beetle-shaped mandibles.

His hair grew to match the rate at which the clippers consumed it. He pushed over the undisturbed mounds, and an hour later, he stood in the middle of a vast army of fiery beetles. In unison, they formed swarms of iridescent blue fire that flew in every direction to hunt pemakin.

"The Legion is not going to like this one bit," Lady Jovena said.

His hair grew to its original length, and a short beard graced his jawline.

"Now you look *professory*," Cassandra said. Her smile lit up her face.

"*Professory*? Is that the technical term?" Michael asked with a chuckle.

"Yup."

A beetle landed on each of their shoulders. Four landed on each of the osulves, two facing toward their heads and two facing their tails.

Cassandra screamed and batted it off her shoulder. It buzzed around her and tried to land again. She pulled her staff and swung at it like a baseball player.

DONG.

Neric's head twitched to the side. His muzzle whipped around, and his jaws locked on something invisible. He yanked it from her grasp and growled at her. Cassandra raised her hands palms up.

"Sorry," she said quickly.

"Cassandra," Lady Jovena said, resting her hand on Cassandra's shoulder. "It won't hurt you or eat your hair. It eats only pemakin. It wants to protect you."

Cassandra flinched as the beetle returned to her shoulder. It rubbed the side of her hood and chittered.

"I think it likes you," Michael said, fire spinning around him to once again encase him in his armor. The greater clipper kept its perch on his shoulder, and the armor materialized under it.

as he climbed up behind her on Neric's back.

"It is trying to reassure her," Eímai said.

"Eímai says it's trying to reassure you."

"Okay," she said, drawing out the word.

Neric tapped her leg with the invisible staff, and she took it, returning it to its place on her back.

"You, okay?" Michael asked the osulf. "I've been on the receiving end of her staff, too. Gave me a concussion and nearly broke three ribs."

Cassandra turned in the saddle, glacial blue eyes flashing with indignation. "I was nine and barely knew how to use it."

He shot her an impish grin. "What's your excuse for today? You know how to use it, and you nearly knocked out Neric."

She sent a backhand toward his chest. To his surprise, it passed through the fire and connected soundly with flesh. He grunted as pain gripped his ribs.

"See what I mean?" he said with a cough, "Violent tendencies."

Lady Jovena shot him her own smirk. "You should be careful what you say, El'esh Michael. You should not insult someone who can strike at you through your armor."

"Yeah," his sister said, delivering another bone-jarring slap to his chest.

*I don't get it. Why did she go through the armor? It protected me against Taras and all those other creeps. Why isn't it working now?*

The osulves bolted away, and everyone had to hang on tight. Rugi and smaller gray-skinned creatures with elephant trunks and pointed cat-like ears scattered before them. Some of the gray creatures charged them, but a sharp bark and bared osulf fangs changed their minds.

Miles and hours later, Chalab's setting rays painted the sky in a collection of oranges, blues, pinks, and purples as they reached a floating mountain. It hung a quarter of a mile above the trees and rolling fields. The jagged bottom looked like it had been ripped from the ground. A covered the cluster of four snowcapped peaks, and caves dotted the mountainside. Monolithic buildings made of white stone and trimmed with gold and silver rose from the base and center of the peaks. Waterfalls poured from the base of the snow, disappearing into the forest and cities below. The sparkling flow reflected the sky's light, turning bright pink and purple.

"We will camp here for the night," Lady Jovena said.

"This is incredible. What is this place called? It didn't have a name on the map," Michael said.

"If it had a name, it has been forgotten. The only floating mountain name I know is Evike, and I know that because El'esh Miklos fought a battle there against the Legion."

The three worked together to set up three tents with warm bedrolls and pillows. The greater clippers formed a perimeter around the camp, facing outward. While Cassandra pulled out the food, Michael approached the shadow of the hovering mountain.

"Stop. Do not go any closer to the mountain," Lady Jovena said.

Her words stopped Michael in mid-stride. "Why not?"

"Anyone who enters the perimeter is lifted to the mountain. In ancient times, Talah shapers went up to sell their work to the Hikaru living in the peaks. The races worked for the mutual good of all as Eímai created us to do. But after the War, the Talah were banished from the mountains."

"What are shapers?" Cassandra asked.

"Shapers are those who use songs to create with stone, wood, metal, glass, cloth, and words. For example, a stone-shaper takes a piece of stone and sings a song that makes it flake off. The deeper the notes, the larger the flakes. Eventually, the stone takes the form of a statue or whatever the shaper envisioned. When I was younger, one of my favorite things to do was to wander the shaper's quarter."

"I'd love to see that," Michael muttered as he turned from the mountain and returned to their camp.

# Chapter 10: Cassandra

***Rün, Citali Province, Aras: Spring, Day 12, Year 1, 5th Age***

The city of Rün lay spread out before the travelers, a vast collection of stone buildings with domes of orange and forest green, encircled by giant stone towers bearing the telltale scars of fire and claws. Catapults and ballistae sat on guard duty atop each turret. Around these stood Hikaru soldiers armed with spears, bows, and swords. Behind them, winged people left the city and flew north. In the plains, scores of people flooded into the city.

*The towers look like something from a European castle. If the city needs that kind of protection, why don't they have a wall? I wonder if those marks happened during the Dragon/Drás War.*

Ten figures riding puffins left the city and headed their way. They wore leather armor accented with gold and kilts of different tartan patterns. Black tonfa sat tucked into either side of their belts.

"Those are Hod'ji Elites," Lady Jovena said, "and Captain Cynyr leads them."

The Hod'ji saluted with arms crossing their chest and moved their puffins to encircle the riders. The captain's eyes drifted to the greater clippers perched on their shoulders and the osulves.

Cassandra raised her right hand, moved it in the sign of a cross, brought it around clockwise in a circle, and held it up palm facing the captain. Lady Jovena smiled and nodded. Cassandra had executed the

Talah greeting correctly. Captain Cynyr gave her a small nod and turned his attention to Lady Jovena.

"It is good to see you alive, Lady. You have arrived just in time."

"What news, Captain?" Lady Jovena said.

"The Legion is coming from the southeast and will be here within two hours. They number at least two thousand, with fifty Sundered dragons flying ahead of them. They will most likely raze the city, and the army will pick off anyone who is left."

Fear gripped Cassandra. *Dragons on their way? How will they defend themselves? What will happen to Mike and me?*

"Where are Father and Todor?" Lady Jovena said as they entered the city.

The crowd of Talah in kilts and leather armor entering the city parted before them, but not because Captain Cynyr shouted for them to make way. They looked in the captain's direction, and their faces grew pale.

Cassandra leaned forward and whispered in Neric's ear, "Are they afraid of the Hod'ji? That doesn't make sense. They're supposed to be protecting the people."

"It's not the Hod'ji they're afraid of. It is your litter-mate and the greater clippers with us. El'esh are usually the king's servants, and that brings fear. Though not as much fear as the King's Scelto caused. But the greater clippers declare El'esh Michael as one who has not taken the oath because those loyal to the king never travel with these."

"So, they're afraid of him because the king will be after him?"

"No. They're afraid of the power your litter-mate wields. The Talah tell stories of powerful El'esh with greater clippers. Those are the ones who can destroy entire armies. Even the packs of the southern plains tell of El'esh who walked in the power of Eímai, and none could stand against them."

Two fish-like beings in vaporous robes stood beside the street and called to the crowd in gargling voices.

"You have gone from the Path. Eímai disciplines those He loves," said a green-scaled male with the face of a catfish and four tentacles for arms. His flippered feet slapped the cobblestones as he spoke, as though to emphasize his words.

"Gaze into Eímai's Writings and Water to find out what you are meant to be. The time is at hand, it is not too late," said a blue-scaled female with a hammerhead shark head and an eel lower half. Her two lanky arms ended in lobster claws.

*They look like mutants from one of those cartoons Michael used to watch.*

"Those are Gwenfrewi," Lady Jovena said when she looked in Cassandra's direction. "They live in the holy rivers and the Sea of Siana in the Siana province."

"The Chief and future chief are at the main house waiting for you," Captain Cynyr said, not paying any attention to the Gwenfrewi. "Sage Braith arrived early this morning and was in council with the chief for two hours. When they came out, the chief ordered preparations for your wedding, which is to take place as soon as you arrive. She will perform the marriage and succession rites."

"If Sage Braith is here, then she bears news from the throne of Eímai."

"What do you mean?" Cassandra said.

"Sage Braith is Eímai's chief messenger. It is said she was chosen in the first age to deliver Eímai's messages and has done so ever since. She only gives the most serious messages."

"If she lived in the first age, that would make her…" Michael said.

"Over eighty thousand years old," Lady Jovena said.

"What?" Cassandra and Michael exclaimed together.

"Lady Jovena, I am giving my report," Captain Cynyr said in a tone that told everyone he was not happy about being interrupted.

"That you are, captain. I will hear the rest when I am finished talking to the Speaker and El'esh. Do not give me that look. Do not forget I am more than a Hod'ji Elite," Lady Jovena said, her eyes flashing.

But the man did not quail before her majestic presence. Instead, he continued his report as though she had not spoken.

"Captain Ragnar and eighty Outcast Clan appeared after the chief's council with Sage Braith. This led to another two-hour council. But this time I was allowed to participate. A great host of the Clan is coming to give aid against the Legion. They wait for someone to cleanse the city square, whatever that means. The tiger and his eighty waits for these two," he gave a dismissive wave toward the siblings, "to take them to Ker'an. There was a great deal of talk about Savelis' prophecy. Supposedly, this girl is part of its fulfillment."

*I don't like the way he looks at me. It's not contempt, but there is definitely something off about him. I wouldn't want to be alone with this guy.*

A male and two female lions ran by. They wore silver armor and leather kilts held up by wide belts. They wielded double-bladed axes. The male's mane was braided into at least fifty braids ringed by ivory beads.

"Those are Vidarr," Neric said.

"Vidarr are lions?" Cassandra said.

"The Vidarr consists of five different cats: lions, tigers, cheetahs, lynx, and clouded leopards. Of all the races, the Legion hates the Vidarr the most because they are their fiercest enemy," Xesa said.

"The Outcast Clan," Cassandra said.

Xesa nodded. "But those three don't belong to the Clan. The Clan wears a shattered four-claw slash on armor the color of stone."

At that moment, the group passed through the city center, and Cassandra saw a black marble platform with a limestone statue of a headless man in a robe. Cassandra saw splotches of green, silver, yellow, and orange on it before Neric turned down a side street.

The Hod'ji guided them to a modest stone building with a green dome. The wooden door had shiny bronze metal strips in a curved tribal design. The Hod'ji guards snapped to attention the moment they saw Lady Jovena and Captain Cynyr. The captain jumped from his puffin and helped Lady Jovena dismount from Xesa.

The house's door opened and out stepped a stocky elderly man with a plaited white beard that reached to his round middle. He had Lady Jovena's nose and moss-green eyes.

"Be prepared to get as many into the escape tunnels as you can if the battle goes against us. Make for the Brenus. The abominations cannot stand the holy water," he said over his shoulder.

"Father," Lady Jovena exclaimed as she ran to him.

Chief Ewan swept his daughter into a tight embrace.

"Praise Eímai. We prayed constantly for your safe return."

The chief set down his daughter and called into the house, "Ilka, Todor, Jovena is here."

An elderly version of Jovena exploded out of the house. A lanky man with a profusion of freckles on his cheeks followed close behind her. His ponytail of red hair swished like a horse's tail.

"Mother," Lady Jovena said, hugging her mother.

"Praise Eímai. I was worried sick," Lady Ilka said between sobs.

Lady Jovena caught sight of the man, and her face lit up even more. "Todor, my love," she breathed, letting go of her mother.

"Beloved," Todor said before laying a long kiss on her lips.

"Mother, Father, Todor, I present El'esh Michael and Speaker Cassandra," Lady Jovena said, waving a hand at Michael and Cassandra.

Cassandra gave the Talah greeting. Chief Ewan returned it and gave her a crushing hug. He turned to Michael and hugged him despite his flaming armor. He gave him three hearty slaps on his back.

*He doesn't seem to mind the greater clippers at all. Maybe because he's so old, he's not bothered by them. Did he see these bugs in action when he was younger?*

"I am forever grateful to you both. I have provided all provisions for your journey to Ker'an. I gave them to Captain Ragnar."

"Thank you, sir," the siblings said in unison.

The chief turned to his family and began discussing details of the wedding.

"We will now travel with you, Speaker. You and your litter-mate. Inform the Talah chief," said Xesa.

"Why do you call him my litter-mate?"

"Are you not sired of the same parents?"

"Yes. But we weren't born at the same time."

"Obviously."

"Sir," Cassandra said, tapping the chief's shoulder. "I'm sorry to interrupt. But Xesa wanted me to tell you that she and Neric are going to travel with us now."

Chief Ewan approached the osulves and scratched them between their ears. "I am grateful to you for your service. May Eímai bless you with many pups and a long life running the plains."

Hod'ji began to unbuckle the saddles. The chief held up a hand. "Leave them. They will need saddles, and there is none better in all of Aras. A last gift to you all."

"Thank you," Michael and Cassandra said together.

"I hate to cut this short," Captain Cynyr said. Cassandra doubted he was sorry. "But the wedding and succession…"

*He is so pushy.*

"Of course," Chief Ewan said. He looked at his daughter and blinked. "Are you wearing armor?"

"Yes, Father. The Armorer's Forest gave it to me."

She returned Michael's jacket to him. It grew to fit him and fastened itself when he put it on. The chief and Hod'ji gaped at Lady Jovena's glittering armor.

"These are unprecedented times," the chief said. "The Legion in Aras, the Armorer's Forest, awakens again, and a new Speaker walks among us. I wish I could speak with you both. I have many questions. But time does not permit. Go with Eímai."

"Go with Eímai and may you all be richly blessed beyond measure," Michael said, giving them a deep bow.

Chief Ewan's eyes went wide, and he grinned. "I like you, young man. I am glad Eímai brought you here. Eímai wills, we will meet again."

"I look forward to it," Michael said.

Lady Jovena took Todor's arm, and the two led the Talah into the house, the door closing behind them.

"I hope they have a happy marriage," Cassandra said.

"Me too. So, what now?" Michael said.

"Speaker Cassandra cleanses Rün," a rumbling male voice said behind them.

A nine-foot-tall white tiger with off-white stripes materialized before them. Three wide, ragged scars ran across his face from his left ear to the right side of his jaw. He wore the mottled gray armor of the Outcast Clan. On his left side hung a scimitar in a black scabbard. The scabbard had a wide silver band around its throat and tip, with four broken claw slashes pressed into it. Down its length ran silver cuneiform saying, "Consecrated by Eímai, Captain of the Outcast Clan." Captain Ragnar's paw rested on the round pommel at the top of a long handle wrapped in strips of white leather.

*He's enormous. How do you greet a Vidarr? I can't remember. Eímai, please help me remember.*

Revelation dawned. She tapped a fist against her chest and held out her hand.

He returned the gesture and engulfed her forearm with a paw. It felt warm and soft.

"It is a pleasure to meet you, sir," Cassandra said.

"Likewise. Long have we waited for your arrival."

Michael's visor split to reveal his face, and he gave the tiger the same greeting. "Where are the rest of your forces?"

Cat warriors materialized on the street and surrounding roofs. Each saluted with a paw to their chest. An orange tiger with black stripes wearing two scimitars on her back stood on the captain's right, and a second with orange fur with white stripes stood on his left. She had two long daggers with bronze tiger head pommels on either hip.

"I am Maja, Ragnar's mate. This is Frida, one of our cubs," the orange and black tiger said, giving the humans a warm smile.

"I am Cassandra, Michael's sister," Cassandra said as she tapped her chest and held out her hand.

"I can see the resemblance," Maja said, returning the gesture.

"Where is Lady Achima?"

"She will join us after you cleanse the city square," Captain Ragnar said.

"You mean where that statue is?"

"Yes. It is a place of execution. Most of the blood spilled there was innocent. If not purified, the Legion will use it to open a portal to Kabas. We need to use it to open a portal to bring our forces into Rün."

"How do I cleanse it?"

"Ask Eímai. He knows."

*Eímai, how do I cleanse a city?*

"Walk up to the statue, drive your staff into the platform, and shout, 'Eímai cleanse this place.' I will take care of the rest."

Hikaru soldiers stood around and on the platform with the headless statue. They looked warily at the cats. Cassandra walked up the platform steps, and four Hikaru stopped her with drawn swords.

"What are you doing?" one demanded.

"Cleansing this place."

"Get back. You are not allowed here."

"I have to cleanse this spot, or the Legion will use it."

"Leave or die," the soldier barked.

*Where's Michael? Why isn't he helping me?*

"You need to depend on me to care for you, not your brother. Follow my instructions," Eímai said.

*How do I get around these guys?*

"Diplomacy."

Cassandra drew a deep breath and let it out slowly. "I understand you are doing your job. But I have a job to do too. I have been sent to cleanse this place of all the innocent blood that was shed here. If I don't, the Legion will use it to open a portal to Kabas. You know what will happen if they do. I need to get to the statue to do my job. May I please pass?"

The soldiers looked at each other, and one by one they stepped aside.

"Thank you."

She pulled her staff and walked to the statue.

"Eímai purify this place," she screamed as she drove her staff into the marble next to the statue.

A column of gold lightning flew from the cloudless sky and slammed into the platform, using the staff like a lightning rod. She found she could not let go of the staff or move. The power held her in place as it consumed the statue, platform, and the ground under them. When it ended, a yawning abyss lay beneath her, and she dropped into it.

Glowing water spiraled upward to fill the pit. A dragon with metallic-looking purple and silver scales flew out of the pool below her. A name popped into her mind. Lady Achima.

The dragon snatched her from the sky with her mouth and placed her between the spikes on her back.

"Hold on, little one," Lady Achima said.

Cassandra slapped her staff to her back and grabbed the long spikes in front of her as the dragon leaned to the right. Dragons and

Hikaru shot out of the pool and filled the sky above the city. After them came Vidarr, Talah, Drás, Hikaru, Gwenfrewi, and a strange being with an L-shaped body and four arms. All but the dragons wore mottled gray armor with a broken four-clawed slash across their breastplates. They poured into the city, and none stopped them.

"Who are those four-armed people?" Cassandra asked.

"Ichtaca. They live in the underworld of Aras. Only in the Clan do the races above and below live in harmony. But with your help, that will change."

Thirty dragons moved to cluster around Lady Achima.

"Prevent the Sundered from burning the city. Draw them into range of those on the ground. Remember, if Miseó is among them, capture him alive. But do not risk the lives of others to do so."

The dragons nodded and flew away. Lady Achima descended toward where Captain Ragnar and her brother waited outside the city. Michael packed supplies into the osulves' saddlebags.

"Who's Miseó?" Cassandra asked.

"My brood-mate," Lady Achima explained, her tone firm.

# Chapter 11: Michael

***Central Citali Province, Aras: Spring, Day 12, Year 1, 5th Age***

"And that brings us to now," Michael said as he finished the summary of his life.

He rode east among a group of two hundred Outcast Clan with Captain Ragnar loping next to him on all fours. Half their number flew above them in a loose diamond formation. The wings of the Dragons, Hikaru, and winged Drás beat a steady rhythm that kept time with Neric's paws on the hard earth. No longer in his armor and without wings, Michael felt vulnerable even though he had so many protecting him. But Captain Ragnar had insisted as they left Rün that his fire would bring unnecessary attention. He assured Michael he could recall both if the need arose.

"You did not tell me how you came to be burned," Captain Ragnar said, looking at him. "Such an injury should have been included in your tale."

Michael's eyes widened. When asked to tell his story, he had hoped not to include that part. "How do you know I was burned?"

"You carry the scent of burnt flesh. I know it well. It clings, and only Eímai's water can remove it. But for some reason, he did not remove it when he brought you here in his river. How did it happen?"

"Hide nothing from him," Eímai told him. "Your transparency will build trust. It will also prevent the enemy from using secrets to bring strife between the two of you."

Michael sighed. "I was supposed to take a different way home. I knew deep down I wasn't supposed to go to the bus station. But I rationalized away the feelings and thoughts because I was tired from my trip to Syria and wanted to get home. The feeling grew stronger, and by the time I decided to obey, it was too late. Three buses pulled into the station and exploded. Many were hurt or killed. I rushed in and saved five before a second explosion doused me with burning fuel. I almost died."

The tiger nodded. "Eímai tried to keep you from harm. Why did you rush into danger?"

*What kind of question is that?* "I couldn't just let them die. I had to do something. Besides, I'm a Jenkins. We help people in need. Why do you ask?"

"Your motives are more important than what you do. Doing good for the wrong reason is as wrong as doing evil for the seemingly right reason. Eímai judges us by our motives. As you memorize Eímai's Writings and commune with him, you will see what is in your heart. When your motives are correct, and you are connected to Eímai, his power will flow through you. Then even the most powerful of Ba'rel's slaves will not be able to defeat you."

"You mean like Vold?" Michael asked, shuddering, as he remembered Umoni tiger's scarred face.

"Yes. What did your encounter with *him* teach you?"

*Good question. What did it teach me? I'm way out of my league. I need people to rescue me whenever I face him. I was two seconds away from becoming a meal.*

"Don't give place to such thoughts," Eímai said. "They undermine your connection with me and breed fear. Fear is a weapon of Ba'rel. Analyze Vold as you would any other opponent. What are his strengths and weaknesses?"

"He loves using fear and intimidation," Michael said, stroking his beard. He had wondered why men stroked their beards when they were thinking. Now he found the tactile experience helped him focus. "He's fast and depends on overpowering and crushing his victims with every attack. He enjoys combat and drags it out instead of finishing you off quickly. Chief Ewan says he's vindictive and will avenge any perceived wrong. He also likes eating people. If not for your fighters showing up, I'd be a goner."

"Goner?"

Michael mimed the motion of someone being consumed, as if his hand was devouring his arm.

"Ah, yes. He has fallen far from where he once stood. What else did you learn?"

"He called you Fléau. It means 'scourge' or 'plague' in a language in my world. Why did he use that name?"

"Long ago, the white tiger El'esh named Rasmus had a great-grand-cub named Bergr who was also white. Bergr was a captain of captains in the Ridarri."

"That's the Vidarr order of knights, right?"

"Correct. It is good to see you have been learning something since arriving here."

"I got a lot of information from Lady Jovena. I think she got sick of all my questions."

"Bergr fought in the Dragon/Drás War and became corrupted by Ba'rel. He did not become Sundered, but he committed many crimes against Eímai. While murdering innocents, he was captured and renamed Fléau. A thousand years later, Eímai forgave his crimes, and I was born."

"Born?"

"All I know is Fléau died and was buried. The life I now live, I live in Eímai. But Vold will never acknowledge Eímai's work. He will always see me as Fléau. Remember, the slaves of Ba'rel will never acknowledge what Eímai has done in you. They will focus on failures and anything that condemns you."

"How old are you?"

"Since the birth of my former self or since my rebirth?"

"Both, I guess."

"Bergr was born 2,750 years ago. I was born 1,523 years ago."

Michael whistled. "You look good for nigh on three thousand years."

Captain Ragnar chuffed and smiled. "That is Eímai's doing."

"If I may ask, how did you get those scars on your face?"

"Fléau fought a fenrir," Captain Ragnar said, looking straight ahead.

"What's a fenrir?"

"An osulf Ba'rel has corrupted. They are extremely hard to kill. Beheading is the best way. Their infection and venom are toxic and can turn you into a Sundered. Had it not been for Lady Achima freezing him and dropping him in the Miwa River, I would not be here today."

"She froze you. But how?"

"She froze Fléau, not me."

"Right. Sorry. It's going to take some time getting used to that way of seeing things."

"Lady Achima breathes ice, not flame. She is the only Dragon with that ability."

"Really? That's awesome. I'd love to learn how that's possible."

"Ask the other dragons. Lady Achima will have nothing to do with you."

Michael felt as though he had been slapped. "Why?"

"You are El'esh, and that means you will fight and slay Sundered."

"I thought she'd be okay with that."

"Achima's brood-mate Kephas joined himself to Ba'rel when Rasmus did. He is now called Miseó."

"Brood-mate?"

"They were of the same sires and hatched at the same time."

"Oh. We call that brother and sister. Wait. Her brother is Sundered?"

"Correct. While I see the slayer of Vold as a dispenser of Eímai's justice, in Achima's heart Miseó is still her brother, and she will do whatever it takes to bring him back to Eímai's light."

"Oh wow. That's crazy."

The tiger shot him a sharp look, and Michael's heart skipped a beat. He held up his hands palm out.

"I don't mean she's crazy. I mean, this situation is crazy. To think I'm traveling with someone who's family member I might have to kill. But don't you want Vold to come back?"

"Of course. But remember what Eímai told you. El'esh who surrender themselves to Ba'rel will never want to come back. They walked with Eímai, spoke with him in person, served as conduits of his awesome power, and knew his Writings. This kind of betrayal permanently severs them from Eímai."

"When I was in the Forest, a couple of lynxes said you were immortal. Is that true?"

Captain Ragnar chuffed, and it took Michael a moment to realize it was the tiger's version of laughter. "No, I am not immortal. But Eímai will not let me go to his rest until I complete my mission."

"What's your mission?"

"To train the one who is Fire."

"Me?"

He inclined his head. "If you learn your lessons well and make the right decisions."

"And if I don't, then what?"

"That is up to Eímai," the tiger said grimly.

*So much depends on me being this Fire guy. If I fail, it will really mess everything up.*

"Eímai, please help me not to mess this up," he said under his breath. "I am so in over my head. This is bigger than me. Please give me the strength I need to do what you brought me here to do."

"Open my Writings to the sixth chapter of the Book of Wisdom, line fifty-two," Eímai said in his mind.

Michael pulled the book from his saddlebag and opened it to the first page. Glowing blue cuneiform rose off the page and hovered above the book. It was the table of contents. The entire volume had been separated into four books: Wisdom, Governance, Calling, and Worship.

*I wonder if Governance is the laws necessary for running Aras, like the Law of Moses was for the Israelites. I'll have to check that out later.*

He flipped the pages to the desired passage, and the hovering text changed. When he reached his destination, the text spun and coalesced into the face of Eímai.

"Be strong, courageous, and do not be frozen with fear," the face said. "You can do everything through me, who gives you strength. I am with you; I will never leave or forsake you. I will be with you even to the very end of time. Therefore, fulfill all the duties I have given you."

"Thanks," Michael whispered. He held the book out to Captain Ragnar and said, "How does the writing hover above the book like this and become a talking head?"

"You are a word-shaper," the tiger said with a smile.

"Lady Jovena mentioned the shapers. What does a word-shaper do?"

"They speak, and their words take on a life of their own. I have seen them walking through a city with a book or parchment floating beside them. As they speak, the pen writes their words."

"Seriously? That's awesome. How do they do it?"

"I do not know. But we have some word-shapers in our ranks. They can teach you."

"I wish I had that when I was in college. I wouldn't have gotten hand cramps from trying to write down everything my professors said."

Captain Ragnar chuffed and nodded. "When I was younger, I wished for that ability as well. But hours of holding the stylus in class made my paws strong for battle."

Michael flexed his hand and smiled. "I'll have to remember that when I'm teaching, and my students complain about taking a lot of notes."

"El'esh Miklos told me something similar."

"I'd love to meet him."

"Perhaps one day you will. For now, we must begin your training." The tiger rose to his back paws and pulled a scroll from a pouch on his belt. "El'esh receives training in seven regimens, each taught by a different member of the races. Eímai will teach you throughout the day. He is your greatest instructor."

Michael unrolled the scroll, and the cuneiform hovered over the parchment. He whistled when he saw the following:

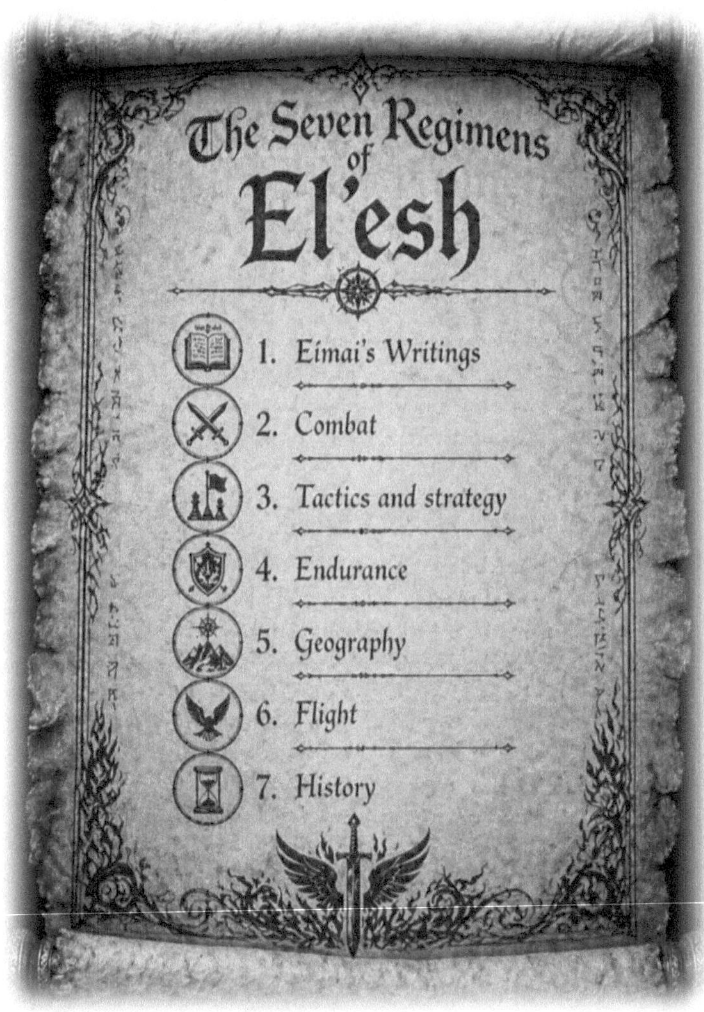

*I get to learn from beings from another world. How awesome is that?*

"Each session lasts three hours," the tiger said as Michael processed the list, "and you will have a five-minute break."

*That gives me about twenty-one hours of training. This'll push me harder than I've ever gone before. I don't know how I'll do this without collapsing. But maybe the enhanced strength Eímai gave me will help. I cannot fail. I will not fail.*

"Alright. When do we start?" he said with a nod.

Captain Ragnar shot him a surprised look. He chuffed. "You are the first to accept the training regimens without complaint."

"Why complain? It is what it is. Complaining does nothing to change things. I'll do my best not to let you down."

Captain Ragnar's face became sad. "When Bergr was younger, he tried to live up to the expectations of others. White tigers are rare and usually become great heroes of the Vidarr. In every Arasian age, there are two born. He was the third born in the fourth age. All expected him to surpass his predecessors. When he fell short of absolute perfection, he was persecuted for it. That is a heavy burden for a cub to bear."

"I know what you mean," Michael said, his grandmother's face filling his mind.

"But Eímai's opinion is the only one that matters. Learn that lesson early, and you will live a much more peaceful life. Read the first five chapters of Wisdom, and I will question you when you are finished."

An Ichtaca with an L-shaped body covered in a deep red shell rose out of the ground next to Captain Ragnar. His angular antennae-less ant-like head had two large green eyes. He had four arms on his vertical torso, the top pair larger than the bottom pair, and the three-fingered hands held two swords and two round shields. His horizontal thorax had four legs ending in two-toed feet. He crossed his swords across his shields. Michael watched them as they conversed.

"Qualoc. Greetings. What is your report?" said the tiger.

"Captain, the enemy is moving to attack the Mushroom Forest. They have at least one dragon with them."

"When will they reach the forest?"

"Two, maybe three at most."

Captain Ragnar shot Michael a sharp look and snarled, "Read. It is rude to listen to the conversations of others."

"Sorry," he said as he flipped to the first chapter of Wisdom, and Eímai's head spoke.

"Listen, my child, and I will give you wisdom to discern between good and evil. My words will give you light in the darkness. They will keep you from the deception of the fallen one and enable you to walk with me blamelessly."

# Chapter 12: Cassandra

*Central Citali Province, Aras: Spring, Day 12, Year 1, 5th Age*

"Clan," Captain Ragnar called with a roar. All talking died. "The enemy moves to seize the Mushroom Forest portal. We have at most three days."

Shouts and roars met his proclamation. The Clan burst forward in a run.

"Hang on," Xesa said as she matched the pace of those around her. Cassandra grabbed the front of Xesa's saddle to keep from falling off. Lady Achima trotted beside her, one stride equal to four of Xesa's.

"While the Clan battles the Legion, we will meet with the council of elders," the dragon said, casting a sidelong glance at her. "They are the first council you will convince to unify. Do not look so horrified. Eímai will guide you and give you the words to say. I will teach you what you need to know."

"How long will it take to get there?" Cassandra asked, her palms getting sweaty in her gloves. She pulled off her gloves and tucked them into the bag at her side.

"At most three days."

"Three days? How am I supposed to learn everything in three days?"

Lady Achima sighed. "Be at peace, Speaker. You will not learn everything in three days. I will teach you what you need for this encounter, and remember Eímai enables you to accomplish this. A scroll in your saddlebag has a list of the regimens you will study."

Cassandra's heart dropped as the list grew with every inch of the scroll she unrolled.

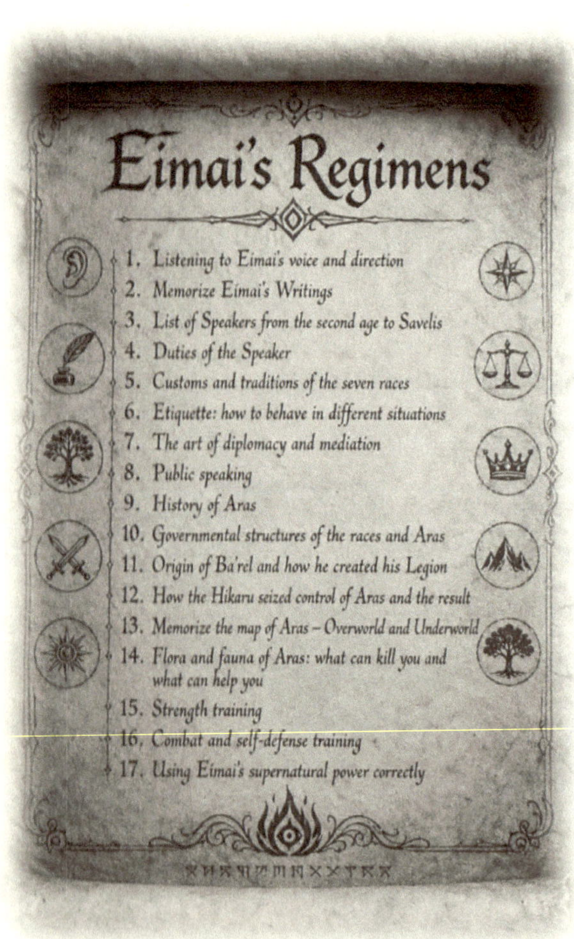

"Sheesh. You got three more to make it an even twenty?" she said, her sarcasm emphasizing her shock.

Lady Achima chuckled. "I could. But these are all Eímai gave me."

"And how long will it take to learn all this?"

"Given our current situation, I do not know. You will learn as you travel and leave the rest to Eímai."

"You really think I can do this?"

The dragon stopped, and Xesa stopped beside her. The rest of the Clan continued their run, flowing around them like a river around a boulder.

"I have seen and done much in the nearly five thousand years of my life. But I would have accomplished nothing if I had not submitted to Eímai's leadership. He makes the impossible possible. While I am used to this, he still surprises me with the way he carries out his will. I had not expected you to be the one I would teach. But here you are, and I am confident that you will achieve all he brought you here to do."

Cassandra returned to the list. She drew a deep breath and sighed. *Eímai, I'll do what you want. You lead, and I will follow.*

"That is all I ask," Eímai said.

"Where do we start? The top of the list?" she asked the dragon.

"I think we should start with the Vidarr in the Mushroom Forest. We will touch on each of the regimens as we do this," Lady Achima said, walking again. Xesa kept pace without direction from the dragon or Cassandra.

*She is one smart dog.*

"When Eímai created Parrésia, he placed each of the seven races in their home. The Vidarr were placed in the Great Forest with its colossal trees whose tops rise nearly as high as the Rogue Mountains on their western border. They are also as big around as two dragons standing side by side. For ages, the Vidarr dwelt there, guarding Aras' western border against the Legion who dwelt on the other side of the mountains. During the Dragon/Drás War, most of the forest was burned in reprisal for the slaughter perpetrated by the Vidarr. When the war ended, there were not enough dwellings for the Vidarr who had survived. Two factions arose. One wanted to stay in the Great Forest and replant the trees even though it would take thousands of years for them to reach their prodigious height. The other wanted to search for new dwellings. The quarrel escalated, and eventually the Vidarr split.

"This is the second schism among the Vidarr. The first was at the end of the second age, when a third moved to the Southern Forest, believing it needed protection. Two ages later, they refused to take part in the Dragon/Drás War because it was in direct violation of Eímai's edict that the races were not to slay each other. They are the second faction of the Vidarr you will need to talk to about joining the rest of the races. Anyway, those who left after the War wandered Aras and eventually settled in the Mushroom Forest. They planted a seedling from the Great Forest, and it grew to maturity in a night. They have their own council of elders, and they accept only their own leadership.

"Kaj is the elder for the lynx clan, Duwalt is the elder for the leopard clan, Vigdis is the elder for the tiger clan, Lennart is the elder for the lion clan, and Suri is the elder for the cheetah clan. I have met with them twice since joining the Outcast Clan."

"Why are you all outcasts?"

"Captain Ragnar is still considered an outcast from his race. Those who join him take on the title of outcast. Though for most of us, we are not truly outcasts. My race still accepts me, and from time to time, I return home to aid my sires. Some who have grieved their sires by joining us include Qualoc the Ichtaca."

"Why?"

"When Sundered Ichtaca pulled the mountains from the sky during Ba'rel's fourth invasion, the surface races accused all the Ichtaca of being Sundered. This is the first time such an accusation has been leveled against an entire race. The Dragon/Drás War is the second when the surface races accused both the Dragon and Drás races of serving Ba'rel. When the surface races rejected the Ichtaca, the Ichtaca established their own king and government. That was also the start of the idea of separate racial governments. Qualoc is the Ichtaca king's son and will take his place when his father returns to the earth from which he was drawn."

*Is it like humans being made of earth at the creation?*

"What does it mean to be drawn from the earth?"

"Eímai used a stone-shaping song to create the Ichtaca."

"Wow. That's awesome. When they get an arm cut off, do they grow a new one by touching the ground or putting dirt on it?"

"We are getting off topic. You will have to ask one of the Ichtaca when you get a moment."

Cassandra laughed. "Yeah, right. When am I going to get a moment?"

Lady Achima flashed her a fang-filled grin. Snowflakes swirled around her muzzle when she breathed out of her nose. "You will. Of all the Vidarr elders, Lennart and Vigdis are the most stubborn. They will be the hardest to convince to let go of past grievances. Vigdis tends to follow Lennart's lead, so if you persuade Lennart, you will have Vigdis as well."

"Great," Cassandra said with sarcasm. "How do I do that?"

"Honestly, I do not know. Depend on Eímai to show you when the time comes. Now, when you enter the council chamber, wait for them to acknowledge you. Then greet them in the Vidarr fashion."

"I just stand there and wait for them to speak to me?"

"Yes. It is considered rude to enter the presence of a leader and interrupt them."

"And if they're just sitting there not doing anything, I still have to stand there silently?"

"Yes."

"And if they don't acknowledge me at all? Then what?"

"Do whatever Eímai tells you to do."

"You're not being helpful."

"If you speak out of turn, they will reject you outright. You currently have no rapport with the council. When you have earned their trust, you will be able to enter their presence and speak, no matter what they may be doing.”

Cassandra sighed. *I wish I were fighting in the battle. It would be easier than this.*

“No, it wouldn’t,” Eímai said. “Since I didn’t call you to fight it would be infinitely harder than standing before the council.”

“The Vidarr have a rich military tradition. They honor valor in battle. They will want to know about your battles. What battles have you fought?”

“I haven’t been in battles. I fought some Matu in the Armorer’s Forest when they tried to jump us. Michael came to our rescue and wiped them out. Oh, I fought a Sundered named Lusare. I defeated her. Lady Jovena wanted me to kill her. But Eímai wanted her to come back to him and told me I couldn’t kill anyone. She escaped before Lady Jovena could kill her. Other than that, I got in a few fights back home. Nothing major.”

The dragon’s eyes widened. “Lusare is here? That is a complication we do not need.”

“She said she’d do everything to stop me and then eat me. She’s got some serious issues.”

“I knew her before she fell to Ba’rel. She had a wise and gentle spirit. But losing her loved ones during the War broke her. She became bitter. In her grief, she made some bad decisions. She blamed everyone but herself when she received the consequences of her choices. Having fought Lusare will give you some influence. Praise their strength and remind them that their full strength can be found in unifying with the races, especially the Vidarr factions."

"There are so many different groups. Three Vidarr and the Eastern and Western dragons. That's two dragon factions. No, three with the Dragon/Drás Confederation. The Talah have the Savelins and those who follow Lady, uh, Chief Jovena. What about the other races?"

"The Drás have the Confederation. I know of no factions among the Gwenfrewi and Ichtaca. Qualoc would know of any among the Ichtaca. The Hikaru has those loyal to the king and those who wish to return to the former Aras."

"Why don't they just change things?"

"The Hikaru opposition are not willing to risk their lives to challenge the king. Did Chief Jovena tell you about King's Scelto?"

"Yeah," Cassandra said with a sigh. "She said they'd come after me."

"They will. They will most likely wait until you are at Ker'an and no longer have a bodyguard."

"Seriously?" Cassandra exploded. This drew the attention of the warriors around them. "I just can't get a break."

"It is the world we live in," Lady Achima said in a sad tone. "But if you fulfill your role, it will change forever."

"No pressure."

"Exactly," Lady Achima said, smiling at her. "If it were easy, we would not need Eímai to empower us. Let us continue the lesson."

The hours passed as the dragon pumped Cassandra with more information than she thought she could learn in one chunk. But to her surprise, her mind absorbed every detail and amazed her teacher by passing every test she gave her. But the real test awaited her in the Mushroom Forest and that dampened Cassandra's enthusiasm.

# Chapter 13: Michael

***Central Citali Province, Aras: Spring, Day 13, Year 1, 5th Age***

Michael's sore rear end caused him to glance at his clock.

"Sixth hour of Second Half-Dark, Day 13."

*I figured years of riding horses would prepare me for this. Yet two days on an osulf and I'm ready to call it quits. I hope we stop for the night soon.*

The clan marched through the hills north of Theitai, and to Michael, the hills looked like miniature grass-covered mountains. Master Kardeiz, a Talah scholar of Arasian History, rode on a puffin next to him, his deep voice pontificating about Ba'rel's origins. The man looked like a blend of professor and knight. His white beard stuck out at random angles. His eyebrows danced like hairy caterpillars over his eyes as his eyes widened and narrowed in time with his undulating voice. The large pack on his back jingled as his mount trotted just out of Neric's reach. Domestication had apparently not overridden the bird's desire to stay as far from its natural predator as possible.

"Eímai created five crystal dragons to stand before his throne and sing his praises. The chief of the five was Teleiotes. Each of his seven heads sang in a different octave. He was a word-shaper and crafted some of the most beautiful hymns we still sing today. But over time, he grew arrogant and thought he could overthrow Eímai. A third of the races joined him, and the gifts he had given them became twisted for evil. They became the first Sundered and the first soldiers in his Legion."

"What gifts?" Michael asked.

"The Vidarr can become invisible, and their acute senses can pick out the faintest smells, sights, or sounds. The Dragons can see the song Eímai used to sing everything into existence. The Ichtaca can move through stone the way a Gwenfrewi can move through water, and they can also shape it in ways that boggle the mind. The Drás pass their memories on to their offspring in a ritual called The Passing. Therefore, a single Drás could possess the memories of their ancestors going all the way back to the first age. Though how they keep it all straight is a mystery to me. Oh, and some can fly and breathe fire like the Dragons. The Gwenfrewi are exceptionally wise and can use their voices as weapons. I have seen Gwenfrewi's scream send enemies flying. They can also shoot poisoned barbs from their hands. Talah can enhance a blade, making it nearly indestructible and capable of cutting through almost anything. Most of the various types of shapers come from this race as well. Is that all of them?"

He muttered to himself as he counted on his fingers. "Ah, yes. The Hikaru. Yes. The Hikaru have wings, of course, and have above-normal dexterity due to their flying ability, no doubt. They also have enhanced sight and a long memory. Their long memory makes them the best scribes in Aras, as they can still remember what they heard thirty or forty minutes ago. Legend has it that a Hikaru can remember things they heard throughout their lifetime. I have not had the opportunity to test the legend to see if it is true."

A flicker of movement in the hills to Michael's left drew his attention. He studied the hills but saw nothing. *Why is my heart racing? It's like my senses have kicked into overdrive. Where's this fear coming from? Am I being paranoid? Where's Captain Ragnar? Oh, that's right. He's walking with Maja and Frida, further back in the ranks. I've seen too many movies where someone dismissed something odd, they saw, only to get eaten.*

"Excuse me, Master Kardeiz, but I saw movement over there," Michael said, pointing toward the movement.

"I do not see anything," the wizened scholar-warrior said as he looked through a spyglass he had pulled from his pack. "But that means nothing. We'd better let the captain know."

Michael's flaming armor erupted around him, and he called the white tiger on the talking disk in his vambrace.

"Captain Ragnar, I saw movement among the hills, and something feels very wrong. I feel afraid, but that could just be me."

Suddenly, parts of the surrounding hillsides rose on poles, while others fell forward like drawbridges, revealing caverns filled with darkness. Akzari, Isoni, and Sundered swarmed out to hit the Clan from every side. Behind them came creatures that looked like they had once been osulves. Huge sores protruded from among the patches of dark fur, and the green pus oozing from them burned everything it touched. Green saliva poured from between broken brown fangs, and more green fluid dripped from their claws. Their howls made Master

Kardeiz's puffin squawk and bolt, his rider screaming at it to stop. He disappeared into the hills. Two of the creatures took off after him.

"Fenrir," Captain Ragnar's floating head roared. "Stay away from the venom and infection. They will corrupt you into a Sundered. Only beheading kills them. Clan, form up. Vidarr, hide in Eímai's shadow. El'esh Michael, take to the sky."

His head disappeared as the tiger used his ability to become invisible. As Michael activated his armor, the Vidarr around him melted into thin air. But through his visor, they appeared as orange shadows moving into formation. The Talah warriors drew their weapons, and the edges of their blades glowed with different colors.

*I wonder if they hum or make a crackling sound when they're used. It's like a medieval version of an energy sword.*

He spread his wings and launched himself into the sky. He spoke the words that appeared inside his helmet.

"Eímai's perfect love casts out all fear. No weapon of the Legion will succeed against us for we are under Eímai's protection."

"Pemakin" a Talah screamed to his right.

A swarm of large black beetles poured out of one of the tunnels. Their mandibles opened and closed, the motion releasing a shrieking sound.

The man yanked the stopper from his canteen and threw the glowing water on the carnivorous insects. The pemakin sizzled and melted, releasing the smell of sulfur and tendrils of black smoke.

Two bright blue blurs shot from Michael's shoulders into the swarm of beetles. Four more launched from Neric.

*Greater clippers. I forgot about those guys.*

A fenrir snatched one out of the air as it passed by. A blue fireball enveloped its head. Its decapitated body dissolved into black smoke. When the smoke cleared, the greater clipper fluttered at the same level as the fenrir's head. It looked unfazed by the fenrir's attack. It turned and joined its comrades in devouring pemakin. Flaming mandibles tore them apart, and their shrieks took on a different tone before stopping abruptly.

Michael summoned a spear and threw it into the side of a fenrir grappling with a Vidarr lion that was not invisible. The fenrir howled and jerked away from the lion. Michael pinned it to the ground with another spear and dropped to deliver a double-handed cut to its neck. The head thudded to the ground. The grass and dirt sizzled with contact with its venom and blood.

Growling and groaning came from the staggering lion. He had long gashes across his chest, arms, and face. The wounds festered at a rapid rate. The lion's body transformed. His golden mane turned crimson, and curved horns grew from his shoulders and joints. His claws doubled in size, and green venom dripped from them. He roared and locked obsidian eyes on Michael.

"El'esh," he roared and charged.

Michael's wings carried him to the right, and the lion missed him. He slammed into two Isoni who held down a Gwenfrewi with a goldfish face and purple fins on her head and forearms. They raised their glaives for a killing blow.

The impact of Michael's body with the Isoni sent them flying. He chucked a spear at each and swept her into his arms. One took an Isoni in the shoulder, and the other punched through his stomach. A tiger-shaped shadow removed their heads before they could pull out the spears.

You, okay?" he asked as he carried the Gwenfrewi to the top of a hill away from the battle.

She gasped and nodded.

"Good. Hopefully you'll be safe here. What's your name?"

"I will not stand by while my pod fights," she said in the gargling accent of her race.

"I'm sorry, I don't understand. What is a pod?"

She waved at the battlefield, and Michael realized she referred to the Outcast Clan.

"You don't have a weapon. Do your barbs work outside of the water?"

Just then, the Sundered lion rose, shook himself, and looked around. His eyes locked on Michael.

Yes!" she shouted, raising webbed hands toward the Sundered lion charging up the hill. Six long white barbs shot from her palms and formed a tight cluster in the lion's chest.

*Holy cow. There's got to be only a couple of centimeters between each barb. Amazing shot.*

The lion kept coming, and Michael stepped between them, shield and sword raised.

"That will not be necessary," she said. "The toxin will take effect now."

The lion staggered a step, black foam poured from his mouth, and he fell forward. The impact of his body sent shock waves through the hill.

"That was a great shot," he said, turning to her.

"Thank you. Every Gwenfrewi spends years practicing. Unfortunately, I spent all my barbs, and it will take three days to regrow more."

"Good thing there's plenty of weapons lying around."

Her face hardened. "Those weapons belong to the slain Outcast Clan. That is never a good thing."

"I'm sorry. I didn't mean it that way."

She stalked past him, scooping up a trident from where she had been lying moments before.

"Way to go," Michael muttered to himself as he launched into the air, gaining enough altitude to see the entire battle. He could not tell who was winning. Smoke masked most of the battlefield. Outcast Clan littered the ground. Some stumbled to their feet, transformed as the lion had, and turned on their comrades. The Clan's flying forces attacked from the air with fire, arrows, and spears.

Lady Achima, with Cassandra on her back, fought a swarm of Sundered Hikaru and Drás. The purple and silver dragon froze anyone who came near, and Cassandra shattered their arrows and spears with bolts of lightning. They looked to be holding their own. He flew toward them to help.

"You haven't mastered aerial combat yet," Eímai said. "You will be a hindrance and not a benefit. Focus on those below. They need your help more than your sister."

"But—"

"No buts. Do as you are told."

Eímai's firm tone left no room for argument. But he did not move.

*What if someone gets in close and hurts or kills Cassandra? I can't let that happen. She needs me to watch her back.*

Eímai appeared before him, brilliant body blocking his view of the fight. His burning eyes pierced him, and he shook before the stern gaze of his lord. "Michael, you must obey me. The Clan warriors will die or be corrupted if you do not act now. I will protect your sister. You must trust me. Go protect my children. That is why I brought you here."

"Yes, Sir. Sorry."

"Maja and Frida are below you. They are tiring fast and have returned to visibility. Drop between them and use your sword and shield to defend them."

Eímai vanished. Michael took a quavering breath, shot one last glance at his sister blowing up enemy weapons, and looked down. Sundered Vidarr encircled Maja and Frida. The two fought to keep them back, but the circle steadily got smaller. Michael tucked his wings and dropped feet first into the circle. He spread his wings and sent two Sundered leopards on either side of him flying.

"About time you got here," Maja yelled over the din of her scimitars knocking away, stabbing spears, and slicing them in half. A lynx spear wielder tried to stab her with what remained of the handle and fell to Maja's cross slash.

"Figured I'd drop in," he said and moved his shield to block two axes aimed for Frida's head. The blows drove the shield down onto her shoulders. She grunted and shoved the shield, knocking the axes away. She slammed her daggers into the Sundered lion's chest.

"Where's Captain Ragnar?" he asked, smashing his shield into the face of a Sundered leopard and finishing them off with a diagonal slash.

"I do not know. He ran to give aid against the fenrir, and we were overrun," Maja said, deflecting stabbing spears with her twin scimitars. "Where did they all come from?"

"Holes in the hills. They must have been waiting for us to come by."

"That means they have been here for some time and did not come through the enemy portals."

"Yup. They infiltrated and waited for the signal to attack. Guerrilla warfare. Tiger on your right."

Maja pirouetted and blocked the glowing scimitars of a black tiger with orange stripes. Akzari stepped in to fill the gaps made by the slain Sundered Vidarr. Attacks continued to come from everywhere.

"Eímai, help," Michael yelled as he failed to be everywhere at once.

The world around him slowed. An Akzari crept forward to stab Maja in the back with a notched sword. A Sundered lynx jumped into the air and brought a spear down to impale Frida through her right shoulder. Four Akzari brought their swords down to finish Maja, who knelt holding a deep gash in her side. Orange blood poured from under her paw to cover her armor and the ground.

Past the tangle of attackers, Michael saw the panic, desperation, and fear on the faces of the nearest Outcast Clan warriors. Each scrambled to block oncoming attacks and hold the little bit of ground they stood on. One by one, they were being cut down.

*Wait a minute. What are we doing? The Clan doesn't fight defensively. They take the fight to the enemy and make them wish they weren't born. They're aggressive fighters, and they fight best as a unified unit. That's it. That was their plan. Surprise us with a fast assault so we'd freak out, and then get us defending ourselves instead of aggressively taking the fight to them. Eímai, can you make sure everyone can hear me?*

"Of course. Go ahead and speak."

"Outcast Clan, listen to me. The enemy surprised us, so we'd be afraid, separated, and defensive. But that's not what we do. We're strong and courageous, not frozen with fear and overcome with despair because Eímai's with us. Remember your training. Regroup and work together to annihilate these guys. You are stronger together. All glory to Eímai."

"All glory to Eímai," shouted his audience.

Maja and Frida started singing, and the song spread. The words scrolled on the inside of Michael's helmet, and he joined in.

No one is as mighty and faithful as you, Eímai.
You fashioned all with the word of your power.
You made us all.
Righteousness and justice are the foundation of your throne.
Mercy and truth go before you.
We walk, O Eímai, in the light of your countenance.
We worship and serve you alone.
You defend us, and we forever rest in your power.

The effect was immediate. A tangible feeling of peace settled over the battlefield.

The Legion stopped fighting. Their eyes widened, and they backed away from those they had been attacking.

Most of the Clan slipped into organized ranks while the remainder tended the wounded. They used Eímai's water and the leaves from the trees that grew beside his water to tend the wounded. Those who could were helped to their feet and given a weapon. All drank from their canteens.

The enemy raised their weapons and roared.

Michael laughed and charged.

# Chapter 14: Cassandra

***Theitai, Southern Citali Province, Aras: Spring, Day 13, Year 1, 5th Age***

Lady Achima landed on the outskirts of the town and lowered herself for Cassandra to dismount. Years of gymnastics and parkour enabled Cassandra to dismount gracefully. The town had stone and wood buildings of varying sizes. Some were big enough for Lady Achima to enter. Most had colorful domed roofs.

"It is up to you to gather the necessary reinforcements we need to save the others," the Dragon told her. "Use what I taught you to encourage their help."

"No pressure," she said. "I hope Mike's okay."

"He is El'esh. They do not fall easily."

The town's main street was large enough for the Dragon to walk down and not hit the hanging signs in front of a plethora of shops. The Snoring Traveler Inn sign featured a Drás with a triceratops head lying in a large bed, squiggly-looking z's rising from his open mouth. It made Cassandra laugh, and she pointed at the sign.

Lady Achima pointed to the wall between the large bay windows. Painted on the wall in vivid color was a red kite shield with a silhouette of a Dragon facing the silhouette of a Drás. She looked at the other buildings, and every one of them sported the crest of the Dragon/Drás Confederation.

Cassandra turned to Lady Achima and said, "Well, this is a bust. We should get back. Maybe you could fly over everything and freeze them all."

"My icy breath is nearly spent," the Dragon said. "I need at least a day's rest to recharge."

"What? You never said it had limits," Cassandra said in irritation.

"The only thing without limit is Eímai's love and power, young Speaker. We are here, and we will not leave until we have secured help for our friends. One thing you must know about Dragons and Drás is that we pass our memories down to our brood in a ritual called The Passing. The purpose is to transfer the lessons we have learned so broodlings will not repeat them. However, during the Dragon/Drás War, the ritual was corrupted due to Ba'rel's deception. The corrupted version passes on the worst of one's memories. The Confederation uses it to make sure that the atrocities of the War are never forgotten."

"That means they're programmed to hate."

"Yes. They no longer depend on Eímai or anyone but themselves. They blame Eímai for losing the War, though it ended with no real victor. They do not acknowledge his sovereignty. Their contact outside of the Confederation is minimal and usually hostile."

Cassandra threw up her hands and paced in front of the Dragon. "That's just peachy. Do you have any other good news for me? How am I supposed to get them to go against thousands of years of brainwashing? That's not something you change in a few minutes."

"First, every audience has leaders. Convince them, and the rest will follow. Second, speak the words Eímai gives you. They will always be the best words to speak, even if they do not appear to be. Third, rest in Eímai. Fear and anxiety cloud your judgment and connection Eímai. Do not let them rule you."

Cassandra closed her eyes and took a cleansing breath. She opened her hands palm out. "Eímai, I don't know what to do. This looks hopeless. Please give me the words to speak. I need your favor, or Mike and everyone will die. Please help."

"Drink my water and eat a piece of fruit," Eímai said. "Regain your strength."

The instructions seemed odd to do at that moment. But she obeyed. Lady Achima also ate some fruit and drank from Cassandra's canteen. To Cassandra's surprise, no matter how much the Dragon drank, water continued to flow out of the container. When she took it back, the canteen appeared untouched. Even after she drank four large gulps, it remained full.

"Eímai always provides for his children," Lady Achima said in response to her awe. "Do you feel better?"

"Yes. I'm not freaking out anymore."

"Good. We will start with this inn. You enter by the front door, and I by the Dragon entrance on the side of the building. Remember, you are the Speaker, chosen by Eímai. Diplomacy, respect, and understanding go a long way."

"Yes, Ma'am," Cassandra said as she opened the door and stepped into the main dining hall.

The stone room had a cozy feel with a fireplace at one end, and Drás and Dragons of every shape and color sat at stone tables. On the right side of the room sat the bar, with the majority of the stools occupied by Drás. Behind the bar stood four rows of stacked barrels, a cork as wide as Cassandra's leg plugging each. In front of the barrels stood a red Dragon with a golden belly and horns that spiraled from the side of its head, pointing forward. Octagonal plates ran down the Dragon's back. Its whip-like tail undulated behind the Dragon as they moved back and forth, helping patrons. The long barb decorating the tail's tip stabbed the cork in a barrel on the second row and pulled it out. Pink fluid poured into a tankard, and the tail plugged the hole as the vessel filled.

The room hummed with at least a hundred different conversations, and Drás and Dragon waiters carried giant platters covered with roasted meat, fresh-baked bread, cheese, and fruit. Cassandra noticed that none of the fruit looked like what grew along Eímai's water.

*Where'd they get that? I didn't know fruit grew anywhere else. Eímai, what do I do now?*

A few of the inn's patrons looked her way, but they quickly returned their attention to their tables.

*I guess that when in doubt, talk to the innkeeper. I wonder whether the Dragon behind the bar is the innkeeper.*

She approached the bar and took a seat directly in front of the Dragon, who studied her with slitted golden eyes.

"What do you want, Talah?" the Dragon asked in a rumbling voice that carried a hint of femininity.

Cassandra flashed her warmest smile and tried to remember the Dragon greeting. It came to her. She dipped her head and opened her arms as though spreading wings. "Greetings, Lady. I have come seeking assistance for friends who are fighting the Legion in the hills north of here."

Conversations died, and she felt everyone's eyes on her.

"The Legion, you say? That would be bad news if it were true. We have not seen the Legion anywhere in our territory."

"They were hiding in holes in the hills. When we passed by, they opened trap doors and jumped out at us. Many have already been killed or corrupted."

"How is it you got here unscathed and not out of breath? If the battle were so treacherous, why is there no mark on you?"

"I was on Lady Achima's back. We fought from the air. Then we came here."

"You abandoned them to death? So much for loyalty. Another example of the fickleness of the Talah. Loyal only to the point of inconvenience."

"That's not true!" Cassandra said, slapping the counter. "We came here looking for help. We wouldn't be here otherwise."

The patrons whispered to each other and watched her with narrowed eyes. Some of the Drás drew their swords.

"Lady Achima," a purple Drás said, motioning to the dragon from a table across the room, his neck frills rising to surround his head. "If she is here, then those in the hills are Outcast Clan. We have no dealings with traitors and murderers. Leave, Talah. Your kind is not welcome here."

Cassandra slid from the stool and strode to the middle of the room. "I am not Talah. I am Human." She gave them the official greeting, her head inclined and her arms spread. "My name is Cassandra. Yes, I give you my name first, for I come to you as a friend, if you will have my friendship. I am new to Aras and Parrésia. Three days ago, Eímai took me from my world and brought me here. In that time, I've tried to learn about this world and its races." Cassandra scanned the room as she talked, turning a slow circle so she could look into the eyes of her audience. "One of the things I have learned is that the Dragons and Drás are two great and noble races who have endured for ages. But now more than ever, you are all in danger of annihilation."

Just then, Cassandra noticed Lady Achima sitting at a table at the back of the room, devouring a gigantic piece of meat. Her stomach gurgled, and she lost her train of thought. She felt her face flush as she looked down at the floor, suddenly at a loss for what to say next.

"You're doing fine. Keep going," Eímai whispered to her.

A new line of thought came to her. She looked up and cleared her dry throat. "The Legion has used innocent blood to open portals all over Aras so they can come in and destroy, no, devour, every adult and broodling. They want your complete annihilation. Ba'rel has worked so hard to divide Aras, and he has succeeded. Instead of standing together for mutual good, the races fought and slaughtered each other. Now, they are so divided that the Legion has little opposition. One by one, they will eliminate those who stand in their way, and Aras will fall to him."

Cassandra scanned the room, observing that she now had the rapt attention of every patron in the inn. She rolled her shoulders back and took a deep breath. "You are angry. You hate the races because of what happened during the War. But those crimes were committed thousands of years ago by beings who are long dead. You see the races as your enemy. But they're not your true enemy. Ba'rel is. He laughed while you fought and died at each other's hands and claws. And what's worse, he got you to believe Eímai was doing it all. He had you turn on the one who created you and provided for you as a sire does their broodlings."

"Why did Eimai allow the war to happen?" a small, plump dragon asked.

"Eímai wept when the War happened," Cassandra explained as she turned to face the one who'd posed the question.

The plump dragon frowned. "Then why didn't he stop it?"

Several patrons chimed in, demanding to know the answer.

Cassandra raised her hands. "He tried," she said, her voice loud. "But the races wouldn't listen." She walked to the table where the plump dragon sat and met his silver glare with a smile. "The time has come to unite and prove to Ba'rel once and for all that Aras will never be his. You were hard-pressed on every side yet not crushed. You were perplexed but not in despair. You were persecuted but not forsaken. You were struck down but not destroyed. In Aras, there is neither Dragon, nor Drás, nor Talah, nor Vidarr, nor Gwenfrewi, nor Ichtaca, nor Hikaru. Instead, there is Aras and only Aras. One country that will rise from the ashes to a glory beyond measure. The choice is yours. But please make it quickly. People are fighting for their lives right now. One of them is my brother. Uh, my brood-mate. He was also brought here. He is the only brother I have, and to lose him… would be as devastating as what your people experienced. Thank you, and Eímai's peace be upon you."

She inclined her head and opened her arms. She met the eyes of those she walked past on her way to Lady Achima's table, but most looked away. She took a chair across from the Dragon.

"Very well done," Lady Achima said. "You were respectful, spoke the truth, and gave them a call to action. From the conversations taking place, your words had an impact."

"I hope so. Do you think they'd let me have some food? My stomach is empty again. That took a lot out of me."

A pink Dragon with a white belly and horns approached and greeted them with spread wings. She looked young, though Cassandra could not pinpoint what it was about the Dragon that made her think this. The Dragon held a large tray filled with roasted meat, a huge chunk of steaming bread, and herb-encrusted vegetables in her large front claws. She set the tray before Cassandra and handed her a fork and a knife.

"Greetings. I am Server Toula. If there is anything else you need, please let me know."

"Thank you very much," Cassandra said, yanking off her gloves and setting them next to her. She dove into the food with reckless abandon. The meat's tenderness and subtle spiciness made her groan with pleasure. The hearty bread had been slathered with a thick layer of creamy purple butter that ran down her chin when she bit into it. The herb-encrusted vegetables topped off a meal that rivaled her mother's. She hummed with delight with every bite.

"Easy, young Speaker," Lady Achima said with a laugh, "You do not want to choke yourself to death. You still have much work to do."

"Sorry," Cassandra said with her mouth full. "This is amazing!"

Server Toula set a large tankard of pink drink in front of her. It fizzed and formed a white froth on top.

Cassandra swallowed her mouthful and said, "I'm sorry, but I don't drink alcohol. Do you have some fruit juice or water?"

"I do not know what alcohol is, Speaker Cassandra," Server Toula said, "This is rabble fizz. We make it from berries that grow in the Southern Forest and store it in barrels until it reaches perfection."

"It's strawberry soda," Cassandra exclaimed after a tiny sip. She took a gulp. "My favorite."

The pink Dragon looked at Lady Achima, and the purple Dragon chuckled. "It would appear that Parrésia is not the only world with rabble fizz."

The pink Dragon nodded and raised her chin in an imperious manner. "Rightly so. No civilized race can exist without it."

"How long will it take to decide if they'll help?" Cassandra asked Lady Achima, wiping her greasy mouth on a cloth napkin.

"They have already decided," Lady Achima said, waving to the inn.

Cassandra turned and found only herself, Lady Achima, Server Toula, and the innkeeper in the room. She had not heard anyone leaving.

"Huh?"

"They went to help your brood-mate," the innkeeper said as she approached. She greeted Lady Achima with a deeper incline of her head and spreading of her wings than Server Toula. "Greetings, Lady Achima, broodling of the great Lord Lysander and Lady Lita. I am honored to have you in my establishment."

"Greetings, Lady Photina, broodling of Master Aquila and Weapons-master Kloe. It has been a long time."

"Two thousand years at least. I believe the last time was when I refused Nakor's proposal." Lady Achima turned to Cassandra. "Nakor is one of her brood-mates."

While the two Dragons caught up on old times, Cassandra finished eating. More than half of the food remained on the platter. Stomach filled, she suddenly felt guilty for eating while the others still fought.

"Excuse me. I don't mean to be rude," Cassandra said, pushing her chair away from the table. "Shouldn't we get back to help the others?"

"There is no need for that," Lady Photina said. "By the time you get there, the battle will be over, and they will be on their way here. I must go and prepare for my new guests. Lady Achima. Speaker Cassandra. I will have Server Toula bring you chocolate truffles for dessert."

# Chapter 15: Michael

*Theitai, Southern Citali Province, Aras: Spring, Day 14, Year 1, 5th Age*

The bed's warmth embraced Michael's sore body. Birdsong told him First-Rising had occurred, while the gentle snoring of twenty warriors urged him to go back to sleep. He groaned and opened his eyes. Stone walls, rough-cut timbers, and a crackling fire in the fireplace made the huge room inviting.

*It's like the ski lodge we stayed at in Colorado. Though none of the rooms were this big or filled with sleeping Talah, Vidarr, and an Ichtaca prince.*

Qualoc sat with his back against the fireplace. Waves of heat rippled over his carapace like a hot sidewalk on a summer day and disappeared into his carapace. His unblinking oval eyes stared at Michael, though his breathing matched the rest of the sleepers.

Everyone else lay on beds or mats on the floor. Thick blankets covered the Talah. The smaller cats slept curled up, and the larger ones rested on their stomachs or sides. Each slept in his armor, even though the inhabitants of the town stood guard outside.

Michael rubbed his eyes and thought about the previous day's events—the Legion's surprise attack, the screams of the dying and wounded, the Clan rallying after his speech, the Umoni Talah arriving with reinforcements for the Legion, and Captain Ragnar's sudden appearance to fight him.

*I don't think I would've been able to follow the fight if not for my enhanced senses. I'm glad I'm on his good side. Good thing the Confederation came when it did. We were so close to losing.*

His mind automatically slipped back to the two hours spent digging graves. He shook his head and pushed down the gory images. *If the bombing still haunts me, how long will yesterday haunt me?* He grabbed his canteen and drained it. The cleansing power of Eímai's water washed away the signs, sounds, and smells of the previous day.

"Good morning, Eímai," he whispered. "Thank you for this beautiful day. Thank you for helping us survive and win yesterday. Thank you for the Confederation. Thank you for helping Cassandra convince these guys to help us. Thank you for this bed and the nice place to stay. It's good to sleep in a soft bed again. Please help me make wise decisions today and get us to the Mushroom Forest on time. Thank you for giving me what I asked for."

He spent an hour studying Eímai's Writings. He whispered his notes to the blank book hovering next to his bed. The stylus scrawled his words in flowing cuneiform.

*I love being able to dictate like this.*

When he finished, he bowed down by his bed and prayed for his family, himself, Aras, Captain Ragnar, and the Outcast Clan, and anyone and anything else that came to mind. As he prayed, the fire within him burst forth, and his wings spread to their fullest length. They lifted him from the floor, and he straightened, arms and face turned skyward. Power, peace, and joy poured into him, and he laughed. The trauma of the previous day melted away, and tears poured down his cheeks.

"Thank you," he whispered as he wiped his face.

He returned to the floor, and the fire and wings faded. He looked around to see if he had disturbed anyone. Not one had stirred.

*Wow, they sleep harder than I do. But after what happened yesterday, I can understand why.*

He pulled on his boots and jacket and slipped out of the room, whistling softly to himself as he descended the creaky stairs to the dining room. The inhabitants of the town sat on one side, and the Outcast Clan sat on the other. His sister sat at the bar holding up a large tankard. A book sat open in front of her, and she held a pen in her other hand.

"May I have some more, please?" she asked, holding up her tin tankard.

Lady Phontina smiled as she filled it.

Michael plopped down next to his sister. "Good morning, Cass. Good morning, Lady Phontina. That was the best sleep I've had in a long time. Thank you for allowing us to stay at your inn. May I have a tankard of blackberry fizz and whatever you're serving for breakfast?" He set a gold coin on the counter.

Lady Phontina picked it up between two talons and dropped it in a stone box behind the counter.

"Is he the one?" she asked Cassandra as she served him the drink.

"Yep."

"The one what?" Michael asked, taking a sip. *I'm so glad Aras has blackberries. A little taste of home in a foreign world. Thank you, Father, for this gift.*

"Nothing," Cassandra said, trying to hide a smirk behind her tankard.

"Uh-huh," he said, taking another drink. "How'd you sleep?"

"Great. The bed is the softest I've ever slept in. The room reminded me of a ski lodge in Colorado."

"Me too. But without the six feet of snow outside and subzero temperatures."

Cassandra laughed. "True that."

"Doing some journaling?"

"Yeah. Lady Achima says every Speaker is required to keep a journal of all their activities, insights, and so on. I'm finishing up writing about what happened yesterday."

The smell of fried dough seized Michael's attention and launched him from his stool. Server Toula strode toward him, holding a platter heaped with pillows of fried dough covered in white powder. Each of the pastries was as big as his hand. Plump blackberries the size of his thumb circled the mountain of doughy goodness. She smiled at him as he gaped at the food she placed on the counter. Cassandra snatched one, blessed it, and took a huge bite. White powder decorated her cheeks and the tip of her nose.

"No way. Seriously? Beignets and blackberries?"

He grabbed one, blessed it, and a third of the pastry disappeared into his mouth. He danced a jig as he chewed. When he devoured the rest, he spread his arms wide and gave Toula a deep bow. "Server Toula," he proclaimed loudly for everyone to hear. "Truly, you are the most blessed of dragons. The generous will themselves be blessed, for they share their food with the poor. You bring food to this poor man, and I will rejoice whenever I think of you."

Her face flushed a deeper pink. "You should not jest about such things. I do not make the food. I only deliver it."

Cassandra laughed, sending a cloud of powdered sugar into the air. She covered her mouth and laughed harder.

"Are you well, Speaker?" Lady Phontina asked, clapping her on the back with a large paw. She handed her a cloth napkin.

Cassandra nodded and swallowed. "Yes, thank you. Server Toula, he's not joking. You brought him two of his favorite foods. We have a saying back home. The way to a man's heart is through his stomach."

"If I knew that, I would have used it a long time ago," Server Toula said, her face scales growing crimson.

"There are more customers to serve. Get back to work," Lady Photina told her.

The pink dragon hurried away, and Michael thought she held her head higher than she had before. *A little boost of confidence? I wonder if there's a dragon in here, she's got her eye on.*

"Food does not work on every male," Captain Ragnar said as he approached arm in arm with Maja. "Prowess and ferocity in combat capture the heart of a Vidarr male."

"Really?" Maja said with a smile at her mate. "And my roasted rugi chops and fried potatoes did nothing to capture your attention?" She looked at the others. "He ate five helpings of both, and the chops are half the size of that platter. He growled with every bite and had to bathe afterward because he was covered in grease."

The tiger captain cleared his throat and smiled. "It affirmed that I had made the right choice."

"Sure, it did," she said, squinting up at him.

Captain Ragnar averted his eyes and focused on Michael, who grinned as he popped blackberries into his mouth.

"It is good to see you are rested. We leave in one hour."

"Any news about Master Kardeiz?" Michael asked, his smile vanishing.

"No. We looked everywhere, except the tunnels, and found no sign of him. Even the osulves could not catch his scent. The fervor of the battle and the stench of the Legion covered all signs of him."

"I hope he's okay. How many did we lose?"

"Half of our party fell, either slain, wounded, or missing. While we destroyed all we could, it is possible some of the Legion retreated into the tunnels. If the tunnels go deep enough, they enter the Ichtaca's realm, and it would take an age to find them down there."

"Maybe Master K went down there."

"If he did," Maja said, "he would not stop until he had explored it from one end to the other. That is, if he survives the dangers."

"I'd love to go down there and explore," Michael said, grabbing another beignet.

"You have more important things to do than wander the underworld," Captain Ragnar said. "Remember, one hour."

He handed Maja a stack of four beignets and took four for himself. The two walked to a table on the Outcast Clan side, and its occupants moved to make room for them.

Cassandra handed Michael a napkin. "Here. You have powdered sugar all over your face."

Michael pointed to her. "You still have a bit on your nose."

Cassandra snatched a napkin and wiped her face.

"Are you and Lady Achima coming with us?"

"Yeah." Cassandra arched a brow. "I have to talk to the Vidarr council of elders."

"Hope that goes as well as it did here," Michael said.

"Do not be deceived, El'esh," Lady Photina said. "We are far from friends with the El'esh and other races. We came to your aid because if the Legion had won, they would have come here. We also did not want the young Speaker to lose her brood-mate. You are here because you are not of Aras and did not participate in the atrocities committed against us. We have chosen at this time not to hold your position as El'esh against you. As for those others, they are here at Lady Achima's request."

Michael stroked his chin and nodded. *When these guys hold a grudge, they really hold a grudge.* "May I take the rest of these with me?" he asked, pointing at the leftover food.

"You bought them. Do as you wish."

"Do you have a bag I can carry them in?"

"I will get you one."

When the dragon left, Michael turned to his sister. "I guess things aren't as nice as I thought."

"It will take them a long time to get over their hostility," Cassandra said, taking two berries from the tray.

"That's for sure. Do you know if they'll let the wounded stay here?"

"I don't know. I'll ask."

"Cass, you shouldn't tell people I'm your brother."

"Why?"

"If the Legion finds out, they'll try to use us against each other.

Lady Phontina brought him a clay box big enough for the remaining pastries.

"Thank you," Michael said, placing a gold coin on the bar next to his tankard.

"Are you always so free with the El'esh's money?" she asked, placing the coin with its partner in her stone box.

"I would gladly pay more for the excellent accommodations and food. Your inn is better than all the other places I've stayed at back home." He raised the box and smiled. "Thanks again."

He hugged his sister and returned to the empty room for the rest of his things. When he went outside, he found Captain Ragnar and the remaining fifty Clan members gathered in front of the inn. Gwyneira stood among them, gripping her trident. She gave him a small nod and turned back to her conversation with her comrades.

Five Dragons, ten Hikaru, and ten Drás hovered above the twenty-five ground troops. Cassandra petted Xesa and Neric, and they nuzzled her with their snouts. Michael put his bags on Neric's back and scratched him behind the ear.

"Lady Achima wants to fly ahead of you so I can get things ready for when you show up," Cassandra said.

Michael's brow furrowed. "What if you get attacked? Who'll be there to watch your back?"

"We won't be alone. The Dragons and Hikaru will be coming with us, and the Drás will stay with you as air support. That's a lot of firepower, no pun intended."

"I still don't like it."

Lady Achima and Server Toula approached. The pink dragon held a bulging saddlebag and an extra-large canteen.

"She is in Eímai's hands," Lady Achima said, "and I will make sure she is safe."

Michael fought down the strong emotions boiling inside him. He forced a smile. "I appreciate that, I do. But she's my sister in a world at war. I don't want anything to happen to her."

"I understand more than you know. But you have your own path to walk, one that is just as dangerous, and she does not want harm to come to you either. You both must trust Eímai to watch over the other. Server Toula has something for you."

"The bag holds blackberries and the canteen blackberry fizz," Server Toula said, holding out the items.

Michael's spirits rose as he took them from her and tied them to the rest of his things. "Thank you very much. These will go great with the leftover beignets. How much do I owe you?"

The Dragon smiled. "Nothing, El'esh Michael." She suddenly sobered. "A dangerous road lies ahead of you. Trust in Eímai's power and love, and you will get through.""Why don't you hate Eímai and the El'esh like the other Confeds?"

"When I was younger, I spent a great deal of time reading Eímai's Writings and the El'esh Chronicles. You act like El'esh Ezrik and El'esh Xipil. It was El'esh Ezrik who said those words I just quoted."

*Ezrik and Xipil? Those names sound familiar. It's too bad Master Kardeiz isn't here. Eímai, are there El'esh records somewhere I'll have access to?*

"Yes. That will be granted when you come to me in my Sanctuary," Eímai said.

*I can't wait. My lessons scratch the surface of all there is to know. I wish there were an El'esh academy or school where I could go and learn everything I need to learn.*

"It has been millennia since the El'esh academy functioned. But I have arranged seasoned instructors for you."

"Clan!" Captain Ragnar roared, causing Michael to jump, "Move out!"

Captain Ragnar and his troops headed toward the hills with the Drás flying above them.

"That's our cue," Michael said. "Eímai's grace to you all."

"Eímai's grace to you as well," Server Toula said.

Michael embraced his sister and rested his forehead on hers. "Eímai, please protect Cass and give her wisdom and favor wherever she goes. Thank you for saying though a thousand fall on her left and ten thousand on her right, no harm comes near her."

"And please protect Michael and give him the wisdom and favor he needs, too," Cassandra said.

"Definitely. See you at the shrooms. I love you, Cass, now and forever."

Cassandra gave him a tight hug, and tears filled her eyes. "I love you too, now and forever. Be careful."

"Always."

They exchanged waves as his sister and Dragon flew away with Xesa running beneath them. Michael jumped into Neric's saddle, and the osulf took off after the Clan. *I hope all this jostling doesn't smash the blackberries or make the fizz explode.*

# Chapter 16: Cassandra

***Mushroom Forest, Western Citali Province, Aras: Spring, Day 14, Year 1, 5th Age***

Mushroom Forest looked as if someone had planted every type of mushroom imaginable in one place and then enlarged them to giant size. Cassandra recognized puffballs, toadstools, shiitakes, morels, bellas, and some that looked like coral. Each had been hollowed out and served as a home for a Vidarr.

In the center of the acres of mushrooms stood a colossal tree with pink rhombus-shaped leaves wrapped in ornately carved staircases leading to balconies with doorways into the tree. Vidarr, in armor the color of the tree and mushrooms, stood guard or moved up and down the staircases. A system of rope ladders ran from the tree's lower balconies to the surrounding mushrooms. More ran between the mushrooms. Vidarr bustled along the ladders on business. They ignored the dragons and Hikaru passing overhead. But the riderless osulf following them drew their attention, and they stopped to watch her pass by.

"This is amazing," Cassandra said. "How'd they grow this big?"

"Eímai made them this way at the beginning of time. Perhaps he knew the Vidarr would need a new home," Lady Achima said over her shoulder. "I will have to drop you off at the balcony leading to the council chamber. It is four levels below the top of the tree. The chamber is not big enough for me to fit. The Dragons and Hikaru will check the portal guard. I will wait for you in the upper canopy. Call for me if you need me."

They circled the central tree twice, and the Dragon stopped in front of the last balcony on the tree. Thirty Vidarr in silver armor with a gold four-claw slash across their breastplates stood around its edge and on either side of the door leading into the tree.

*Those must be Ridarri, the Vidarr knight. Eímai, thank you for giving me favor and wisdom.*

Cassandra climbed off Lady Achima and smoothed her clothes. As the Dragon flew to perch in the branches above them, Cassandra looked for Xesa. The osulf ran to the entrance at the base of the tree, but the Ridarri guarding it refused her entry. She lay down in a yard from the front entrance and refused to move.

"State your business," a lion with a braided mane said, tightening his grip on his battle ax.

"I am Speaker Cassandra. I have come to speak with your council of elders on a matter of great importance. Please take me to them."

"Many claim to be Speaker and are liars. Prove you are who you say you are."

*How do I do that?*

"Your staff," Eímai said. "Extend it and tap him on the left shoulder. A tap on the right is a challenge to combat."

She tapped him with the invisible staff, and it rang as it bounced off the lion's armor.

"I will take you to the council," he said as he led the way into the tree. "But there is no guarantee they will speak with you."

"I am sure they're busy getting ready for the Legion attack."

"What attack?" he asked, whirling toward her.

"The Legion's invaded Aras, and now they're going to try to take the portal from you. They're supposed to attack today."

"We've heard of no such invasion or attack. How do you know this?"

"I've seen the Legion and fought them with my brother, El'esh Michael. As for the attack on the portal, Qualoc the Ichtaca discovered it and told Captain Ragnar, who told us."

"Ichtaca? El'esh? Ragnar? I see now what you are. You are a gullible Talah child who is pretending. You are no more a Speaker than I am, and you should not listen to traitors. They are all liars."

"First of all, I'm human, not Talah. Second, if I'm pretending, why did the broodling of the lords of the Western Dragons carry me here to speak with the council of elders?" she said, pointing toward the watching dragon. Lady Achima blew out a puff of ice crystals. "And why are fifty Outcast Clan coming to reinforce you for the attack?"

The lion bared his teeth. "If they are on their way, we should get ready."

Cassandra nodded. "Yes, you should."

"Not for any supposed attack. But to capture them. Long have we waited for the opportunity to pass judgment on them."

"For what?"

"Treason. A child like you would not understand. Thank you for the information. Now go home."

"I'm not leaving until I speak with the elders. Let them decide if what I'm saying is a lie."

"Fine."

Iridescent moss on the walls lit the way as they walked into the depths of the tree. They exited a corridor dotted with more rooms than she could count and entered the center of the tree. Official-looking Vidarr in robes and armor scamper over the staircases and rope bridges linking the hundreds of levels. Some forsook the stairs and bridges and climbed the sides of the tree. Others sprang down to lower levels, landing gingerly on their paws.

Her guide led her across a bridge that ran diagonally across the vast expanse. They entered a shorter corridor that ended in a lobby. Two floor-to-ceiling windows filled the wall to her left, wide enough for Captain Ragnar to step through without turning sideways. Intricate carvings covered the walls and the double doors before them. The floor looked to be waxed and showed the tree's rings.

A cheetah and a clouded leopard guarded the doors. The lion gave a nod, and they pulled the doors open. The lion waved her forward. She swallowed and strode into the room, careful not to click her staff on the floor. The doors closed soundlessly behind her.

The round chamber had a ninety-foot domed ceiling covered in murals of Vidarr in battle and giant windows. Beyond the windows, the tree's leaves danced in the sunlight, casting spinning green rhombuses on the chamber's floor. More murals, colored by different glowing mosses, covered the walls.

*This is amazing. I wonder how they got the moss to grow on the walls like that.*

Around the room stood Ridarri. They alternated species so that no two of the same species stood together. Each had armor that looked as if it had been in many battles. But the damage had been repaired and accented with gold. They watched her approach, all business. She noticed that a few tightened their hold on their weapon.

*There's got to be at least fifty or sixty of them. If they attacked, I'd be dead before I knew what happened. It's like going to talk to the president with the Secret Service watching you. I guess that's what's happening. Only I'm talking to cats instead of humans.*

In the center of the room sat the five elders in high-backed wooden chairs carved from the tree and covered in leather and fur. Each held the weapon of their species. As she looked at each, she matched names with faces.

Elder Duwalt, the male clouded leopard, sat in the first chair and had a black spiral design on the left side of his face. He wore a forest-green tunic and gold armbands.

*It looks like he's been branded. I haven't seen anyone else with that mark. I wonder if he meant to have that done, or if it was done to him. He's also the only one without armor. I wonder why.*

Elder Vigdis, the female tiger, came next, wearing a purple dress and gold breastplate.

*She looks all business. I don't know if she or Captain Ragnar is more serious.*

Beside her sat Elder Kaj, the lynx, with a long orange tunic and leather breastplate.

*He looks like Lucy's cat. But I doubt he'd enjoy being petted.*

Next came Elder Lennart, the male lion, with his mane platted with onyx beads and a white tunic and silver breastplate.

*There's the leader of the group. He's the one I've got to convince.*

Elder Suri, the female cheetah, sat in the last seat wrapped in a blue dress that reached to her knees and a bronze breastplate.

*That dress brings out the color of her eyes, and she looks pretty. All of them look amazing. But I have to remember they'd kill me in a heartbeat if they thought I was an enemy. I wish Lady Achima were here.*

"You have me," Eímai whispered to her. "I am more powerful than any Dragon or Vidarr. Do not be afraid. You asked for my help. Trust me to give it to you when you need it."

The five conversed with an aged lynx leaning on a staff carved from a twisted piece of wood. Their voices sounded like a hive of buzzing bees.She stopped a few yards away and waited.

"You ignored the Talah chief's warning of invasion," the aged lynx said in a surprisingly strong voice.

"Master Teodr, we have ignored nothing," said Elder Suri. "We have waited until such claims could be substantiated."

"Substantiated? For the past four days, I have received reports of battles raging throughout Aras, and I have passed them on to you. Yet you have done nothing. You must inform the clans. To wait is to doom us to extinction."

"That is hardly a possibility," Elder Lennart said. "We have endured and will continue to endure, though all of Aras burns down around us."

"If it does, we will burn as well. We must act now."

"Yes, you are right. We will mobilize," said Elder Lennart. He nodded to Elder Duwalt.

The lynx pulled a talking disk from under his breastplate tunic and opened it. "Mushroom Clans," he said. "The Legion has invaded Aras. Mobilize. This is not a drill." He closed the disk and returned it under his tunic.

"Our scouts say the Outcast Clan forces are coming here. Captain Ragnar and Lady Achima are with them, along with two Talah, one of which is an El'esh." Master Teodr said.

"They must not be allowed anywhere near our clans," said Elder Vigdis. "Their influence has already poisoned the hearts of hundreds of our warriors, so they abandoned their rightful place among us."

"It would appear they are already here," said Elder Kaj, his eyes on Cassandra. Throughout the entire conversation, he had not stopped looking at her. She smiled at him, and it seemed like he gave her a smile in return. "Come forward, young Speaker. What have you to say to us?"

Cassandra's heart skipped in her chest as all eyes turned to her. *Okay, Eímai. What do I say?* She stepped forward, leaned her staff against her shoulder, and gave them the Vidarr greeting.

"Elders of the Vidarr, I am Cassandra, a human from another world. Four days ago, Eímai brought me. He chose me as Speaker. El'esh Michael and I fought the Legion in the Armorer's Forest to save Chief Jovena from being sacrificed to Ba'rel. We delivered her safely to Run, and since Eímai commanded us to appear before him five days from our arrival in Aras, we set out for Ker'an with a company of the Outcast Clan. We received intelligence from Prince Qualoc that the Legion planned to attack you and seize the portal. So, we made a detour to assist you. Yesterday, we were ambushed by the Legion in the hills south of here. We fought a fierce battle, but they were going to defeat us. Lady Achima and I fought their aerial forces. Once those were defeated, we realized we needed help. So, we flew to the city of Theitai and asked for the aid of the Dragon/Drás Confederation living there. They agreed, and together we won."

She paused to allow her audience to ask questions or make comments. When they remained silent, she continued. "Elder Lennart, you said a moment ago that you have endured. Yes, you have survived. But just surviving is not why Eímai made the Vidarr. He made you to thrive in unity with the other races of Aras. Ba'rel got you all to fight each other and reject Eímai's will for you. The races forgot Eímai and followed their own understanding. Ba'rel weakened Aras, and now he moves to devour it, both literally and figuratively.

"You will not be able to withstand the Legion for long. They will surround the Mushroom Forest and destroy it, whether by entering it or burning it from the sky. You would fight valiantly, but in the end, you would lose. I urge you to lay aside past offenses and unify with the races once again. Only through unity under Eímai's leadership will Aras defeat Ba'rel once and for all. Thank you for considering my words."

While she waited for a response, she looked into each of the elders' faces. But she could not read anything, even with Elder Kaj.

"You make many assumptions," Elder Lennart finally said. "You confess to not being if Aras and yet you assume to tell us what we can and cannot do. You assume that, since the traitors led by the one calling himself Ragnar could not defeat a small Legion force without help, we are incapable of doing better. You assume that we would acknowledge your claim to be Speaker and consider your words. You are a cub with no knowledge or experience. You have no authority here. Now leave and do not return."

Cassandra whirled and stalked toward the doors, eyes straight ahead. A Ridarri tiger opened the door.

"Thank you," she muttered as she walked through.

The moment the door closed, a wave of fear slammed into her. The room looked darker than before. She looked around and saw the two guards slumped against the wall, orange blood flowing from a gash in their breastplates. She tried to call out for help, but the words caught in her throat. Then she heard a voice that sent shivers down her spine.

"Well, well, little morsel. We meet again. I told you that you could not escape me."

# Chapter 17: Michael

*Mushroom Forest, Western Citali Province, Aras: Spring, Day 14, Year 1, 5th Age*

"The time of stealth is over," Captain Ragnar said as the Mushroom Forest lay a mile away. "You must ignite your armor. But stay close to me. It's impossible to predict what will happen when we arrive at the portal. I do not see the enemy, but that does not mean they are not nearby. I wonder what direction the attack will come from."

"I haven't seen Qualoc since those ruins we passed near Theitai. You think he's, okay?" Michael said as his armor ignited around him and he rose on flaming wings to fly above Neric.

"I do not know. I have been petitioning Eímai for his safety. Clan, we will aid in protecting the portal while we wait for Speaker Cassandra to finish meeting with the council of elders. As soon as she joins us, we will go north to Ker'an. We can resupply in Xjin. By Eímai's grace, we will be in Ker'an by nightfall at the latest."

The portal consisted of a bronze disk embedded in a stone platform between the Miwa River and the Mushroom Forest. It was large enough for a full-grown Dragon to walk through. Two hundred Ridarri stood around the platform in three concentric circles. Above them hovered the Outcast Clan Dragons and Hikaru.

A Ridarri cheetah stepped out of the outer ring and approached Captain Ragnar and his forces. She held up a paw, motioning them to stop.

"Outcast Clan," she said, "continue on your way. We do not need your help. We can guard the portal without you."

Michael approached the portal and landed before the first ring of guards. He scanned their faces and marveled at a world that could contain such noble creatures. Some stared at him open-mouthed. Others glared at him with hatred so strongly that he could feel it.

*Why would these guys hate me? Is it because I'm El'esh? Is it a rivalry thing between the orders? No, if that were the case, all these guys would be giving me dirty looks.*

"We will render aid until the rest of our group joins us," Captain Ragnar said.

Michael's eyes drifted up to the disk. A cuneiform inscription formed a vertical rectangle above where the disk disappeared into the platform.

Eímai's gift to speed you on your way.<br>
Never use it to bring harm.<br>
Speak the destination.<br>
Rest in Eímai's arms.

The words rose off the metal, spun around, and became an image of Michael placing a hand on the disk, speaking, and walking into the portal. The surface of the disk did not swirl or change before or after he stepped into it. *I don't think that'll ever get old. I wonder if the 'rest in Eímai's arms' part means you step into the portal believing it's going to take you where you need to go, and not smash your face when you walk into it.*

"We don't want you here, Fléau," the cheetah said.

Alarm bells went off in Michael.

*I thought he stopped being Fléau thousands of years ago. Are these guys old enough to know about his former life?*

A new thought entered his mind, and he grew cold despite the heat of the fire around and inside him. He flew to the tiger's side and hovered as he leaned toward his ear.

"Captain, may I have a word?"

The two moved fifty yards away, and Michael kept his eyes on the cheetah while the captain faced him. He moved inches from the tiger's face, and the tiger stepped back.

"Sorry about getting in your face, but I don't want her to hear us. Do the Ridarri know about your past life?" he whispered.

Captain Ragnar caressed his sword's pommel. "It is possible. Why do you ask?"

"You said the Legion can't acknowledge Eímai's work. The Dragons and Hikaru would have told them you were coming. But they'd use your current name. This could be my suspicious self and watching way too many nineties' cartoons, but is it possible for any of the Legion to shapeshift? You know, change their appearance."

The tiger's eyes flashed, and his lips pulled back in a snarl. "Yes." He turned to look at the cheetah, and Michael turned him back to face him.

"If she's Matu, we don't want to let on that we know. When I looked at those around the portal, some glared at me with intense hatred. From everything you've taught me so far, there's no reason they'd hate me. But I have an idea, and it's horrible."

"What?"

"Back home, we have something called sleeper cells. They are enemy agents among a country's citizens. They look and act like everyone else. However, when they receive a specific message, they leave their normal activities and carry out assassinations or attacks on designated targets. Their purpose is to prepare that country for invasion."

From the look on the tiger's face, he assumed he did not believe him.

"I know it sounds crazy. But what better way to seize the portal than to have agents appearing to be Ridarri mixed in among the guards? At the proper signal, they could kill the guards around them, and they'd be home free. If I were Ba'rel, that's what I would do. Do you think he'd think of it?"

Captain Ragnar's eyes narrowed. "Unfortunately, yes. El'esh Miklos told me about his uncle Vadimus fighting a Matu disguised as a baker. The Matu had lived in the town for decades before he was discovered."

"Is there a way to communicate with the Ridarri without the Matu knowing?"

"Yes. They have signals and codes known only to them. When the attack happens, you will take our fliers and strike the enemy from the air."

Michael blinked. "What?"

"You proved you are a capable leader during the battle in the hills, and now you showed yourself to be a skilled tactician. You have earned the respect of the Clan. Lead well."

The tiger approached the disguised Matu, and as he drew his scimitar, a figure stepped out of the portal. The black flaming armor and wings, along with the dragon helmet, made Michael's stomach drop.

"Vold," Michael said, pulling his sword and activating his shield.

The cheetah's form transformed into that of a Matu. Kris-bladed swords materialized in his hands. Captain Ragnar unleashed a roar so loud it made Michael's ears ring despite the protection of his helmet. His scimitar flashed with white fire as he swung it toward the Matu. The sorcerer tried to block his attack, but the glowing blade split the metal like aluminum foil. The blade continued on its path and split the Matu diagonally. The sorcerer dissolved.

As soon as the tiger roared, the Dragons unleashed a flaming barrage on Vold, engulfing the portal platform in liquid flame. At the same moment, chaos erupted among the Ridarri as they attacked each other. Real and fake Ridarri fell to each other's blades. The Hikaru above used spears and bows to pick off any Matu who revealed their true self. Smoke from the Dragon fire blended with the smoke from the slain Matu.

Those behind Captain Ragnar shrugged off their packs and charged the portal, with Captain Ragnar and his family leading the way. Michael joined the five Drás in the air and flew over the charging group.

"Canteens," Maja ordered.

In unison, those on the ground put away their weapons and pulled their canteens from their belts. When they were ten yards from the portal, they uncapped their canteens. They split into three squads, each led by a member of Ragnar's family. The larger fighters followed Captain Ragnar. The faster and more lithe fighters followed Maja. The lynx, Talah, and Drás, the archers, followed Frida. Captain Ragnar's group hit the combatants from the right, and Maja's from the left. They threw water in the faces of everyone they met. Some screamed and melted into smoke, and some stood straighter as their wounds healed.

Frida and the archers stopped on the outskirts of the battle.

"Archers, shoot at the top of the portal. Shatter angle," commanded Frida as she took a position between the archers and the combat around the portal, her long daggers at the ready.

Arrows slammed into the bronze portal, and while some stuck in the metal, most shattered on its surface. Glowing liquid splattered everywhere.

Michael frowned. "Why are they doing that?"

The red-winged Dras stepped forward. "The arrows are hollow and filled with Eímai's water."

"Brilliant. We'll do the same," Michael said. "Douse them with water and take out any Matu that show their ugly face. I don't see any Legion fliers, but that doesn't mean they're not out there. Be alert."

The Drás saluted, and together they flew back and forth over the battle, pouring water on those in the middle of the fighting.

The dragons ceased their flaming barrage. The smoke cleared. Vold was nowhere to be seen. Michael pulled up and hovered over the scorched platform. Those in his squad formed up around him.

"Where'd he go?" he asked as he scanned the terrain.

The red Drás checked the area and spun back toward Michael. "I don't see him."

"He must have been destroyed," a green Drás said.

"That'd be too easy." Michael shook his head. "He's got to be around here somewhere. Check the back of the portal, but be careful. If he's hiding back there, he'll spring out and attack us." He pointed to the yellow, green, and blue fliers. "You go to the left." He pointed to the purple-and-orange fliers and to himself. "And we'll go to the right. Swing out far enough that you have maneuverability if he comes after you. You don't want to hit the portal."

The two groups circled the portal but again found the space behind empty.

Michael flew toward the river and rotated, looking for the evil tiger without success. "How did he just disappear?"

No sooner than the words left his mouth, a black blur smashed into his chest. A dragon helmet looked down at him, and Vold's chuffing filled his ears.

*Eímai, help me.*

"I told you I would find you," Vold growled as he raised a paw, and long claws extended from it.

Michael struggled to get free, but Vold's hold would not break. The claws repeatedly hammered the same spot on his stomach. The power of each blow sent shockwaves throughout his body. "There's no way this breastplate can survive this. He's going to punch through and kill me," he said, believing every word.

In that moment, Vold's five claws pierced his breastplate and punched into his stomach. Michael screamed. Vold tried to rake his claws downward to rip him open, but Michael's armor prevented it. The Umoni yanked his claws from his victim, and Michael screamed again. Crimson poured from the five puncture wounds. Michael's hands passed through his armor to clutch the wounds. Hot blood flowed through his fingers. His pain-wracked mind struggled to form any kind of coherent thought.

"Father," he gasped. "Help."

"He cannot save you," Vold mocked as he held Michael before him with one paw. "You are mine."

Words appeared inside Michael's helmet. He had to focus hard to read them.

"Eímai is my refuge and strength. He is my ever-present help in my time of trouble. I walk through the valley of death, and Eímai brings me out alive."

Strength fading, Michael's chin dropped to his chest. He watched his blood rain down on the portal beneath them. Rivulets of red wound their way over the portal's shiny surface like rivers cutting their way through a barren landscape. Captain Ragnar, the Clan, and the remaining Ridarri looked up at them. The archers pointed arrows at Vold, and the Dragons formed a circle around them.

"Once again, you failed, Fléau. Another El'esh falls, and you can do nothing to stop me."

Captain Ragnar roared, and an arrow whistled through the air.

Michael's head snapped up, wanting to see the evil tiger impaled on a water-filled arrow.

But Vold caught it before it pierced his neck. He chuffed as he threw it away. "Still a failure," he snarled.

"Play dead," Eímai said.

Michael dropped his hands and went limp, head falling forward. Vold shook him, and his limbs thrashed around, though more from the force of being shaken than Michael's acting. The stab wounds in his stomach screamed. He clenched his teeth to keep from crying out.

His armor extinguished.

Vold roared.

*Now I'm really dead.* Michael braced himself to be mauled or bitten.

Thousands of running feet sounded all around them. Metal sounded on metal along with the screams of the wounded. Michael kept his eyes closed, trying not to look tense but still tensing his body for the raking of claws.

An orchestra of shrill whistles mixed with a deep clicking reverberated around him. All fighting ceased.

Vold growled something unintelligible.

Skittering. Whistling. The sound of a rope or something being shot forcefully through the air. A cry of alarm. The sickening thud of something sharp entering something soft. A gargled scream and metal crashing onto something hard. The sounds came again, and then there were so many that they overlapped.

Something sticky splattered on Michael's back and legs, and he felt himself yanked from the tiger's grasp. Vold's long claws shredded the flesh of his right shoulder and raked his collarbone. Michael screamed as he flew backward. He tried to grab his shoulder and came close to passing out when he touched shredded cloth and flesh. Hot blood pulsed from the wound to flow down his chest and limp arm. More of the sticky substance splattered over him and pinned his right arm to his side. It kept splattering over him until only his face remained uncovered.

"Father," he cried out as tears of pain blurred his vision. The pain surpassed what he had felt after being burned and when he had been cut up with knives.

He stopped falling and gently came to rest on the ground. The whistling and clicking intensified. When he blinked the tears away, he saw a new reason to scream.

The four approaching creatures had the bodies and legs of spiders and the heads, pincers, tails, and armor of scorpions. Red lines ran the length of their bodies as though someone had painted racing stripes on them. Their three tails arched from their rear toward their heads—each tipped with a long stinger. Instead of mouths with fangs or mandibles, they had a cluster of long syringes pointed downward. Their eight eyes never left him as they grew closer. Their stingers folded down as though on a hinge, and webbing shot from the tips of their tails. It coated Michael, pinning him to the ground. Only his head remained free. A bit of webbing slapped his mouth, silencing his screams. He watched as one hovered over his wounded stomach and one over his shoulder. Five of the syringes grew and slid into each of the punctures in his stomach. The other creature's syringes grew and slid into his shoulder wound. He felt suction tugging at his stomach and shoulder. His mind shut down, and he passed out.

# Chapter 18: Cassandra

***Mushroom Forest, Aras: Spring, Day 14, Year 1, 5th Age***

Lusare stepped from a shadow-filled corner and flashed a menacing grin. "How'd it go with the elders? They fawn over you like those Confederation fools in Theitai?"

Cassandra went cold. H*ow does she know about that? Is she following me? I never saw her. Lady Achima never mentioned seeing her.*

Lusare laughed. The sound grated on Cassandra's nerves. "Oh, yes, I know all about that. You'll be happy to know I made sure they won't help you again. They were quite tasty, especially that pink Dragon, so young and tender."

The faces of those she had met in Theitai and the wounded Outcast Clan warriors they had left there passed through her mind. Tears of sorrow blended with tears of rage.

"I told you I'd destroy everything you tried to accomplish," Lusare said, a sadistic grin plastered on her face.

*All those awesome people are dead.*

She twisted her staff, and it split, the halves becoming kama. She unleashed a feral roar as she attacked. Lusare pulled her cutlasses and blocked her attacks with ease.

"Trying to avenge your dead friends? You can't kill me, remember. Eímai wants me to return to him," Lusare mocked.

"I'll send you to him in pieces."

She added kicks to her attacks and landed several blows to Lusare's stomach and legs. Lusare rolled to her feet every time Cassandra knocked her down. She had lost her mocking grin. They fought back and forth across the antechamber. While she fought, passages from Eímai's Writings came to mind.

"Vengeance is mine; I will repay perfectly. Mercy triumphs over judgment. It is not my will that anyone perish. I desire for all to change their mind about what they are doing and come to me so I can cleanse them of their crimes against me."

*If she were going to go to Eímai, she would have done it by now. She had her chance, and she refused. She deserves what she gets.*

Another passage followed. "Do you despise the riches of Eímai's goodness, forbearance, and longsuffering, not knowing that my goodness leads those in darkness to repentance?"

She shoved the passages aside and redoubled her efforts to cut down the Sundered Drás. She slipped into Lusare's guard and carved a gash across her chest. Black vapor poured from the wound. Lusare knocked her kama aside and slashed her right side.

Hot pain shot through Cassandra, killing her rage. She dropped a kama and clutched the wound. Hot blood poured through her fingers. Fear threatened to choke her. She pushed it down and gritted her teeth against the pain.

*I refuse to let this monster win.*

"You bleed red," Lusare said.

"So what?" Cassandra said, as the crimson patch ran from her waist to the floor.

"You're not Talah," Lusare said. "What are you?"

*Like I'm going to tell you what I am.*

"None of your business."

Lusare bared her fangs and moved in for the kill.

"Weren't you going to crush everything I worked for, and after I was thoroughly broken, you were going to eat me?" Cassandra said through gritted teeth.

"I'm done playing with you."

The muffled sounds of combat in the council chamber stopped the Drás. She laughed and lowered her swords as she backed toward the giant windows.

"What's that?" Cassandra asked.

"The attack has begun. Soon there will be no council and or Vidarr."

"What attack?"

"We infiltrated the Ridarri and the council of elders with Matu. It was easy. The flea-ridden vermin see only what they want to see. All we had to do was wait for Captain Vold's signal to start the attack. I guess I can wait a bit longer before finishing you off. It is worth it to make you watch the slaughter of all those you worked so hard to help. Until we meet again."

Lusare swan dived out of the window. Wings sprouted from her back, and she flew out over the Mushroom Forest.

Cassandra ran for the council chamber doors and yanked on the handle. The door resisted her efforts. She yanked, and it still would not open.

"Why won't it open?" she yelled.

"Call for Lady Achima," Eímai said.

Cassandra ran to the window and screamed the Dragon's name. Lady Achima flew down and gripped the tree with her massive claws, their tips poked through the wall.

"What is that red?" the Dragon thundered.

"It's blood."

"Blood? Who injured you?"

"Lusare. But she flew off when we heard the fighting in the council chamber. Matu are attacking the council. I can't get in there. The door's stuck or locked."

"We must take care of your wound first. Remove your hand and bare your side."

Cassandra removed her jacket as slowly as she could, but flashes of pain made her scream. She unclasped her belt and let it join the jacket on the floor. She lifted her tunic high enough to reveal her wound. She ventured a look and nearly vomited. Narrow black ribbons writhed in the gash.

"What are those? Why can't I feel them?"

"They are corruption worms. Lusare coated her weapon with their eggs. They grow in a wound and secrete corruption through their waste as they devour the victim's flesh. Eventually, the victim either dies or becomes Sundered."

"They're eating me?"

Lady Achima inhaled and shot a ball of ice into the wound. The ball stuck to the opening and pulsed with sea blue light. It sucked the ribbons into itself and destroyed them.

"Yes. But the ice will remove them. Did Chief Ewan give you oasis leaves and fruit paste healing balm?"

"Yeah," she said, her eyes locked on the worms leaving her side.

*How many of them are in me? How much of me did they eat? Why am I not dead?*

Terror flooded her, and she began to weep. When she was younger, she had read Acts 12, where worms ate King Herod after he took God's glory. She had nightmares afterward.

"Do not be afraid," Eímai said. "There is no wound I cannot heal. Cluster the leaves on the floor and pour the paste over them. Push them into the wound. Then, command the wound to close. I will take care of the rest."

She forced herself to look away from the ice ball and pulled the required items from her bag. Her hands shook, and tears poured down her cheeks. Try as she might, she could not keep the fear from swallowing her.

"Peace, Cassandra," Lady Achima said in a soft tone.

She looked at the Dragon. This was the only time she had ever spoken just her name.

"It is going to be okay. They will not kill you."

Cassandra took a shuddering breath. She finished preparing the poultice. The ice ball shattered when it fell from her wound. She scooped up the poultice and fruit pulp dripped through her fingers. She took a shuddering breath as it entered her wound. Warmth replaced the cold caused by the ice.

"Close in Eímai's name."

Her wound obeyed.

"I hope I don't have to do this again," she muttered.

"In time, you will be skilled enough to avoid being wounded," Lady Achima said.

"What now?"

"Step aside," Lady Achima said, drawing back her head a second time.

Cassandra scurried from the window and turned in time to see a giant blast of icy streak toward the doors. Ice spread, covering them from floor to ceiling. Cracks split the wood, and after what seemed like forever, the thick doors shattered.

Chaos and death had their way inside the council chamber. Elder Lennart fought back-to-back with Elder Vigdis against thirty Matu. Elder Kaj defended Master Teodr, who lay sprawled with a deep head wound. She could not see Elders Duwalt and Suri.

*They must have been Matu.*

More Ridarri littered the floor than fought the invaders.

"Can you blast them with ice?"

"I can reach some, but not all. The elders must not fall. You must defend them."

"What?" she exclaimed. "I got hacked open, and you want me to fight?"

"Ask Eímai. He will lead you."

"Eímai, what should I do?" Cassandra asked, turning to face the battle.

"Now you choose to listen to me?" Eímai said, tone firm.

"What do you mean?"

"I called to you to stop attacking Lusare, and you ignored me. Had I not intervened, she would have cut you in half."

"I'm sorry. I shouldn't have ignored you. Please forgive me."

"I forgive you. But Lusare now knows you bleed red. Those wishing to destroy you have doubled."

"Why?"

"Speaker Savelis' prophecy. 'Theirs is the crimson river.' No one was to know you filled the role of Lightning until your training was completed."

"I really messed up."

"We will deal with the consequences later. For now, you must purge the council chamber of this infestation."

"I'm not supposed to kill anyone."

"You will not. You will position yourself between the elders and the Matu. You will stand still and see my salvation."

She scooped up her fallen kama and returned her weapon to its staff form. A Matu saw her enter and tried to cut off her head. But an ice blast from Lady Achima froze him. An icicle the size of Cassadra's arm pierced his side, and he shattered.

*She shoots balls and icicles. What else can she do?*

More Matu attacked her and met a similar fate. She stood before Elder Kaj and looked over her shoulder at the other two elders.

"Please stand by Elder Kaj."

The two elders and the remaining Ridarri fought their way to Elder Kaj's side.

"What do you intend to do, cub?" Elder Vigdis asked.

*Still her charming self.*

"Stand still and see Eímai's salvation," Cassandra said, turning to face the elders.

The Matu surrounded them and raised their swords. Their blades ignited with purple fire. They flashed sharp teeth and crouched.

"Thus is the end Vidarr," they said in unison.

"What? We are supposed to stand here and do nothing?" Elder Vigdis said, her ears flattening.

*That's a sign of aggression. She's going to attack me. Then what do I do?*

"Do not let her intimidate you," Eímai said. "Stand your ground. Vidarr value courage above all other virtues."

"No. We are to stand still, see Eímai's salvation, and be silent," Cassandra said,

"You dare tell us to be silent? You are more arrogant than you appeared." Heavy footfalls approached from behind Cassandra.

"Vigdis," Elder Lennart snapped. "Do as she says and—"

"But," Elder Vigdis countered.

"Be silent," Elder Lennart roared.

No further protests came from the tiger.

"Go ahead, Speaker," Elder Lennart said. "We will do as you have instructed."

"Turn so the Vidarr are at your back, raise your staff pointed at the ceiling, and speak the words I give you," Eímai said to Cassandra.

"Eímai saves those who trust in him," Cassandra said, raising her staff. The Matu froze; eyes locked on Cassandra. "Though a proud enemy surrounds us and crouches like beasts eager to tear their prey, Eímai rises and delivers us. Though they spew proud words and celebrate our destruction, they know not that their destruction is at hand. Eímai sent lightnings in abundance and vanquished them. He delivered us from our strong enemy who hated us. He delivered us because he delighted in us."

Nothing happened.

Cassandra kept the staff raised.

A minute passed.

Two minutes.

Three.

Still nothing.

*Did I do something wrong? Shouldn't something have happened by now? Maybe I heard wrong.*

"Is there a time when I gave you instructions, and it didn't go the way I said it would?" Eímai asked.

The Matu laughed their grating laugh and straightened. They sauntered toward the cluster and drew their swords back to strike.

*No.*

"Then why would you doubt because I didn't act the way you expected. Your job is to do as I instruct you. Mine is to make my words a reality. I watch over my words faithfully to perform them, and they never fail."

A white bolt of lightning blasted through the ceiling and slammed into the raised staff. It split into dozens of smaller bolts that pierced the chests of the surrounding Matu. They disintegrated with an echoing wail. The smell of sulfur and ozone made Cassandra wrinkle her nose. The smaller bolts moved from where the Matu had stood to the fallen Vidarr. They pierced their wounds and closed them. One by one, their chests rose, and they woke. Even the two dead guards in the antechamber came to life.

A tendril arched down to Cassandra's side. She shook as the power surged through her abdomen. Her stomach grew warm, as though she had eaten a bowl of her mother's soup. The warmth gave way to the sensation of something moving inside her.

*What's happening to me?*

"I am repairing your organs. There. It is done."

The lightning stopped as though a switch had been flipped. Cassandra crumpled. Strong paws caught her and lowered her to the floor. Elder Kaj pulled his paws from under her and gave her a warm smile.

"Easy, Speaker. Rest."

Cassandra released her staff and touched her stomach. It felt normal. She touched her side. A puffy line marked where she had been wounded.

"Never have I seen anything like what I witnessed today," Elder Lennart said. "What do you have to say now, Vigdis?"

The tiger met Cassandra's eyes and bowed her head. "I was wrong, Speaker. I ask your forgiveness."

"I forgive you," Cassandra said. "Now, about joining with the other races…"

Elder Lennart and Elder Kaj broke into rumbling laughter, and Elder Vigdis chuffed, her strong form shaking with mirth.

"You truly are a Speaker," Elder Lennart said. "Yes, we will join with the other races."

"I'm glad. Do you mind if I lie here a little bit? I don't have the strength to get up just yet."

"I will take you to more comfortable accommodations," Elder Kaj said as he scooped her up and headed for the ruined chamber doors. "We will also see about getting your clothes mended. We have a few cloth-shapers among us."

"That'd be great."

She remembered her brother and the Outcast Clan defending the portal.

"I've got to get to the portal. Everyone is waiting for Lady Achima and me. They're probably being attacked right now."

"You are in no condition to travel, let alone enter battle with the Legion. You must rest here and let us handle the Legion. I will see that they are cared for."

"Listen to him," Lady Achima said from the windows. "I will watch over you. Where will you take her?"

"The tenth level. The room faces the north and has a balcony large enough for you outside the room."

"Pass her to me. I will carry her to the room, and you can meet us there."

"You do not trust me? That hardly promotes goodwill."

"The Speaker is under my protection and tutelage."

"As you wish."

He handed Cassandra through the window, and Lady Achima took her with her right forepaw. She released her grip and dropped away from the tree. She circled the tree and landed on the chosen balcony. The door grew by itself as Lady Achima approached. When she strode into the room, it expanded to comfortably fit the Dragon. She laid Cassandra on the bed, and before she could speak her thanks, she slipped into a deep sleep.

# Chapter 19: Michael

***Mushroom Forest, Western Citali Province, Aras: Spring, Day 14, Year 1, 5<sup>th</sup> Age***

Whistling.

Clicking.

Garbled screams.

A deep voice spouting gibberish.

Something soft stroked his cheek.

Wetness poured down his throat.

Power coursed through him.

Sounds became clear.

"El'esh Michael, wake up," a growling female voice said. "You're not dead. Wake up."

Michael's consciousness fully returned. He opened his eyes and looked into Frida's worried face.

"Hello," he said weakly.

"Thank Eímai." Frida bowed her head for a few moments. "Father will be pleased you are still alive."

He tried to remember what had happened before Frida woke him. But his mind could not bring the memories to the surface.

"Still alive? What do you mean?"

"Don't you remember what happened?"

"No. I'm having trouble remembering anything past blackberries and beignets."

Frida chuffed. "Of course, you would remember food."

He tried to sit up but found he could not feel anything past his neck. "Why can't I feel anything past my neck?"

"The skepna webbing is still holding you down."

"Webbing?"

He looked, and his mouth dropped. Red stained the web cocoon on his shoulder and stomach. The two spots tingled, as though they had fallen asleep. He felt lightheaded and weak.

"Frida, what happened to me? Why am I bleeding?  Why do my shoulders and stomach tingle? I feel woozy and weak. Am I dying?"

She slashed the webs holding his left arm to the ground. Each strand popped like a taut wire.

"Not anymore. Vold pierced you with his claws. You would have died if not for the skepna drawing his evil from you. When they moved on, I packed the wounds with leaves and fruit paste and poured Eímai's water over it all. The wounds closed, but they are still healing."

"Where's he now?"

"He flew off when the skepna tried to catch him. I wish they ended him once and for all."

"It'll happen eventually," Michael said, resting his head on the grass.

"I hope so."

His left arm free, he pulled it out of the webbing and flexed his hand. Dried blood caked it, and he had a hard time moving his fingers.

"I'm going to need a bath."

"The river is not far from here. You can bathe in its healing waters. Maybe full submersion will speed up your healing," she said, freeing his legs and moving to his right side.

He tried to pull some of the web off his chest, but it stuck fast.

"Only Eímai's water can remove the web. I know of nothing else strong enough."

"You mentioned skepna. What is it?"

"Over there." She pointed to his left.

He looked, and his eyes bugged. The creatures were five feet high and long and looked like someone had crossed a black scorpion with a spider. It had three scorpion tails on the hind end of a bulbous body covered in overlapping armored plates. Their stingers folded down, and crystalline webbing shot from the spinnerets behind the stingers. The web snagged Akzari, Matu, and Sundered, yanking them off their feet. Long stingers flipped up and impaled the victim. The victim screamed or howled as the skepna's venom pumped into them and caused them to melt into vapor. The skepna sucked up the vapor using its syringe-like mouth. Others slurped up the vapor rising from those killed by the Outcast Clan, Vidarr, Talah, and Hikaru. Three dragons blasted enemies with balls of fire as though they were in a video game.

"Who's winning?" he asked.

"I am not sure. Even with the skepna's help, we were going to lose until more Vidarr and Ridarri showed up. Then, more Legion reinforcements arrived over the river. They lowered a bridge so they wouldn't get near the water. Then Lord Ewan showed up with a battalion of Talah. More Legion emerged from holes in the ground along with corrupted beasts from the underworld. Then Hikaru came from the mountain, and together they seem to be holding their own. I haven't seen any other Legion reinforcements."

Michael whistled, and a skepna turned to face him. Despite himself, Michael waved, and the skepna's tails waved back. It turned back to the battle and snagged a fenrir lunging forward to bite the head of a fallen red Drás. The snapping jaws stopped centimeters from the Drás' snout. The skepna's tails whipped back so they were horizontal, and the fenrir flew backwards. In a flash, the tails were back up, stingers snapping into place. They pierced the fenrir and the beast howled before turning to vapor. The churning black cloud turned into twisting tendrils, and it spiraled down to the skepna's syringes. In a flash, no more vapor remained.

"That's the coolest and most terrifying thing I've ever seen," he said as Frida cut the last of the web.

"It's a good thing they only hunt Ba'rel's abominations. If you want terrifying, try the lazar-moth. That's terrifying. I'm surprised they aren't here. There's plenty of Legion to feed on."

"Lazar-moths?"

"They look like moths made of ice crystals. They land on a Legioner."

"Legioner?" he said with a chuckle.

Frida shrugged. "What else do you call them? Member of the Legion is too long to say."

"I like Legioner. I'll have to start calling them that."

"Anyway, the moth's touch burns *members of the Legion,*" she said with a smile.

He laughed, and heat flashed in his stomach and shoulder. He groaned.

"I'm sorry. I didn't mean to make you laugh," Frida said, putting a paw on his chest.

"It's okay. It's going away. As you were saying."

"The Legioner smashes the moth. The moth shatters into hundreds of pieces. Each piece becomes a moth. Then they turn into a cyclone of moths around the Legioner. I don't know what they do when they swarm, but somehow the Legioner turns to smoke, and they suck it up kind of like the skepna. Then the moths all come together, melting into one moth. That moth flutters away as though nothing happened, and there you go."

He shook his head. "This world is tripping me out. So, what now? I'm guessing I shouldn't move anytime soon."

"That would be a good idea. I will guard you."

"Thanks."

He lay his head back. The sky grew darker, and the stars started to appear. Khane and its two moons looked down on them. It looked so peaceful up there. He tried to tune out the carnage around him as he focused on the celestial bodies.

*I wish Cass were here to see this. She loves all things astronomy.*

His mind clicked, and the webbing kept him from sitting up.

"Cass. Where's my sister?"

"Lady Achima is with her in the tree at the center of the Mushroom Forest. She is safe."

"Thank you, Lord. Please protect her. When can I be able to be moved? I want to see her."

"After you recovered in the river."

"Thanks for staying and watching over me."

"You're welcome," she said with a smile.

Maja's face appeared above him. "I see you are awake. How are you doing?"

"Healing, I guess. I'd like to see my sister."

"You need to spend time in the river first. Why did you not tell me your blood had the power to activate the portal?"

"Didn't know it did. What happened?"

"The moment it touched the writing at the portal's base, the blood flow changed course and flowed to the portal's center, where it disappeared. Seconds later, the skepna came through."

"Good thing they did."

"Yes. They changed the tide of the battle."

"Is it over? I still hear fighting."

"We are finishing the remnants now. Frida, gather the Clan. We will make a litter to carry El'esh Michael to the river."

"Yes, Mother."

Frida ran toward the battle, blowing a trumpet made from the horn of some unknown animal.

Maja knelt and leaned close to Michael. "I am glad to see you alive."

"I'm glad to be alive. Sorry, I got caught so quickly. Rookie mistake. I still have a lot to learn."

"Being ignorant is not a crime. Choosing to remain ignorant, or worse, refusing to apply what you already know, is."

"Sounds like something my mother would say."

"She is wise."

"That she is. I hate to ask. Did you lose a lot of warriors?"

"I do not think so. We will not know for sure until we are gathered."

Minutes later, Captain Ragnar and the remnants of the Outcast Clan gathered around Michael. Only three had died, and two had been under Michael's command. Michael expressed his condolences, and they told him they were glad he was alive.

They made a litter and gently placed him on it. Four Drás carried him while the rest of the Clan encircled them. The Clan fliers coasted overhead, heads turning back and forth for any sign of trouble.

A lush orchard grew beside the river. Trees with purple oranges and pink pears grew thick along the bank. Bushes with red, black, green, and blue berries grew in rows among the trees. Predator and prey ate fruit and drank from the river together.

"And the lion will lie with the lamb," Michael said.

"I am not familiar with that passage," said one of the Drás.

"It's from the writings of the creator of my world. It means peace will reign so much that natural enemies will live together without wanting to kill each other."

"I like the sound of that," the Drás said.

"Me too."

The litter bearers stepped into the river. Its power shot through the bearers into Michael. He gasped at its intensity. He felt like he was being electrocuted. They lowered him into the water and continued to push down on the litter until the water covered him.

"Hello, Michael," Eímai's voice said. "You have done well. But much more still waits to be done."

"How could I have done well when I'm lying here torn up. Four days here, and I almost died."

"You would not have if you had believed your armor would protect you. Your words weakened your armor and allowed Vold to pierce you. Your words have the power to bring life or death, strength or weakness. Guard your mouth and speak only what I tell you to speak."

"Your words have been harsh against me," Michael quoted from the book of Malachi.

"Exactly. You doubted my ability to protect you. You also did not ask for my help to find him. You trusted in your own abilities. An El'esh must be completely dependent on me for guidance, empowerment, and protection. The one who does this will fear no evil."

"You're right. I'm sorry. I tried to do it all on my own, and I messed it up. Will I have to be in this river long?"

"For an entire day. Three hours after Second-Apex tomorrow, you will be able to leave."

"What do I do until then?"

Eímai's Writings floated out of his satchel, and the book hovered in front of him.

"Read and I will teach you more about myself."

He opened the book to where he left off, and this time the writing stayed on the page.

"Make your mind, will, and emotions wait silently for me. Listen for my voice to guide you. Place your expectations in me. I want to protect, save, and defend you. When I do, you will never be moved. Trust me always and pour out your heart to me, for I care for you."

# Chapter 20: Cassandra

*Mushroom Forest, Western Citali Province, Aras, Spring, Day 15, 5th Age*

A thick, wet tongue drew Cassandra out of a deep sleep. She groaned and pushed the huge furry head away.

"Oreo, stop licking me."

"Who is Oreo?" Xesa said.

Her eyes popped open and came nose to nose with the osulf.

"Xesa. Good to see you. Where's Lady Achima?"

"I don't know. She left two hours ago."

She lifted her tunic and examined her side. The scar no longer looked puffy.

"So glad it's healed. I had such a good nap."

Xesa laughed. "Nap? You have slept for a day. I have never seen anyone sleep as deeply as you. You must be hungry."

"I'm starving."

"Good. We must tell the guard you are awake."

"Why is there a guard?"

"They wanted to keep you safe," Lady Achima said as she strode in from the balcony. "After the infiltration by the Matu, everyone has been on high alert against further infiltrations. Those with a high rank were given a guard of Ridarri who proved to be loyal."

"I didn't know I qualified," Cassandra said with a laugh.

"Oh, you are more than qualified. You saved the council of elders and healed and resurrected the fallen."

"I didn't do that. Eímai did."

"True. But he used you to do it. Your position as Speaker brings certain privileges."

The thought of being treated differently from others made Cassandra uncomfortable.

"I used to feel as you did when I was younger," Lady Achima said with a smile. "I don't like special treatment either. But if you do not misuse the privileges, you will be fine. Before you eat, there is something we must discuss. Xesa, would you leave us for a moment?"

"Neric and I are returning to our osulf pack. It has been too long since I saw my pups and their litters."

Cassandra hugged her neck. "Thank you for carrying me. I'm going to miss you."

"And I you. Perhaps Eímai will allow us to meet again."

"I'd like that very much."

She kissed Xesa's forehead and scratched her behind the ears. She let her out of the room and closed the door.

"Move to the center of the room," Lady Achima said.

The Dragon's firm tone caused her stomach to churn, not from hunger.

*She's mad at me. Mom uses that same tone when she's about to chew me out for something. I could run for the door, but I have a feeling running from a Dragon is stupid.*

She did as she was told, and Lady Achima coated the walls, door, and even the balcony entrance with a thick layer of ice.

"Now we will not be heard," the Dragon said, looking down at her.

She raised her eyes, and the fierceness in Lady Achima's eyes made her look at the floor.

"We must speak about your actions with Lusare," Lady Achima said.

Her mind went blank as she braced herself for the Dragon's lecture.

"Eímai chose you to be his ambassador. He called you to bring the races to him and to each other. He gave you a simple set of rules and told you not to break them. Yet when you were tested, you threw them away without considering the consequences. He wanted to work through you to bring Lusare to himself. But instead of encouraging her return, you tried to kill her. I believe your exact words were, 'I'll send you to him in pieces,'"

Cassandra's head snapped up, eyes wide.

*How did she know that? Did she hear me?*

"A Vidarr heard the battle and ran to find the source of the noise."

"I didn't see anyone."

"You were too focused on murdering the one you were supposed to save. She heard your words and fled at the sight of your rage. She approached me while I watched over you and told me what had happened. Broodling." Lady Achima released a deep sigh and lowered her massive head to look her in the eye. "Cassandra, what you have done is a crime against Eímai. This is no light matter. You broke the code of the Speaker."

"She murdered Server Toula and Lady Photina and everyone in Theitai," Cassandra exclaimed.

"She told you this?"

"Yes. She said Server Toula was tender and tasty. That's when I attacked her."

Lady Achima released another deep sigh. "You are not Eímai's hand of judgement. That is the task of the El'esh. You are his ambassador of reconciliation. No matter what she has done, you are called to bring her to Eímai."

*I can't believe she's saying this. Doesn't she care that those she knows are dead?*

"Of course I care," Lady Achima snapped, stomping her right foot. The room vibrated.

Cassandra scurried backward and flopped onto the bed. A muffled pounding sounded at the door.

"All is well," Lady Achima boomed at the door. The pounding ceased. She returned her golden gaze to the cowering girl on the bed.

"I have consulted with Eímai about the next course of action."

*That's it. I proved I'm no better than Savelis. Grandma L was right. I won't amount to anything, even with what I've done back home. Now she's going to kill me.*

"No, I am not going to kill you. I am to continue teaching you. But you will have to live with the consequences of your actions. Perhaps you will get another chance with Lusare. Only Eímai knows.

But I hope you will learn from this. As for thinking you will not amount to anything, that is a lie of Ba'rel."

*She keeps saying what I'm thinking. Is she reading my mind?*

"Not exactly," Lady Achima said in a gentler tone. "Eímai's Song of Creation resonates in all things. He gave Dragons the ability to see the song's notes. When one is close to Eímai, the song is bright and melodious. When one is upset or, in your case, condemning themselves, it becomes discordant. For Ba'rel's servants, the song is not there. They are an empty void."

Cassandra wiped her face and blew her nose on a handkerchief the Dragon offered her. A gentle knock sounded at the door.

"I have food for the Speaker," a muffled voice said.

"Is there anything else I should know about?" Lady Achima asked.

"I don't think so."

"Then we will have our meal." The Dragon looked at the door and said, "Melt."

All the ice in the room melted. The water flowed over the balcony, leaving no wet marks or signs that it had been there.

Four Ridarri entered and saluted, snapping to attention. One was the lion who had led Cassandra to the council chamber.

"Lady Achima, Speaker Cassandra, the elders request your presence after you have dined," the lion said, his eyes fixed on the human attempting to make herself presentable.

"Very well," Lady Achima said. "I will see that she gets there in a half an hour."

The Vidarr saluted again and exited. The lion stayed behind. He looked as though he wanted to say something.

"Is there something else?" Lady Achima asked.

"I… apologize for my treatment of you upon your arrival. I was rude," he said to Cassandra.

"It's okay," Cassandra said in a small voice. "I didn't ask your name. I'm sorry."

"I am Tryggyr, Elder Lennart is my sire.

*I can see the resemblance.*

"What has upset you? Is there anything I can do to…?"

"Thank you for your kind offer," Lady Achima said, cutting him off. "But it is a private matter. We will arrive in the council chamber shortly."

The lion saluted again and rotated on his paw. He strode from the room, shutting the door behind him.

As much as she wanted to ask why the Dragon treated him the way she did, she was afraid to say anything.

"There is nothing he could have done," Lady Achima said, "and the source of your tears was none of his business."

*You didn't have to be that cold to him.*

"Would you want him to know your failures?"

Cassandra shook her head.

Two tigers entered bearing large trays. The first held roasted meat and vegetables. The second held fruit, a pitcher of pink fizzy liquid, a plate, a knife and fork, and a wooden goblet. They looked for a place to put them and found none.

"You can set them on the floor," Cassandra said. "I don't mind."

The servers did as they were instructed and left, closing the door behind them.

"Eímai, for this food we thank you and ask for your wisdom in all we have yet to face," said Lady Achima.

She blew a thin layer of ice over the contents of the trays. Steam rose from the food as the ice melted.

"Why did you do that? Is it too hot?"

"No. I am checking for poisons or corruption. It is safe to eat."

They ate in silence. The food was excellent, and the pitcher contained rabble fizz. But the meal reminded her too much of the one she had at The Snoring Traveler Inn, and she found she could not enjoy it.

"I will leave you to wash your face and prepare yourself," Lady Achima said when they had finished.

Cassandra washed her face and hands in a basin sitting on a side table. Her jacket lay draped over a chair along with her satchel and belt. When she examined the jacket, she saw no sign of a tear or bloodstain. When she put on her jacket, her right pocket vibrated. Inside sat her talking disk.

*Maybe it's Mike. I wonder how the battle went. Lady Achima didn't mention anything about it. If something had happened to him, she'd tell me. Unless she was so focused on chewing me out for my mess up that it slipped her mind. I hope he's not dead.*

She popped the lid and a pink dragon head appeared before her.

"Speaker, it is good to see you."

"Server Toula? How? What?"

"You are surprised to see me. Did you not think I would call? I suppose with being as important as you are, a server is not the type of being you'd expect to call you."

"No, it's not that at all," she shouted, tears of joy replacing tears of sorrow. "It's just… I heard you were dead and…"

"Oh, that. Well, the news of my demise has been exaggerated. I and all of us in Theitai are well. Well, except for fifteen. They got fifteen of us before we got them."

"What do you mean?"

"After you left, we were attacked. They tried to assassinate all of us when we weren't looking. They got fifteen, as I said. Most of them were your Outcast Clan friends, I'm sorry to say. But we took care of them. I got five. I smashed a jug of rabble fizz over an Akzari's head. Sad way for a good drink to go. But it took care of the scum. He melted away in a flash."

Cassandra could not hold back the laughter that bubbled out of her at the image of the Server Toula smashing the jug over the would-be assassin's head.

*It's like those old westerns Dad watches. I wonder if it was a brawl.*

"I'm glad you're okay. Is Lady Photina okay too?"

"Oh, yes. She roasted a good number of them. I've seen her mad before, but nothing like this. She nearly burned the inn down around us. The main framework of the inn is intact. But the rest was toasted.

She says now she has an excuse to do the renovating she's wanted to do for ages."

Cassandra fought for air as she laughed harder.

"What is going on here?" Lady Achima asked, poking her head into the room.

Cassandra held up the talking disk.

"Lady Achima," Server Toula said with a bow of her head. "It's good to see you. Are you well?"

"Yes, I am," Lady Achima said, eyes narrowing.

"Is something the matter?"

"We heard you were dead."

"Well, I'm still alive. At least I think I am. I was telling Speaker Cassandra about a little attack that happened after you left. I regret to say we lost fifteen. Most were among the injured Outcast Clan. They were slain while they slept. But we took care of the murderers. The Snoring Traveler burned, but Lady Photina plans to rebuild."

"Were the slain Clan buried?"

"Yes. We took them to the outskirts of the Southern Forest and buried them there."

"Thank you."

"You're welcome. I must go now. Lady Photina is calling me. Goodbye."

"Goodbye," Cassandra said, shutting the disk and hanging it around her neck.

"What have you learned?" Lady Achima asked.

Cassandra wiped her face and sat on the edge of the bed.

*What have I learned? I don't know.*

"There is no way Lusare could have taken part in that attack and gotten here in time to speak with you," Lady Achima said. "She lied. She overestimated the Legion's ability."

"Yeah."

"Are you ready to meet with the council?"

"Yes. Let's go. I hope it's not another verbal beating."

"Verbal beating? I did not verbally beat you."

"It's an expression back home."

"I see. Well, climb onto my back. I will lower you through the hole in the ceiling."

# Chapter 21: Michael

*Mushroom Forest, Western Citali Province, Aras, Spring, Day 15, 5th Age*

"Our time here is done," Eímai said as the floating book closed and went into Michael's pouch.

"How's that possible? I just got here."

Eímai laughed. "When you're with me, time passes without you noticing."

The light around him faded, revealing a vast underwater world of bright, colorful coral, fish, and other underwater creatures. He half expected to see a shark swim by. But none did.

"Why are saltwater fish and corals in freshwater?"

"My water gives life to all creatures. It doesn't matter what type of water they live in on Earth. I show this to you so you will understand my power. I will make the impossible possible. I am your shelter and your strength. I sustain and empower you. In this time with me, you have neither slept, eaten, drunk water, nor expelled waste. I supplied you with everything you needed. My fire dwells within you. My presence is with you, and I give rest when you need it. I will never leave or forsake you. I have given you everything you could ever need. You have only to learn about it, believe it is yours, and receive it. You have many challenges ahead of you. But if you remain true to me through it all, you will receive a reward for your faithfulness."

"Why do I feel like I've been given a pep talk before heading off on a suicide mission?"

"No, you are not going on a suicide mission. But I am sending you on a mission that is of utmost importance. In the third age, an El'esh named Xipil entered the Blue Forest in southern Emer Province to hunt Ba'rel's abominations. He carried with him a vial of Ba'rel's blood. The fallen one had been wooing him, promising him the fulfillment he thought he lacked with me. When he reached the skepna hive, he rejected Ba'rel's lies and smashed the vial against a tree. Though the skeplings, that is the name for infant skepna, sucked up the darkness emanating from the blood, the blood's poison entered the tree and ground. Since the trees had one root system, the poison caused all the roots to withdraw from the underground springs that sustained them. Removed from my sustaining power, the forest slowly died. Now the region is a wasteland. The place where the vial shattered is now the main hive of the skepna, and its evil causes the skepna to love darkness instead of light. They withdraw from the light of the suns and hide in the tunnels that link their pits."

A basketball-sized sphere materialized before him. White light swirled with strands of deep crimson.

*It's like the marbles I used to play with as a kid.*

"What is it?"

"A mixture of my water and your blood."

"My blood? What's it for?"

"I want you to bury it at the bottom of the hive pit. Just as the blood of one man cleansed many and brought freedom from the dominion of darkness, so too will the blood of one-man cleanse and bring freedom from darkness."

"With all due respect, that man was pure and not contaminated by evil. I'm not like him. I had to have him cleanse me."

"Exactly. And as one of the cleansed, you bring cleansing, for just as he is, so are you in this world."

A different kind of numbness washed over him as he realized the implications of Eímai's words.

"Are you saying I'm going to die to save this world?"

"I didn't say you would save this world. I said my water and your blood together would cleanse the southern portion of Emer Provence."

"And the water and blood agree," Michael said.

"Exactly."

Michael opened his right hand and called for his map. His heart skipped when he saw the skepna pits were directly across from Cluster Falls, hundreds of miles east of his original destination.

"What about the mountain? It's already Second Half-Dark. I have just enough time to get to the mountain and stand before you before Final-Set."

"Be at peace, son. You have until First-Rise tomorrow to stand before me. Use the portal to go to the pits. You will then use the portal to return here and continue on to my Sanctuary."

"Do I have time to see Cass before I go?"

"No. As you said, time is short. Besides, she has her own mission to accomplish. You can use your talking disk to communicate with her."

Michael sighed and took the floating sphere. It vibrated with power. The swirls shifted enough for him to see a plethora of oblong objects in the sphere's center.

"Seeds?" he guessed.

"Yes. I will replant the Blue Forest, and the latter will be greater than the former."

Michael laughed and called for his armor. As it formed around him, he remembered a question he had in Rün.

"Why was Cass able to touch me through my armor?"

"You trust her and have a relationship with her. The armor allows those you trust to pass through it. This is how Vold was able to murder the El'esh council of elders. They trusted him, and he used that trust to destroy them. Be careful with whom you enter into friendship. Things are not always as they appear. It's time to be on your way."

The river's current shifted and launched him skyward. He erupted from the river, and his wings carried him high into the air. From his vantage point, he could see the mountain of Ker'an with its waterfalls flowing down into the sacred rivers. Terraces filled with houses and fruit trees encircled the mountainside. Hikaru soldiers encircled the stone edifice like bees guarding their nest. Other Hikaru, some in armor and some without, flew to and from the mountain in every direction.

The Outcast Clan camped outside of a double ring of skepna guarding the portal. He landed next to Captain Ragnar, who sat tearing chunks from a large piece of meat. Juice dribbled down his chin as he smiled at Michael.

"Is that one of Lady Maja's legendary rugi chops?" Michael asked.

The tiger nodded and swallowed.

"It is good to see you whole again. What are you carrying?"

"It's a mixture of water and blood. Eímai wants me to bury it in the skepna's hive pit. He's cleansing the land and replanting the Blue Forest. I'm supposed to take care of this and then use the portal to come back here. Then I'm do go to Eímai's Sanctuary."

"I will go with you and stand guard while you complete your quest."

"I'd appreciate that very much."

Captain Ragnar called a passing cheetah and said, "Pass the word to be prepared to leave when we return. I am not sure when that will be."

The cheetah saluted, shot a glance at Michael and his sphere, and zipped away.

"Where's Neric?" Michael asked, looking for the osulf.

"He had one of the Clan unload him, and he and Xesa ran southeast. They are probably rejoining the osulf packs."

The tiger had a whispered conference with Maja. Michael went on to the portal, not wanting to intrude on their conversation.

The skepna whistled and bowed when they saw Michael approach.

*Why are they bowing?*

"They recognize your authority and give you honor," Eímai said.

*What authority?*

"You bear the cleansing blood, and my power resides within you. When they look at you, they see me."

Red streaks and splatters decorated the portal. He touched its smooth surface. Dried blood flaked off and fluttered to the pavement. Captain Ragnar came up to stand next to him and drew his scimitar.

"Skepna pits," Michael said.

Together they stepped into the disk. Red filled his vision. Then Michael stepped into a barren wasteland. Holes covered the landscape as far as he could see. Dwindling sunlight made the webs between the pits shimmer. He saw no signs of skepna.

*I wonder how many skepna are in those pits. Scorpions and spiders can have up to a hundred or more babies in a birthing. I wonder if they have natural predators that keep their numbers in check. Eímai, where's the hive?*

An orange dot appeared in the distance with an arrow pointing toward it.

He turned to the tiger, who scanned their surroundings, body tensed and sword at the ready.

"You see anything?" Michael asked.

"No. But that does not mean the enemy is not here."

"Wouldn't they want to stay as far away from here as possible with the skepna around?"

"Not necessarily. They may risk it in order to seize control of this portal. Go quickly."

Michael gave him a nod and flew in the direction the arrow pointed.

His heart thundered in his chest as he flew high above the pits. He had seen what these creatures could do, and he wanted to give himself enough room for maneuverability in case they attacked him. His enhanced sight helped him see that each pit contained at least one skepna, and others entered the pits through hidden tunnel openings.

"Why don't they have red stripes?" Michael asked. "These are solid black."

"They didn't pass through your blood. Only those who pass through the blood have the mark of the blood on them," Eímai said.

"When the Outcast Clan goes through the portal, will they be streaked too?"

"They do not need cleansing. They are already clean."

The closer he got to his destination, the more uneasy he felt. Fear and hate radiated from that place, and Michael started praying. The sphere's brightness and his armor blazed brighter. The sensation of fear lessened. He stopped over a yawning chasm filled with darkness so thick that the light from the sphere and his armor could not penetrate it more than a foot.

"That's the place?"

"Yes," Eímai said.

"I'm not going to have to fight an evil version of myself, am I?"

"No. But you will have to face the skepna queen."

Every science fiction movie he had seen with a giant queen alien or creature popped into his mind. He groaned. He had no desire to fight a forty-foot-tall skepna.

"How big is she?"

"Eight feet tall at the shoulder and ten feet long."

"That's a relief. At least she's not ginormous. Am I going to have to kill her?"

"That is not your mission."

"But she's going to try to stop me, isn't she?"

"Yes."

"This just keeps getting better," he muttered.

"I wouldn't send you here if you couldn't succeed. Remember, I am your strength. Rely on my power and wisdom to see you through."

"Yes, Sir."

He prayed harder as he tightened his grip on the sphere and descended into the hive. Skepna of every size whistled and scurried over a complex network of web bridges stretching from wall to wall. He weaved his way through the gaps around the bridges, and scores of skepna watched his descent with more scrutiny than his dog Oreo did the mailman. He descended two hundred yards to a solid layer of web with no holes or visible way through it.

"Is this the floor?" Michael said.

"You are twenty feet from the bottom. You will need to land and cut a hole large enough to enter."

"Won't my armor burn through it?"

"Not fast enough given your time constraints. The cover is three feet thick."

"Just slightly thinner than the length of my falcata."

Michael set the sphere near the pit's wall and drew his falcata. The sword's handle grew so he could grip it with both hands, and he pushed it into the web cover. The web sizzled as the blade split the fibers. He shuffled backward as he cut a wide circle. The incision glowed orange as though he were cutting metal.

"What's this made of? It looks crystalline, but glows like metal?"

"It's a mixture of both," Eímai said.

"How does that work?"

"It's my secret recipe."

Michael laughed. "Proprietary information, huh? Cool. This cover's really thick. I guess with the thousands living here, it didn't take long to make."

"The first skeptic queen affected by Ba'rel's corruption places the first layer. Each Queen after her added a layer, deepening the darkness underneath."

"So, she's sensitive to light. That'll be an advantage."

"She has not yet become a creature of darkness. The light streaming through the hole will not be as powerful as it could be because of the bridges across the pit. Your actions today will save her and the rest of the skepna from bondage to complete darkness."

"This is a rescue mission," Michael said as he realized the deeper purpose for his mission.

"Yes. It breaks my heart to see what my beloved creations have become. It is time to restore them."

When Michael finished cutting the hole, its center dropped. A loud thud reverberated beneath him. A cacophony of whistles and shrieks rose from the darkness. He grabbed the sphere and stepped to the hole's edge.

"How do you want me to do this?" he asked.

"Drop down and use your sword to chisel a hole for the sphere," Eímai said. "The queen will try to capture you. Dodge her and keep cutting the hole. When the hole is deep enough, place the sphere, bury it, and fly out of the hive as fast as you can."

"And if I'm not fast enough?"

"You don't want to know."

*Okay. So, failure is not an option. Good to know.*

He took a deep breath, spread his wings, and stepped into the darkness. He drifted toward the floor, and the light from the sphere and his armor cast a black-light effect. The exoskeletons of the thousands of skepna covering the walls, floor, and bottom of the lid glowed neon blue-green. More of the creatures entered the pit through side passages.

*I'm glad my armor will protect me if they try to sting me. I don't see the queen. But that doesn't mean she isn't here. It'd be nice for Eímai to be wrong, and I won't have to deal with her. But he's not been wrong yet.*

# Chapter 22: Cassandra

*Mushroom Forest, Western Citali Province, Aras: Spring, Day 15, Year 1, 5<sup>th</sup> Age*

The top of the council tree looked like it had been hit by several hundred pounds of explosives. Lady Achima lowered Cassandra into the council chamber with her tail. She kept her tail next to Cassandra while she gripped the ruined ceiling. All signs of the previous day's battle had been removed except for the scorch marks Eímai's lightning had made on the walls and floor. The council sat in their respective chairs. A different clouded leopard and cheetah occupied Elders Duwalt and Suri's seats. Twice the number of Ridarri lined the walls. Captain Trygyrr and his warriors stood several paces behind Cassandra like an honor guard.

"Speaker Cassandra," Elder Lennart began, "we are pleased to see you are healed and on your feet."

"Thank you for your kindness," she said, giving them the Vidarr salute.

"Let me introduce the new members of our council. This is Elder Havard."

The clouded leopard inclined his head, and his olive-green tunic rustled as he saluted her. His claws clicked on his gold breastplate.

"And this is Elder Fredrika."

The female cheetah in a light pink tunic and silver breastplate saluted her.

"I am honored to meet you," Cassandra said, returning the salute.

"We requested your presence," Lady Vigdis said, "because we wanted to inform you of the latest developments with the Vidarr. After the battle, we contacted the Vidarr in the Great Forest and the Southern Forest. We informed them of the Matu incursion into our ranks and the attack on the portal. They had similar incursions and suffered heavy casualties. All the elders, along with their chosen successor and most of their Ridarri captains, were slain. The Southern Forest Vidarr lost one of their elders and ten of their Ridarri captains."

*Oh no. How can they unify with the races when their leaders are dead?*

"Do not fear," Elder Fredrika said. "We have contingencies for such losses. The new elders and captains have already filled the leadership gaps. They wish to meet with you to discuss reintegration into one unified race and unifying with the other races."

"That's great news," Cassandra said. "I'm sorry to hear of the losses. My deepest condolences to everyone."

"There is a condition to this," Elder Havard said. "You must appear before them in person. They will not discuss unification by talking disk."

"Do they want to meet separately, or all the leaders in one place?"

"Separately first, and then all the leaders together in one place."

"No doubt they'll want to meet at a neutral, secure location. Did they mention any possibilities, or is it too early for that?"

"Too early," Elder Lennart said, "but we already have some ideas. The Southern Forest elders want to meet with you three days from now."

*Eímai, is this, okay?*

"Yes. You have enough time to get there."

*Do I need to go to Ker'an first?*

"Yes."

*Where are their elders located?*

"Two hundred miles into the forest along the Miwa River."

*If you say I'll make it in time, then I believe you.*

"You're learning," Eímai said with a chuckle.

"We also wanted to warn you," Elder Kaj said, cutting into her conversation with Eímai.

*Uh oh.*

"King Tarin has issued a warrant for your arrest."

"What is she accused of?" Lady Achima said.

Cassandra jumped at the sound of her voice. She had forgotten she was beside her, even though she took up half of the room.

"The usual charge for anyone who is a Speaker. Treason," Elder Vigdis said.

"And what proof has he given that she has conspired against the crown?"

"He hasn't given any," Elder Fredricka. "But we all know it is because she is Speaker that the king wants her arrested."

"Aras is under siege by the Legion, and he is worried about one broodling. This is foolishness," Lady Achima boomed.

"We agree that now is not the time for this," Elder Lennart said. "But he is the current ruler of Aras."

*He said "current". Is he hoping Taras'll get killed as the king did during the Dragon/Drás War? If so, does he have in mind who would take his place? Is he looking to rule Aras himself, or will he try to put a Vidarr on the throne? How many other people are hoping to rule Aras?*

"The Speaker is not here to overthrow the king," Lady Achima said. "She is here to unify the races and lead…"

Lady Achima stopped short, not finishing her sentence. Cassandra shot a glance at the Dragon.

*She was going to say I was supposed to lead Aras in defeating Ba'rel. Surely everyone here knows Savelis' prophecy, and they saw me use lightning to destroy the Matu and heal the Vidarr. They saw me bleeding red. It doesn't take a genius to figure out I'm Lightning from the prophecy.*

The Vidarr Elders nodded in unison. Elder Kaj leaned forward and placed his paw tips together as though he were steepling fingers.

"We know Speaker Cassandra is the fulfillment of Speaker Savelis' prophecy. We accept her with gladness. However, the king also knows about what happened here, and he will strive to remove her as a potential threat to his reign."

"I don't want his throne. I just want to do my job and go home," Cassandra blurted.

"We understand," Elder Lennart said. "Lady Achima has informed us of your origins outside of our world. We do not want to see any harm come to you and will do what we can to protect you while you are with us."

"How can I help the races unify when people are fighting because of me?" Cassandra said, her voice rising to reflect her frustration.

"That is a good question," Elder Havard said. "As of right now, we have no answers."

"Only Eímai knows the best course of action," Lady Achima said. "If we are through here, we take our leave to rejoin Captain Ragnar and the Outcast Clan. We will seek Eímai's counsel at the river."

"Captain Ragnar and the Outcast Clan have broken camp and are preparing to go through the portal," Captain Trygyrr said, taking a step forward.

"Did he say for what purpose?" Lady Achima said.

"Word among the Clan is they have a mission in Emer Province in the skepna pits."

"That is back the way we came. Eímai gave this mission?"

"I don't know. But El'esh Michael did leave the river carrying a sphere, which he carried through the portal."

"We must leave at once," Lady Achima said.

The elders nodded and saluted.

"Farewell, Speaker Cassandra. Farewell, Lady Achima. Eímai's grace be upon you," they said in unison.

"And to you," Cassandra said, returning the salute.

She climbed onto Lady Achima's back, and the Dragon leapt through the hole in the ceiling. She spread her wings as her massive bulk passed the shattered treetop and, with several flaps, gained altitude. She turned toward the portal.

Smoldering remains of campfires marked the remains of the Clan camp. Strange creatures with three tails guarded the portal.

"I don't remember you mentioning monsters like those. Are they a new abomination?" Cassandra asked over the wind blowing in her face.

"No, those are not abominations. They are skepna. They feed on the Legion."

"They must've gone through the portal already. Why didn't they tell us they were leaving?"

"I do not know. But we can catch up with them fairly quickly."

She dove for the portal.

"Skepna pits," she yelled.

"No," Eímai's audible voice boomed around them.

Lady Achima pulled up with such force that Cassandra grabbed the spikes in front of her to keep from falling off. She hovered above the platform, and the skepna turned to watch her.

"What do you command?" Lady Achima said.

"Bring her to my Sanctuary."

"How will we get past the King's Scelto?"

"Head to the top of the mountain. I have taken care of everything."

"Yes, my lord."

Lady Achima rose into the air and turned toward the mountain in the distance. Cassandra looked east.

*Eímai, please protect Michael. Bring us back together.*

She turned her attention to the mountain and forced herself to look beyond the swarm of soldiers guarding it. Terraces ran along the slopes, and houses sat among the fruit trees. Each terrace sported a giant doorway into the mountain. Thick doors stood open, and Cassandra could not tell if they were made of stone or metal. Jewels and swirling designs decorated the door jams. Waterfalls flowed from cave openings at the top of the mountain into the sacred rivers.

"Wow," she said.

"Indeed. But the outside is nothing compared to the inside," Lady Achima said.

Cassandra tightened her grip on Lady Achima's spines as they neared the soldiers. But they gave no indication of seeing them. They passed through their ranks, and still the soldiers made no move to stop them. She looked over her shoulder, expecting them to suddenly give chase. But they faced away from the mountain, gripping their weapons as though waiting for an attack.

*It's like when God blinded the soldiers so Peter could leave the prison without them seeing him.*

"I told you I took care of everything," Eímai said.

*I'm sorry for doubting you.*

Lady Achima flew into the southern-facing cave, and the light of the holy water removed all traces of shadow. Cassandra expected to be deafened by the roar of the rushing water. But there was no roar, only the sound of a melody so beautiful that it wrapped her in its warm embrace and held her spellbound.

*I've never heard anything more beautiful in my life. It makes all the music of Earth seem like banging on pots and pans.*

The light of the water illuminated the cave. The e entirety of the Book of Worship had been inscribed on the walls and ceiling,

"Do you know how long it took to carve all that into the walls?" she asked Lady Achima.

"Eímai spoke the words, and they wrote themselves in the stone," the Dragon said. "Remember, he is the originator of all the shaping gifts. He can use them better than anyone. We are expected."

A doorway, columns, and a platform made of clear stone filled the back of the cave. Water flowed from the edge of the stone floor, but Cassandra couldn't see an opening.

*It's as though it's flowing out of the rock.*

A tall man in a white robe, with a silver-and-gold sash around his waist, stood in a doorway large enough for Lady Achima to enter. His silver hair, beard, wings, and gold staff glittered in the light radiating from the floor. He smiled at their approach, but to Cassandra it looked forced.

"That is Jattir, the Grand Sage," said Lady Achima.

"He doesn't look happy to see us," she whispered to the Dragon.

"Perhaps not. While he is the head of Eímai's Sages, he is also in close friendship with King Tarin. In some ways, he has shown that he cares more for King Tarin's will than Eímai's."

"Will he hand me over to the king?"

"It is more likely he will urge you to swear allegiance to the king."

She landed on the platform, and Cassandra dismounted. Grand Sage Jattir approached and flashed another smile.

"Welcome to Ker'an, Lady Achima and Speaker Cassandra."

"Greetings, Grand Sage Jattir," Cassandra said, pulling her chata staff from her back and elongating it. Its tip clicked on the stone floor.

"Thank you, Lady Achima, for escorting the Speaker here. I will lead her from here."

"With all due respect, Grand Sage, I am led by Eímai alone. Lady Achima is my protector and instructor until Eímai releases her. These orders come directly from him."

Hot rage flashed for a moment in the man's eyes. His smile looked as though he gritted his teeth.

"I was referring to leading you into Eímai's Sanctuary," he said in a sickly-sweet way.

*This guy's dangerous. I'm glad Lady Achima's next to me. I'm going to have to watch my back while I'm here. Hopefully, whatever I need to do can be done quickly so I can get out of here.*

"I apologize for the misunderstanding," Cassandra said, bowing slightly.

Grand Sage Jattir gave a sharp nod, turned on his heel, and walked through the doorway down a corridor decorated with engravings of Eímai singing stars, planets, and the races into existence. Dragon and human followed at a distance.

"You could have handled that more diplomatically," Lady Achima whispered.

"I know. But I wanted him to know I wasn't anyone's pawn."

"Well, you made that abundantly clear. But you made an enemy when you could have made an ally."

"Is it wrong that I don't care? I don't like him."

"You represent Eímai, so your own opinions mean nothing. Your opinion should be Eímai's opinion. Grand Sage Jattir is the leader of Eímai's Sages. That places him in a position of authority. For the sake of his position, he should be treated with respect. Next time, consider how your words will affect your audience."

# Chapter 23: Michael

***Skepna Pits, Southern Emer Province, Aras: Spring, Day 15, Year 1, 5th Age***

The moment his feet touched the smoldering remains of the chunk of cover, all sound ceased. No whistles, clicks, or even the sound of feet on dirt. He tightened his grip on his sword and turned to scan the pit. He let out an undignified shriek as he came face to face with the largest skepna he had ever seen. The queen towered over him. Her six tails waved like cobras waiting to strike, and her two sets of pincers clapped out an agitated rhythm. Her red eyes locked on him as she let out a low trill. Cat-sized skepna scuttled up her legs and over her back. Her stingers snapped down with a loud click, revealing her spinnerets. A drumroll of clicks told him that every assembled skepna followed her example.

He swallowed.

"Remember your authority," Eímai said.

"No," Michael said, and his voice cracked.

*That was impressive. Try again without sounding like a scared kid.*

He cleared his throat and tried again.

"No." This time, the word came out with the same firmness he used when he stopped Oreo from chewing on furniture or his socks. "Put those away."

Another drum roll told him everyone had obeyed. Everyone, except the queen. Her trill grew deeper, more threatening.

*Eímai told you she'd attack. But at least the smaller ones won't attack.*

He backed away, eyes locked on the queen. He picked up his feet, not wanting to trip over the edge of the round web chunk he'd cut or an inquisitive skepna. The queen silently watched him. Everyone silently watched him.

He stepped down onto the floor of the pit and drew his sword. The queen released an ear-shattering whistle, and her tails fired six jets of webbing at him. He dropped the sphere as his wings rocketed him above the jets. The web splattered over a cluster of skepna on the other side of the pit. The snared creatures expressed their extreme displeasure at being pinned to the wall and floor. He returned to the floor and drove his sword into the ground next to the sphere. He stabbed at different angles, chiseling chunks from the packed earth. Another blast of web came his way, and he rolled to the right.

*Prof. B would get a kick out of me using his training to avoid an overgrown spider-scorpion.*

He rolled back and found his sword covered in web. But it sizzled and burned away under the sword's extreme heat. He snatched it up and continued chiseling.

"When am I going to hit soft ground?"

Six more globs of web came his way, and he rolled to the left. He rolled back and kept working. He did this several more times before he had a hole big enough to bury the sphere. As he placed the sphere in the hole, web smashed into his chest, knocking him off his feet and slamming him into the wall next to the entangled skepna. The queen walked toward him, pouring layer upon layer of web over him.

"Well, that puts a damper on things," he said, pushing his arms against the web.

Tendrils of smoke wafted between the web's strands. Blue fire burned a circle over his right hand, melting the web. He opened his hand, and his sword flew past the queen's third right leg into his waiting palm. He hacked through the layers, and it filled him with satisfaction to see the queen scuttle away as he freed himself.

"Let's finish this," he said, kicking dirt over the sphere.

As soon as he finished the job, he bolted to the center of the hole, spread his wings, and saluted the queen with two fingers.

"Have fun," he said.

He blasted through the hole in the cover and streaked toward the surface as an explosion erupted under him. A path through the maze of bridges appeared in orange before his eyes.

*It's like a heads-up display in a sci-fi game. I guess all that gaming is going to pay off.*

He followed the path, reveling in the way his body rocked back and forth on its zigzag trajectory. Shrieks and whistles filled his ears as the pit shook like a wet dog. The web bridges rippled, dropping their occupants into the pit.

"Getting crowded," Michael said as he struggled to keep moving forward without getting smashed by falling skepna.

The roar grew louder.

*That's not an echo. What's going on down there?*

He chanced a look down. A churning wall of white and red surged toward him at incredible speed. It devoured webs and skepna as it sought to consume him too.

"Go," Eímai commanded.

Michael turned to the sky and willed his wings to fly as fast as they could. The pit blurred around him as he blasted toward the surface. Yet the surge continued to nip at his heels. It slapped at the bottoms of his feet.

"Come on, wings. Go, go, go."

Finally, he burst out of the hive and rose hundreds of feet into the air. He looked down, expecting to see the gushing flow rise a few yards into the air and pour out over the barren land. Instead, it blew into the air and nearly crushed him. He zipped sideways, and it stopped twenty feet above where Michael hovered. Water, blood, dirt, stone, and the blue tree seeds rained over the landscape. His armor sizzled under the downpour but did not extinguish. The ground between the hive and the nearby pits rippled and collapsed, spilling red and white fluid into the pits. The fluid filled the tunnels that connected the next set of pits and collapsed them as well. Skepna fled out of tunnels and pits in a desperate attempt to escape the cataclysm. But the ground crumbled under them, and they fell shrieking into the churning flow. The destruction rippled outward, taking out each successive ring of pits.

"What are you doing?" Eímai said. "You have to pass through the portal before the flow reaches it."

"What happens if I don't?" Michael said as he flew toward the distant portal.

"The foundation of the platform is going to disintegrate, and the portal will drop into the ground. The destruction will continue, tearing up the remaining ground between the pits and the Brenus River. The portal will be tossed about and smashed. Its remains will be hurled into the Brenus River, never to be used again."

"Oh snap," Michael exclaimed as he counted only five sets of tunnels before the portal.

He rocketed toward the portal, eyes on the devastation below. He shot a glance toward the portal. He didn't see Captain Ragnar anywhere.

"Where is he?" Michael shouted.

"To your left, fifty yards from the portal," Eímai said.

"Oh, you got to be kidding me," Michael said when he saw the white tiger locked in frenzied combat with Vold. "I'm really starting to hate that guy."

"Hate is unbecoming of an El'esh," Eímai said in a firm tone.

"It's just a figure of speech."

"It is words coming out of your mouth," Eímai said. "Figure of speech or not, they create avenues for either Ba'rel or me to operate in your life. Death and life are in the power of the tongue, and those who love it will eat its fruit. Your words will always have consequences. Saying you hate Vold, whether in jest or not, plants the seeds in your heart that can grow into a murderous mindset because hate in the heart is the same as murder. That reduces you to Vold's level, and that is a place no El'esh should be."

"You're right. I'm sorry. I shouldn't have said what I did. I'll work on being careful what I say. I got to warn him without distracting him from the fight. I know, the talking disk. Captain Ragnar, do you hear me?"

The tiger's face appeared for a second over Michael's vambrace. Then a blur of brown and black replaced it.

"I hear you. What is it? I am busy at the moment," the tiger said through gritted teeth.

"You have to get to the portal now. Thousands of gallons of bloody water are ripping up the ground and heading toward the portal. It's going to destroy it in a matter of moments. We've got to go now. I'll be there in about a minute or so."

"Go through the portal. Do not wait for me," Captain Ragnar commanded.

"But…"

"Go. Finish your mission. Eímai's grace be with you," the tiger said, and the transmission ended.

The white tiger threw aside his sword as he leaped on Vold and grabbed him in a crushing hug. His evil opponent thrashed and pounded his captor in an attempt to break free as Armageddon sped toward them.

Michael landed on the platform and slapped his hand against the portal. But he could not bring himself to activate it.

"I can't leave him," he shouted.

"Fear not. Captain Ragnar is in good hands," Eímai said.

With a growl of frustration, he turned to the portal.

"Mushroom Forest."

With a different kind of roar at his heels, he stepped into the portal.

He stepped into a stampede of skepna as they ran into the portal.

"Wait," he called, but they didn't listen.

The last of the skepna vanished, and a boulder the size of a dragon erupted from the portal and tore a wide path into the Mushroom Forest. The portal teetered and fell backward. Its landing sent a resounding sound echoing for miles.

"Where's Ragnar?" Maja yelled, thundering up to him.

Michael stared at the fallen portal, unable to make his brain or mouth work. He suddenly felt exhausted. He crumpled to his knees.

"What happened to Ragnar?" Maja roared into his face as she grabbed him by his shoulders.

"He… he's gone," he said, tears pouring down his cheeks. "He grabbed Vold, and the whole thing blew up."

"Vold? What whole thing? Tell me everything."

Michael looked down at his hands and realized they were shaking. His whole body shook. Maja's fierce expression softened, but only a little.

"Tell me," she snarled, his armor crackling as her talons dug into it.

"I planted the sphere and got out of there. I didn't think the whole place would blow. It was a ripple effect of water pouring into the pits and destroying the tunnels. Each circle of pits was filled and destroyed. It headed for the portal, and Eímai told me we had to get out because it would destroy the portal's foundation. It'd drop into the ground and be destroyed. I called him on the talking disk and told him. He told me to go and finish my mission. Then he grabbed Vold and wouldn't let him go. I didn't want to do it. But Eímai told me he was in good hands. That's when I came through. It sounded like the world was ending as I did."

Maja yanked her talking disk from under her breastplate and snapped it open.

"Ragnar," she said.

Nothing happened.

"Ragnar," she said louder.

"I'm sorry," Michael muttered.

"Eímai said he was in good hands. Therefore, Eímai is taking care of him. I will rest in that knowledge. We will escort you to Ker'an and then go to find Ragnar." She turned to the gathered Outcast Clan. "Gather everything. We leave for Ker'an immediately."

Michael trudged to where Neric's saddle and bags lay in a heap. He knelt beside the pile and shook his head.

"How am I going to carry all this?" he muttered.

He untangled everything and draped the bags over his shoulders. He grabbed Neric's saddle and stood. The weight was considerable, but not overwhelming.

"I'm glad I'm stronger than usual. Otherwise, this would be rough."

He fell in line with the rest of the travelers and focused on putting one foot in front of another. He could not keep his mind from thoughts of the brave Vidarr captain who had taught him so much in so little time.

*I wonder if he's buried under tons of rock or adrift in the river. I hope Lady Maja finds him quickly.*

# Chapter 24: Cassandra

***Eimai's Sanctuary, Ker'an, Aras: Spring, Day 15, Year 1, 5th Age***

Grand Sage Jattir led them into a room the size of a football field. Twenty-four pillars, each large enough for four people to circle holding hands, stood in three rows of eight down the center of the room. Each column was cut from a colossal gem, and the light radiating from the floor used the pillars to create a stained-glass effect. In the center of the room stood a cluster of sculptures, one for each of the seven races. They were the same size. Their arms were raised while their faces watched the column of fire rising from the altar they surrounded.

Soft orchestral music played in the background, but Cassandra could not see where it came from. She stopped and closed her eyes, letting the music wash over her. It surpassed every symphony performance she had heard or seen. The melody filled her with a longing to go deeper into this magnificent place.

I'd love to learn this music. It's too bad I don't have my violin or drums here. It would be amazing to join whatever orchestra is playing.

Members of all the races except Ichtaca filled the space between the pillars. Some knelt in alcoves. Others stood and sang songs that sounded to Cassandra like passages from the Book of Psalms. Others headed from one end of the room to the other on business. Some carried artwork in metal, wood, stone, glass, and precious stones. Many wore the same type of robes as the Grand Sage, and some had more ornate sashes than others.

"Are the ones in robes Sages?" Cassandra asked.

"Yes," Grand Sage Jattir said. "Novices, apprentices, and masters. Their sash reveals their station."

He walked with head held high and made no response when Sages with plainer sashes bowed or greeted him. Their looks of disappointment made heat flush Cassandra's face and ears. She gripped her staff tighter.

*He's a jerk. His ego's so big it'd fill the entire mountain.*

"Calm yourself, Speaker," Lady Achima whispered. "Learn from what you see."

Cassandra drew several deep breaths and loosened her grip on her staff. She smiled at the crestfallen Sages and greeted them with their racial greetings. They returned her smile and greeting gestures.

Grand Sage Jattir led them to a thick magenta curtain embroidered with flames. On either side stood a burly Hikaru Sage with gold armor over their robes. They wore helmets with lowered visors, but the lower half of their face showed. One had a neatly trimmed brown beard and brown wings. The other had a short blond beard and green wings. Each held a staff with two curved blades at the top and a sharp point at the top and bottom.

"This is the Inner Sanctuary," he said.

The curtain rustled as she pushed it aside, and she caught the sweet scent of incense. The music became so loud that Cassandra winced. But before she could say anything, its volume softened to a bearable level.

Columns ran the length of the hexagonal room, and inside them burned metallic-looking fire: gold, silver, bronze, and copper. The combined light of the floor and pillars blotted out all shadows. There was not a spot or speck of darkness anywhere.

*How can there be no shadows?*

"The light shines at so many angles it is impossible for darkness to exist here," Eímai said.

The smell of incense came from censers swung by Vidarr Sages as they walked back and forth through the room. They spoke under their breath, and their voices sounded like humming.

Blocks of clear stone with padded benches dotted the room. Some bore books or scrolls, and the light from the floor rose, making them glow. Others held plates of bread and fruit, and crystal pitchers and chalices decorated with gold or silver filigree, full of different-colored liquids. Sages ate and studied, giving no need to the newcomers. She saw no regularly dressed people.

*This must be a Sages-only section. That must be what the guards were for.*

Before them stood two colossal gold doors bearing the rotating crest of Aras. It had no guards, yet it was the most intimidating thing Cassandra had ever seen. The hair on her arms and the tingling she felt intensified the closer she got to the doors.

*What am I doing? I can't go in there. Out here is good enough.*

"Do not be afraid. Come to me," Eímai whispered in her ear.

Her head whipped to the side to see him, and she saw nothing.

Lady Achima's paw rested around her shoulders. "Steady, Speaker. It is good for you to be filled with awe and reverence because he created and rules all things. But do not be terrified of him. He is good. You have seen him face to face and spoken with him."

The doors opened when Grand Sage Jattir reached them. Blinding light and a cacophony of music and singing burst out between them.

All of Cassandra's strength vanished. She crumpled to her knees and bowed with her face to the carpet. She shook violently as overwhelming power filled every atom of her being. She clenched her eyes shut as she gripped the carpet and thought, *I'm going to die. I'm going to die.*

"Cassandra, welcome," a thunderous voice said. "Jattir, thank you for bringing my daughter to me. You may go about your duties. Achima, please bring Cassandra here."

Cassandra barely registered the Dragon scooping her up and carrying her into the light. She did not know how long Lady Achima carried her before she was set down on something soft. Strong arms wrapped around her and warm lips touched her forehead. She let out the breath she had been holding in a long sigh as the shaking in her body lessened. She curled up and found the lap she sat in big enough for her to sit comfortably She still did not dare to open her eyes.

"I'm so glad you're here," Eímai whispered, and his breath tickled her ear. His hand caressed her cheek the way her father did when he told her how much he loved her. "You don't have to be afraid. My desire is not to harm you but to give you an eager expectation of good and to bring you to a victorious end. I love you with all I am. Open your eyes and look at me."

She forced her eyes open and looked into his glowing eyes. He radiated power, authority, and a level of goodness she knew in an instant she fell utterly short of measuring up to. Tears blurred her vision.

"I've messed up so much," she said, sobs choking off any more words.

"Shh. I have forgiven all your failures, beloved. I don't remember anything you did wrong. But this I do know, I love you, and I am proud of you."

"How can you be proud of me? I tried to kill Lusare, and I hated my brother and…"

Eímai put his finger to her lips.

"You kept moving forward, and you strive to not repeat your failures. But you don't have to be like your brother. He is his own person. If you were meant to be a copy of him, then you would have been born a copy of him. You are Cassandra, and that is the best person you could ever be. You have accepted the perspective of the wrong people. Your grandmother knows nothing about you, and yet you have believed what she says you are. Oh, daughter, I made you more wonderful than you could ever imagine. Not because of anything you have done or will do, but because of the way I made you."

"Made me?" she asked in a small voice.

Eímai's grin made laugh lines crinkle in the corners of his eyes. "Yes."

*Is he who I think he is? If he is, does Michael know?*

"You have much to unlearn and even more to learn. To that end, Lady Achima will take you to the Speaker Archive. It will be a more suitable classroom for you to learn in."

"What about going to see the Vidarr? How will I learn here and get there in time?"

"You will fly, but not on Achima."

He set her on her feet and motioned over her shoulder. "Look."

She looked and gasped. Golden wings made of arcing energy spread from her back. The energy formed feathers that ruffled as her wings opened and closed at her mental command. She laughed and gave the wings a mighty flap. She rocketed off the floor and soared high above Lady Achima. She spun through the air and let out a whoop. Eímai remained beside her, teaching her how to fly. She did circles, spirals, hovered, and flew backward. She didn't know how long the lesson lasted before she descended. To her surprise, Lady Achima stood talking with Eímai. She looked to where he had been next to her, and he was still there.

"How can you be with her and me at the same time?"

"I'm Eímai," he said with a grin as though that explained everything. "I will always be with you. Even when you don't see me, I'm there."

She landed next to the Dragon. She opened her mouth to tell her about the exhilaration of flying and stopped. Large tears poured down Lady Achima's cheek, and her armored form shuddered.

*She's crying. What does she have to cry about? Her brother? Or something else? Yeah, Eímai, I know. Focus on myself.*

"It is right for you to be concerned for your friend. When the time is right, you could ask her. But for now, standing silently by her is the best thing you can do."

Cassandra rested a comforting hand on the Dragon's side. Lady Achima wiped her face with her wings. She rested a paw on Cassandra's shoulder. She smiled down at Cassandra.

"Thank you," she said.

Cassandra smiled up at her.

"The time has come for you to go to the Speaker Archive. I will speak with you both soon," Eímai said.

She did not know how it happened. One second, she stood before Eímai and the next she stood on the platform where they had met Grand Sage Jattir upon their arrival to Ker'an.

"What?" she said, looking around.

"Eímai moved us to where we need to be," Lady Achima said with a smile. "Follow me."

They flew out of the cave into darkness.

"Why's it dark?" Cassandra asked. "It was still light when we got here."

"We have no awareness of time when in Eímai's presence," Lady Achima said. "Hours or even days could go by without us noticing. I would not be surprised if a thousand ages passed and we thought we had been there only a few minutes."

Lady Achima turned to the left. She tilted her body, so she headed diagonally down the mountain.

The Dragon circled the mountain twice and stopped where she started.

"What are we looking for?" Cassandra asked.

"The hidden door to the archive. It has the crest of Aras on it and you have to look at it from the right angle to see it. It is easier to see in Full-Light."

"Eímai, please help us find the door," Cassandra said.

She looked straight down, and there was the rotating crest, directly in front of them.

"Found it," she yelled.

"Shh. You do not want to wake the mountain. Place your hand on the crest. When you hear the lock open, press against the wall, and the door will swing open."

Cassandra flew to the rock wall and placed her right hand on the crest. The rock slid away from her hand, and warm light shone in her face. The wall slid back into place when they entered the archive. Around the walls ran ten streams of glowing water that emptied into each other in little waterfalls. The bottom stream emptied into a pool that flowed under a round central area with tables and benches like those in the Inner Sanctuary. The light from the water was bright enough to illuminate the entire cavern without being too bright or too dark. The cavern had been divided into three sections that looked like giant stairs running up the left, right, and back of the cavern.

"Welcome to the Archive," Lady Achima said. Her voice rolled through the cavern and returned in a rumbling echo. "As you can see, the eight levels to your left are the library. The five in front of you are the living area with a kitchen, bedroom, and area for relieving yourself. The last two levels are the garden. Lastly, the area to your left is the physical training area with an obstacle course, target range, and a padded area for hand-to-hand combat training. This is your home when you are not traveling Aras. You have access to everything here. Nothing is forbidden to you. Eat what you wish, look at what you wish, go wherever you want."

Cassandra flew from one area to the other, investigating everything. One section was a bedroom for Lady Achima, and the other had one for her with a king-sized four-poster bed with a soft mattress, six pillows, and warm green blankets. A wardrobe sat near the bed filled with clothes that were her size and favorite colors.

*I'm looking forward to sleeping in that bed. I feel like I could sleep forever.*

The bathroom had a flushable toilet, sink carved out of the side cavern wall, a big tub that filled with water when she turned a nob, and a wardrobe with plush towels and washcloths. The water came out of the faucet at a perfect temperature and radiated light.

*Of course it'd be Eímai's water. I don't think there's any regular water here or anywhere else in Aras or this whole world.*

The kitchen had an oven, a stove, a sink, and cupboards filled with dishes and cookware.

*Mom would love this kitchen.*

She yawned and drifted to the bedroom.

"Sleep well, Speaker. We will begin training at First-Rise," Lady Achima said.

# Chapter 25: Michael

*Ker'an, Aras: Spring, Day 15, Year 1, 5th Age*

Michael's clock read minutes to First-Rise when they reached the mountain capital. Hikaru, in silver armor with a white wings crest on their breastplates, refused them access through the lower gates.

"These are Scelto," Maja whispered to Michael.

"Come back at First-Rise. Then you may enter the mountain."

"This El'esh must get to Eímai's Sanctuary by First-Rise," Maja said.

"Then he can fly there," the guard said.

Michael walked away from the gates, and when he was fifty yards away, he dropped his load.

"That didn't go according to plan. Where's the door to the Sanctuary?" he asked.

"Near the top of the mountain," a red Dragon said. "I will lead you there."

"This is where we part ways," Maja said. Without warning, she scooped him up into a tight embrace. Her arms passed through his armor, and he felt her fur against his cheek. "It has been a pleasure fighting alongside you. Your valor and ferocity in battle will be remembered."

"Thank you," Michael said as he fought for breath. He felt like a little child given the size difference between them. He wrapped his arms around her and gave a small squeeze. "I'm glad to have gotten to know you all some. I've learned a lot from you all. Thank you."

She set him on his feet, and Frida gave him the Vidarr greeting. He returned it. The others gave him hugs or greetings. The Dragons did not try to embrace him.

"I hope you find Captain Ragnar, and I hope we see each other again."

"Eímai willing we will," Maja said.

They gave one last wave and headed east. The red Dragon grabbed his gear and headed for the top of the mountain. Michael followed, and in minutes, he entered a cave from which a river of glowing water flowed. It illuminated the cave and the carvings of Eímai singing everything into existence.

"This is the headwaters of the Brenus River," the Dragon said. "They flow from Eímai's throne and keep all of Parrésia alive."

At the back of the cave stood a platform and a doorway made of clear stone.

"The water flows out of the rock," Michael said. "I wonder if someone had to hit it with a rod first."

"I do not understand your words," the Dragon said.

"Back home, we have a story of water being supernaturally provided for a million people when a prophet, you'd call him a Sage, struck a rock with his staff."

"I don't think this rock needed to be struck. Eímai's water flows where he wills, and nothing can stop it. This is where I must leave you. Enter the mountain, and at the end of this passage is Eímai's Sanctuary. May Eímai's grace be with you."

"And with you," Michael said. "Thank you for everything."

He didn't watch the Dragon leave. Instead, he busied himself with gathering up his bags and the saddle.

*I wonder how much it costs to send these back to Chief Ewan. Though I guess he'd be Lord Ewan now.*

His movements grew slower as the fatigue of two days without sleep and his ordeal with the skepna caught up with him. He yawned and shook his head.

*I really don't feel like carrying these right now. I'll come get these later.*

He put them against the wall out of the way of everything and headed down the passage. The farther he went, the more tired he felt. He forced himself to put one foot in front of the other. He made it halfway before doorways opened in the walls, and twelve large Hikaru soldiers with winged crowns on their breastplates stepped out to surround him.

"And you'd be King's Scelto," Michael said with a groan. "I was wondering when you'd show up. I figured it would be at the least opportune moment."

"King Tarin commands your presence," a Hikaru with dark brown wings said.

"Of course he does. I'd love to meet him. However, Eímai commands me to stand before him before First-Rise, and that's in a few minutes. As soon as I finish meeting him, I will go to the king."

The knights drew their swords. "You will come now," a white-winged knight said.

Michael sighed and straightened. "This is not necessary," he said. "I told you I'd go with you to the king. But first I must stand before Eímai."

"No. You will come now," repeated the white-winged knight.

"To clarify, you're saying your king has more authority than Eímai?"

That made the knights pause, and Michael took that opportunity to drain the last three mouthfuls left in his canteen. Strength replaced fatigue.

*I should have filled this before I came in here.*

"You will do as your king commands," the brown-winged knight said.

"First," Michael said holding up a finger for emphasis, "I'm not from Aras or Parrésia. I'm a human from the planet Earth. Therefore, King Tarin is not *my* king. Second," a second finger went up, "I gave Eímai my allegiance before I landed in this crazy world. Third," a third finger went up. "I will meet with your king after I meet with the one to whom I owe first allegiance. You can follow me into the Sanctuary and stand guard or whatever while I meet with Eímai. Then we can go together to your king. This way, everyone is satisfied."

*Please don't be dumb and try to stop me. Eímai, what do I do if they insist on their way? Would you change these guys' minds?*

The knight with the brown wings gave a sharp nod, and the King's Scelto sheathed their swords.

"Very well. But do not try anything. We know how to handle your kind."

"Dude, I doubt you've ever faced one of my kind before," Michael said as the knights formed a circle around him and they proceeded down the passage.

"Do not provoke them," Eímai said. "Remember, your fight is with Ba'rel and the Legion, not the Arasians. They represent King Tarin the way you represent me. An attack on them is an attack on the king, just as an attack on you is an attack on me. That is why they are allowing you to come to me. Do not give them cause to change their minds."

*Yes, Sir. Do you want me to apologize for my words?*

"No. They needed to know you are not what they are used to dealing with. But do not be arrogant about it."

They led him into the Sanctuary, and Michael caught snatches of his surroundings and the music playing in the background as they hurried him to a curtained door at the end of the room. A Hikaru with brown wings and one with green wings stood on either side of the door. Their gold armor and white robes gave them an air of authority. As the group approached, they stepped forward and crossed their staff weapons.

"Only the elect may enter here," the green-winged Hikaru said.

The knights stepped aside, and the two guards motioned Michael to enter. He pushed through the curtain and soaked in the details of the room. The columns filled with metallic fire, the glowing tables filled with books, scrolls, and food. Arasians in white robes studying, singing, and muttering under their breath as they paced the room. The music grew louder, and it lifted his spirits.

"This is amazing," he said.

A Gwenfrewi male with a round head capped with a jagged fin and tentacles hanging around his mouth approached him with a wide smile.

"Welcome, El'esh Michael. We have been expecting you. Please, come and refresh yourself. You must be tired and hungry from your journey. Sit and eat."

Michael's stomach rumbled. He could not remember the last time he ate. The food pulled at him, and he took a couple of steps toward a table with bread and roasted meat on it. His eyes drifted from the scrumptious food to the golden doors at the end of the room. He stopped and sighed.

"I need to speak with Eímai first," he said.

"Very well," the Gwenfrewi said, and he retreated to a table loaded with bread, fruit, and shrimp.

Again, the food pulled at him. He balled his hands into fists and stormed toward the doors.

"Food can wait," he said under his breath.

As soon as he reached the doors, they opened. Blinding light, deafening music, and overwhelming power hit him. He lost his strength and fell to his knees with his face bowed to the floor. His armor faded, and he felt warm stone against his forehead.

"Welcome, El'esh Michael," a male voice boomed from the light. "You made it in time. Rise. Come in."

The words made his body and the floor he knelt on vibrate. He stayed down, shaking with fear. While he had felt Eímai's power in the past and seen him briefly, this surpassed all his experiences. He realized that those other times had been dampened for his benefit. Now, in the unhindered, full presence and power of Eímai, Michael felt tiny and insignificant. His failures returned to him, and he pressed his head harder against the floor.

"Michael, son, you can rise now," Eímai whispered in his ear. Michael still vibrated with the sound, but not as intensely as before.

A large hand rested on the top of his head and slid down his hairy cheek to cup his chin. It raised his head. He saw feet the color of hot metal and the bottom of a white robe. The hand continued to lift, and his whole body rose until he knelt. Eímai stood before him, his smile going all the way to his eyes. Michael saw no disappointment or judgment. He barely noticed the gold sash wrapped around Eímai's chest and waist and the flashing crown on his head. Eímai's fiery eyes had swallowed him.

"Why do you focus on past failures?" The gentleness in Eímai's voice wrapped him like Nana Sophie's quilts. "I forgave you of those long ago. In fact, I don't remember what happened. Come, my son. We have much to discuss."

Eímai held out his hand, and Michael took it. Live current flowed into him, and he shot to his feet. He felt like he could run from one end of Aras to the other a thousand times. Eímai led him by the hand into the light, and the doors closed behind him.

The light lessened, like fog melting in a rising sun. He saw a dais with twelve steps. At its summit sat a massive gold throne, covered in jewels. Shimmering water flowed down the front and sides of the dais, dancing over the steps and disappearing into the floor.

*So the rivers really do flow from his throne. Awesome.*

The light dimmed further, and before the throne on either side of the middle river stood two crystal Dragons with seven heads. They surpassed Lady Achima in size and majesty. Their bodies refracted the light shining from Eímai into a rainbow of color that made all the laser shows Michael had seen on Earth look like a child waving a laser pointer. All the Dragons' mouths moved, singing a song Michael could not make out. He could discern that every head sang at a different octave, making each Dragon a walking choir. The beauty of the melody and song tugged at the depths of Michael's heart.

*Their hitting notes and octaves I didn't know existed.*

Their golden eyes caught his attention next. They seemed to follow every move Eímai made. Michael stopped walking to test his theory. When Eímai released his hand and took his place on the throne, all twenty-eight eyes focused on him. Suddenly, he saw what he had missed. The light from Eímai shone into the eyes of the Dragons the way Lady Jovena's blood had filled the mouths of Ba'rel's idol in the Armorer's Forest. But instead of bringing darkness, Eímai's light flowed into their bodies and blazed out of them in an explosion of rich colors.

"The lamp of the body is the eye," Michael whispered. "If, therefore, your eye is good, your whole body will be full of light. But if your eye is bad, your whole body will be full of darkness. If, therefore, the light that is in you is darkness, how great is that darkness."

"Very good," Eímai said with a smile. "Come. Sit with me on my throne, and we will talk."

*Is that allowed?*

He felt dumb thinking the thought. Eímai would not have told him to do it if it wasn't allowed.

Michael walked up the steps and to his amazement, Eímai's size increased. When he reached the top step, Eímai stood twelve feet tall. He scooped Michael up and sat him on his lap. Memories of sitting on his dad's lap while he played cards at family reunions popped into his mind. The feelings of safety, security, and immense love returned to him.

"You should always feel this way in my presence," Eímai said. "Now, to more serious matters. The Legion is gaining ground every day. The Arasians are having minor successes in holding them off because the Legion brings reinforcements into Aras as fast as the Arasians slaughter them. Those portals must be closed. You are to take a small force and close the portals as you did in the Armorer's Forest. The Legion will not expect you to attack the portals directly."

"But I told Chief Ewan how to close them. I'd be surprised if he didn't pass the info on to the other racial leaders. Didn't anyone try to attack them?"

"No. The enemy ensured the races could not carry out any such plans. All the races lost members of their councils when the Matu sleeper cells engaged."

"What are the chances King Tarin will listen to me when I talk to him?"

"King Tarin's reign is coming to an end."

"What?"

"In an attempt to protect his throne, he will do something that will end his reign forever. Then a king I choose will take the throne."

"If I may ask, what will he do?"

"He will eliminate the one who brought hope to Aras in its darkest hour."

Michael's heart dropped.

"Are you talking about me?"

"Yes. After you close Ba'rel's portals, you will appear before the king."

"How would killing me end his reign? Everyone knows he's killed El'esh and has done nothing. Is Cass going to go after him? There's a prophecy in my world that if a human is slain, it's by a human's hand that the killer will be slain."

"No. All of Aras will see what you have done and the king's response to it. Your sister will be nowhere near Ker'an when it happens. And Michael, he is not going to kill you. But take heart and do not be afraid. I am with you."

*Uh, okay. I'm not sure that's comforting. What's he going to do to me? There are a lot of ways he could—*

"You are focusing on the wrong things," Eímai said, cutting off his thoughts. "I told you I am with you. You witnessed my power moments ago. It is not limited to this room. Nothing is coming your way that is greater than me."

"You're right. I'm sorry. So, who's on my team?"

"They wait for you in the Inner Sanctuary. One last thing before you eat and prepare for your mission. Once you have destroyed the statues and altars, drive your sword into the ground and command the ground to be purified. No blood required this time."
"What about the Scelto guys waiting for me?"

Eímai laughed.

Suddenly, he found himself sitting at a table filled with food. The Inner Sanctuary looked dim in comparison to the brilliance of Eímai's throne room. A male tiger approached him. He wore the armor of the Outcast Clan and a Roman gladius on each hip. He gave Michael the Vidarr greeting and his extended claws looked to be at least two inches long.

"Greetings, El'esh Michael," he said in a rumbling voice. "I am Hákon, cub of Bergr and Maja."

# Chapter 26: Cassandra

*Speaker's Archive, Ker'an, Aras: Spring, Day 16, Year 1, 5th Age*

"Speaker Cassandra," Lady Achima's echoing voice said from far away. "It is time to rise and start the day. Your breakfast is ready."

*No. I don't want to get up.*

"Get up. You have much to learn before you meet with the Southern Forest Vidarr."

Cassandra caught the faint smell of frying bacon, and her stomach commanded her to get out of bed. Her eyes popped open, and she closed them again as the sunlight streaming in through skylights carved into the high ceiling blinded her. She turned away from the ceiling and opened her eyes again. This time, she saw the warm light cast by the rings of Eímai's water on the archive walls. She threw aside the inviting covers. Her pajama tunic and pants felt like silk against her skin as she sat up and threw her legs over the side of the bed. The cavern floor felt like ice, and she yelped, yanking her feet onto the bed. She whipped herself around, so she lay on her belly and looked for the slippers she had found in the wardrobe the previous night. She found them to the left of where she had put her feet. She banged them on the floor to knock out of them anything that may have crawled in during the night. Finding nothing, she looked into them to make sure nothing was holding on. Finding nothing, she slipped them onto her bare feet. Their warmth dispelled the chill. She stood and stretched.

"Thank you, Eímai, for this new day. Thank you for getting me here safely and providing this place to stay and learn."

Remembering her wings, she looked over her shoulder to make sure they were still there. They opened and shook, energy feathers crackling near her ear.

"Thank you for the wings, too. Please help me to learn and understand today. Please give me wisdom and help me to make the best decisions."

She prepared for the day, washing her face and dressing. She picked out a long green tunic with flowing sleeves, brown leggings, a brown vest, a brown belt, and her boots. She combed her hair and examined herself in the full-length mirror in the bedroom.

"I look like Robin Hood."

"You look very beautiful," Lady Achima said. The Dragon's head poked up from the level below.

"Thank you. What's for breakfast?"

"Eggs, toast, fried strips of pig meat, and juice from Eímai's fruit."

"Fried pig meat?" Cassandra said with a laugh. "You mean bacon?"

"I am not familiar with that word."

Lady Achima turned and flew down to the central ring where their food waited for them. Cassandra joined her, reveling in her newfound ability to fly. She stumbled forward as she landed and caught herself on the stone table before she planted her face in a large tray of green eggs.

"Green eggs," she said with a laugh, "and bacon. I mean fried pig strips."

"Call it bacon if you wish," Lady Achima said. "But do not mock our names for things."

"Sorry. Did you make all this?"

"No. One of the Sages who tend the archive. Now sit and eat your pig strips. I mean bacon."

Cassandra sat, blessed the food, and piled her plate with food.

"Do not eat too much," Lady Achima said. "You have physical training later, and it would be most unpleasant if you lost your breakfast."

Cassandra scanned the archive as she ate. Sages in colorful robes worked on each level.

"Eímai has had the Sages tending the archive since the second age when he called the first Speakers," Lady Achima said.

"If there hasn't been a Speaker since Savelis, what's there to do?"

"The garden needs constant tending, and they eat the produce. Things can fall into disrepair from lack of use. Even here, things can get dusty. So there is always something to do."

"What's on the schedule for today?" Cassandra asked after washing down a mouthful of eggs and bacon with a swig of fruit juice.

"We will continue with the regimens. Added to that, you must practice flying and lightning control."

"Am I going to be in here all day?"

"We will spend today with lessons, and at First-Rise tomorrow we will begin our journey to the Southern Forest. You will get plenty of fresh air as we fly south."

"Okay," Cassandra said, popping the last bit of toast into her mouth. She wiped her mouth on a napkin and rose. "I'll go thank the cooks and study Eímai's Writings."

"Take heart, young Speaker. You are learning your lessons well. In time, you will not need my teaching."

The thought made Cassandra sad. While the line between teacher and student was clearly drawn and Cassandra didn't consider her a friend, she enjoyed spending time with the Dragon.

*It'd be nice to have a friend here. I wish Lucy were here.*

"Do not despair. You will make friends," Lady Achima said. "But until then, you are stuck with me. Off with you."

"Are you sure you're not reading my mind?"

"We have discussed this already."

"Mm hmm," Cassandra said with a smile, then flew to the kitchen level where five Ichtaca bustled around the kitchen, their four hands doing different tasks at once. "Excuse me," Cassandra called.

Heads turned her way.

"Thank you for the meal. It was very good."

"You are welcome, Speaker," said an Ichtaca, kneading two loaves of bread with her larger hands and holding and stirring a bowl with her smaller hands.

Cassandra returned to the bedroom and plopped onto the bed. She took her copy of Eímai's Writings and her journal from the nightstand next to her bed.

*I still have to write down everything that's happened since Theitai. Ugh. That's going to take a while. But I'll have to do that later.*

"Eímai, thank you for your Writings. Please help me to learn what you want to teach me today."

She opened the book and picked up where she had left off.

Two hours later, she completed her study of Eímai Writings and dove into recording all that had happened since leaving Theitai. It took her three hours of continuous writing to get everything down.

She closed the journal and set it and her pen on the nightstand. She flexed her hand.

*I'm surprised the pen didn't run out of ink. I wonder where Lady Achima is.*

She stood and stretched. She walked to the edge of the bedroom level and scanned the cavern. Lady Achima's silver horns stuck out from between the bookcases in the library.

*There she is. I think I'll walk. Sitting so long really hurt my back.*

She picked up a warm, buttered slice of bread with strawberry jam from the kitchen and strolled to the library.

"No food in the library," a lynx Sage said from the row of bookcases ahead of her.

She finished her meal in the central ring and washed her hands and face in the water flowing around the platform. A Talah Sage brought her a towel, and she thanked him. She ascended the stairs and saw no sign of Lady Achima. But an aerial view revealed her in the center of the bookcases on the top library level.

Lady Achima lay on a cushion reading *The Dragon Lords of the West, Fourth Age*. She looked up as Cassandra landed clumsily before her.

"We need to work on your landings," the Dragon said.

"Yeah. But this time I didn't nearly face plant in a plate of bacon."

"Considering how much of it you ate, you do not see that as a bad thing," Lady Achima said with a smile.

"True. Good reading?"

"I was reading about my sires. It contains information I did not know about them."

"You miss them."

"Yes. It has been over a thousand years since I saw them."

"A thousand years? Why so long? I'm sorry. I shouldn't stick my nose in your business."

"It is all right. I have been with the Outcast Clan fighting the Legion. The days blend, and one misses the passage of time."

"But a thousand years? Sorry. I'm prying again."

"Be at peace, Speaker. I am not offended."

The Dragon set the book aside and moved to a sitting position. She motioned to a cluster of high-backed chairs.

"Take a seat. Recite the Speakers you have memorized so far."

Cassandra sat in a chair with a pink plaid cushion.

"Clopis, Renald, Nicette, Vrandil," she said in a singsong voice.

She sang names for twenty minutes before she couldn't remember any more.

"Very good," Lady Achima said. "Putting them to music is an ingenious idea."

"It's how I memorized stuff when I was in school."

"These shelves contain the journals of every Speaker," the Dragon said, spreading her forelegs to encompass the library. "One day, yours will be here for future Speakers to learn from."

"But if I'm going to fulfill Speaker Savelis' prophecy, then darkness will be defeated forever. Won't that mean there will be no more fighting among the races?"

"I do not know," Lady Achima said. "We have only the day that is before us. Go find the journals of the Speaker who was present when the Vidarr divided, and the faction moved to the Southern Forest. It will be helpful to know the full details of why they split in the first place. While the Vidarr are not as long-lived as Dragons, their memory for offenses is."

"Is there some kind of index or catalog I can look at to find out who it was?"

"First, you need to know the date of the schism. Then, you can look for the Speaker."

"Okay. So how do I find out the date?"

"Do you not have a book containing the history of Aras?"

"Oh, yeah. It's in my satchel."

She retrieved the book and returned to the library. She flipped to the table of contents. She scanned ten pages of entries until she found what she was looking for.

"Here it is, in the second age section. First Vidarr Division. Page 371," she muttered.

She flipped through the book and put her finger on the desired entry.

"Okay. In the year 18,022 of the second age, the Vidarr quarreled amongst themselves about whether or not the Southern Forest should come under their protection. A third of their race took the position that since Ba'rel had proven to be a dangerous and resourceful adversary, all borders needed to be heavily protected. The debate grew so heated that Speaker Kelda was sent to mediate. The Vidarr fractured despite her mediation."

"Now that you have the date and a basic understanding of what happened, find her journals and any additional records to learn the full story. The library levels are for different ages. The first level is the second age, the second is the third age, and this one is the fourth age. The shelves are alphabetized."

"This makes me wonder," Cassandra said as they rose from their seats. "Since Speaker Kelda was Vidarr, did that make her not a good choice to mediate the argument? Wouldn't she have a conflict of interest?"

"Speakers learn to put their own personal opinions and feelings aside because they represent Eímai. To represent him is to speak, think, and act the way he would in a given situation. You have chosen to forfeit your own opinions in exchange for his. You speak on his behalf. If you do or say anything contrary to his purpose, will, or character, you deliver a false message to those you interact with. But yes, perhaps she may have been conflicted. Only her journal will tell."

"What if she purposefully left stuff out?"

"That is a good question. In that case, it would be up to Eímai to reveal it. He makes sure hidden things are revealed."

"And another thing," Cassandra said as they walked down to the bottom level. "What was the big deal? Why did it matter that some of the Vidarr wanted to protect the southern border? It seems a no-brainer. Ba'rel had done all sorts of horrible things and wanted to conquer Aras. Not protecting all the borders would be dumb."

"One thing I have learned about the Vidarr is that they are tied to their ancestral home. The Great Forest is where Eímai put them when he created Aras. They are not the same when they are away from that forest for extended periods of time. Put a Vidarr in the Great Forest, and they will suddenly be stronger, bolder, and more powerful. It is like we Dragons being away from the floating mountains and the sky."

*She's really got to get home. I wonder if I can talk her into going home after we meet with the southern Vidarr. I'm supposed to meet with every racial leader anyway.*

Lady Achima settled onto a cushion similar to the one she had lain on on the fourth level and kept reading her book.

"Let's go to the north to talk to the Dragon leaders after we see the Southern Forest Vidarr," Cassandra called as she hunted for Kelda's journals.

"You have to meet with the Great Forest Vidarr before we can do that," Lady Achima said.

"But it could be a really long time before I'm able to meet with them."

"One thing at a time, young Speaker. Going north could endanger the good thing you have going right now. I appreciate what you are trying to do. But you must not rush ahead of where you need to be."

It took until three hours into Full-Light to find the journals. The shelves were not as clearly labeled as she thought they would be. After lunch, Lady Achima taught Cassandra how to form balls of lightning and shoot them from her hands. Then the Dragon had her run the obstacle course. Cassandra changed into some loose-fitting clothes to make it easier to maneuver.

"Avoid the obstacles, hit the targets, and run the maze. You have one hour to finish."

She was halfway through the maze when she pulled her talking disk from under her tunic and said, "Lord Lysander and Lady Lita."

# Chapter 27: Michael

*Ker'an, Aras: Spring, Day 16, Year 1, 5th Age*

Michael stood and returned the greeting.

"Greetings. I didn't know Captain Ragnar had a son."

"He doesn't," Hákon said coldly.

*Okay. Obviously, something is going on between them. Should I tell him what happened to his dad? Nah, better not.*

Michael sat at the table, blessed his food, and began filling a plate with fried fish, fried seasoned potatoes, roasted vegetables, and a large chunk of hot bread. He tried a bit of bread with purple butter. It tasted like Earth butter. He slathered the chunk of bread in butter and bit a large chunk.

"Slow down," a familiar voice said behind him.

Qualoc strode toward him, a broad smile on his ant-like face.

"Prince Qualoc," Michael exclaimed, jumping to his feet.

"Just Qualoc," the Ichtaca said, pushing him down onto the bench. "I do not know that word."

"Prince means son of the king," Michael said.

"Ah. Offspring of rulers are called Lord or Lady, and the heir is called Future King."

"Future King Qualoc," Michael said.

"Just Qualoc, please." He sat next to Michael and filled his own plate. Hákon sat across from him. "Hákon, it is good to see you again. How are you?"

"Well," Hákon said. "It is becoming more difficult to hold the mountains. The Legion is attacking from in front and behind. They are determined to wipe us out so we can't hinder them. Destroying the portals will prevent their two-sided attacks. How is King Ueman?"

"He is in Eímai's Rest."

"I'm sorry for your loss," Michael said.

"What loss?" Qualoc said. "He is better off than I. The body returns to the stone from which it was taken, but he is more than stone."

"When will you ascend the throne?" Hákon asked.

"I'm not. Now that the Speaker is here, we will once again unite with the surface races and be one country again."

"What does Amoxtli say?"

Qualoc chuckled. "He is upset. But that is to be expected. He had hoped to be an adviser to yet another king. But he will soon be in Eímai's Rest as well."

"And Ohtli?"

"Ohtli. She wants me home and not fighting. She is the reason I was so late in coming. She insisted on becoming mates before I returned. She was furious."

"Is it okay to say congratulations?" Michael asked.

"Yes," Qualoc said with a smile. "She is disappointed at not being queen. But she agrees with me that the time of the Ichtaca kings needs to come to an end."

*It would be funny if Eímai chose him to be the next king. His willingness to give up the forfeit the throne to follow Eímai's plan of unification shows strong character and humility.*

"How is Kari?" Qualoc asked.

"The last I heard she was well. She commands our forces in the northern regions."

A lean blond Talah man with chocolate brown eyes, brown tunic, leather armor, green plaid kilt held up by a wide belt, knee-length boots, and a bulging satchel over his shoulder approached the table. He set the satchel next to the table and sat next to Hákon.

"Hello. I am Ry'lek, son of Ke'lek of Rün."

"Hi," Michael said. "I'm Michael. This is Hákon and Qualoc. Welcome to the party."

A Hikaru as broad as Hákon came next, his mottled white and blue armor covered in dents and gouges. A double-bladed battle ax hung from his belt, and he held a spear in his right hand.

"Greetings," he said, pulling off his helmet, revealing skin as coppery as Michael's. His purple hair matched his wings.

*The guy looks like he hasn't cracked a smile in millennia.*

"I am Chegar."

"Welcome," Michael said. "Pull up a seat."

Chegar set his helmet on the tip of his spear and leaned them both against a pillar with silver fire. He grabbed a bench from a nearby table and set it at the end of the table Michael occupied.

*Enter the muscle.*

A Drás with an angular face and snout materialized next to a column with gold fire. His scales seemed to mimic his surroundings like a chameleon. His helmet, breastplate, greaves on his shins, and his sword's scabbard had the same attributes as his scales. His pale, round eyes never stopped moving, and they scanned the room constantly.

*I don't see the crest of the Confederation. I wonder where he's from.*

"I am Baldoin," he said, sitting next to Chegar.

"I'm Michael. That's a cool talent you have."

"Thank you."

"Where are you from?" Michael asked.

"The region near Perrin."

"That's the racial capital of the eastern Dragons and Drás, right?"

Baldoin nodded and started eating.

A blue and black striped Gwenfrewi with a harpoon and white coral-looking armor over a water vapor robe approached next. Jagged fins tipped with long barbs ran up his arms, the outside of his legs, and along the top of his head. Small, pointy teeth filled his mouth, and he had round eyes with a thin band of green around black irises.

"Greetings," he said. "I am Gweldig."

They went around the table and introduced themselves.

"Is a Dragon joining us?" Ry'lek asked.

Everyone scanned the room. None of the five Dragons looked up from their reading or moved to join them.

"This must be it," Michael said, resting his right-hand palm up on the table. "Map."

The map of Aras appeared and enlarged filling the space above the table.

"We have seven portals to shut down," Michael said, pointing to each on the map with his left hand. "The statues should be fairly easy to destroy. My sword cut through the one in the Armorer's Forest easily enough, and the Matu who tried to stop me took some chunks out of it as well. The biggest challenge will be the distance between the Arasian and Ba'rel portals. It's going to take a long time to travel from one to the other. And with the portal by the skepna pits destroyed, we're one portal short."

Hákon's brow furrowed. "What do you mean by destroyed?"

"It was destroyed when Eímai purified the skepna hive."

"How can a portal be destroyed?" Qualoc asked. "They can endure Dragon fire."

"It fell into the ground, got bashed, and its remains were chucked into the Brenus River. I can tell you about it later."

"Travel is no longer of consequence," an elderly female Drás said in a quavering voice as she approached the table. Tiny silver horns ran up either side of her long snout, over her head, and down the back of her head and neck. Her white scales blended with her robe, and silver scales covered the front of her neck. Her amber eyes had vertical silver pupils. She leaned heavily on a twisted staff and carried a censer from which rose tendrils of incense smoke. She had four long fingers on each hand and four toes.

"Have my seat, great elder," Baldoin said, taking the censer from her, rising, and motioning to the bench.

Chegar slid over to give her more room.

"Thank you." She settled herself on the bench and rested the staff against the table. "Much better. This bench is harder than I remember."

"We could find you a cushion," Ry'lek said.

"No need. I will not be long. Eímai has made a way to instantly move from one place to another. Therefore, you can strike the enemy and vanish before they know what hit them."

"A teleporter? Where is it? Do we need an activator to make it work?" Michael blurted.

"One question at a time, young El'esh. The impatience of youth. Don't know how to ask one question at a time. I do not know what a teleporter or activator is. But I do know you need no object for it to work. When you are prepared, you will immediately leave here and go to the first portal. When you are finished, you will appear at the next."

"But we would immediately be seen by the enemy. Seven against hundreds or thousands are not good odds, even for us," Chegar said.

"We can thin them out quickly," Ry'lek said with a smirk.

"True. But Eímai has taken care of that as well." She held up the censer. "This contains an incense that will shroud you from the enemy. As long as you are not attacking, you will be hidden. The moment you attack, you will become visible. Young Baldoin, take this and slowly walk around the table ten times. Swing it gently so the smoke covers you and your companions."

"Why ten?" Gweldig asked.

"It is the number that represents responsibility," she said with a smile.

"I can already move unseen," Hákon said.

"This is different, Hákon son of Ragnar."

The Vidarr bristled at the name but kept silent.

"This will stop the enemy from seeing and hearing you."

"That takes stealth to a whole new level," Michael said. He deactivated his map and looked over his team. *Seven. The number representing perfection and completeness.*

"Are we able to choose which portal we attack first?" Hákon asked.

"I do not know," the Drás said. "But I'm sure you will find out soon enough."

They ate in silence while Baldoin circled the room holding the censer.

When she finished eating, she pushed herself up and took the censer from Baldoin. "Go in Eímai's grace," the elderly Dras female whispered before disappearing through the curtained door.

When she was gone, Baldoin sat and continued his meal.

"Ry'lek," Michael said. "You said we could thin them out quickly. What did you mean by that?"

"I know the secrets of Ky'lek," Ry'lek said. It sounded like a boast, but his face showed no pride.

"I don't know Ky'lek."

"He is my ancestor who lived at the beginning of the fourth age. He was a wood-shaper who used wood to create explosions that wiped out scores of Legion."

"I have heard of this," Chegar said. "The Talah claim Eímai gave this knowledge. Supposedly, it was passed down to his successor, who took his name. Only the Ke'lek knows it. But no one has ever seen it be used. It is just a story used to make the Talah appear dangerous."

"We are dangerous," Ry'lek said.

"Then why didn't you use it in the insurrection?" Chegar said in a smug tone.

"That's enough," Michael said.

"It's to be used against the Legion," the red-faced Ry'lek said through gritted teeth.

"A convenient excuse."

"Says the King's Scelto."

Surprise flashed briefly in Chegar's eyes.

"Yes, I know what you are. Every Talah knows Chegar the butcher. Do you still keep a tally of your victims on the inside of your shield?"

"Knock it off," Michael said.

"I left that life fifty years ago."

"Fifty or fifty thousand, it doesn't matter. You're still a murderer."

Michael jumped up, and his armor flashed around him.

"Enough," he yelled, his helmet making his voice resonant. "You dare to quarrel in Eímai's house? Strife is a tool of the enemy. This is why Ba'rel is wiping the floor with Aras. He divided you, and now he is conquering you." He stepped away from the table and stood at the end without a bench. "Eímai chose us for this mission. It doesn't matter what our past is or how we've failed. Right here, right now, we are men-" He paused and looked at the nonhuman-looking beings at the table.

"We know what you mean," Qualoc said with a smirk. "Please continue."

"Thanks. Where was I? Right. We are… beings… who have what is necessary to cut off Legion's supply route. Whether you like it or not, and it doesn't matter, so get over it, we need each other. Aras needs you, us, to work together. This isn't for our glory, but Eímai's. Now, we're going to leave whatever drama's going on in our life for another time, out there, kick butt, and succeed in this mission."

Heads nodded around the table.

"Good. Finish eating so we can get going."

"If we can choose the order," Hákon said, "I say we strike the portal in the southwestern corner of Siana Province. The Legion has pinned my litter-mate between two forces."

"Eímai, we ask that we can go to Kari's aid," Michael said. "But if you want us to go somewhere else first, then so be it."

"So be it," everyone at the table said.

Together they rose from their seats and gathered their things. When they were ready, Gweldig said, "We should stand together and face outward with our weapons at the ready."

"Good idea," Michael said. "Ry'lek, you get your bombs ready. Are there any objections to you covering me while I chop up the statue? My sword won't dull as your blades will."

"I have no objection," Baldoin said. "Ry'lek, would your wood harm the statue?"

"I don't know. They're designed to send a spray of water-soaked darts when they burst."

"Then use them on the Legion," Michael said.

They formed a circle with weapons ready. Ry'lek held a wooden cube in each hand.

"What do we do now?" Hákon asked.

"I don't know," Michael said. "Maybe we say we're ready."

The world around them blurred, and the last thing Michael saw of the Inner Sanctuary was the King's Scelto bursting through the curtain. Their shouting voices sounded distant. They rushed forward and slashed at Michael with their swords. But the blades passed through him without harming him.

*So that's why Eímai laughed.*

# Chapter 28: Cassandra

*Ker'an, Aras: Spring, Day 16, Year 1, 5th Age*

Two orbs appeared above the disk. The left orb contained a purple dragon with four horns protruding back from the top of their head, while the right orb had a silver dragon with a collection of small horns protruding forward from the side of their head.

"Greetings, Lord Lysander and Lady Lita. I am Speaker Cassandra. I hope you are doing well."

"Greetings, Speaker," the silver dragon said in a rumbling male voice. "Yes, we are well. You have not finished negotiations with the Vidarr. Why are you contacting us?"

"How do you know I'm negotiating with the Vidarr?" Cassandra asked.

"There is little that happens in Aras that we do not know about."

"I am contacting you to see what your schedule is in order to set a time to meet with you as the new Speaker. Also, Lady Achima is here with me at the Speaker Archive. She misses you horribly. I was wondering if you were nearby so she could see you. She isn't willing to go home until we finish with the Vidarr. I was thinking, if we happened to be in the same place at the same time, you could see each other. A thousand years is a very long time to not see family."

"You *are* Speaker," the purple Dragon said. "Though we are on good terms with our broodling and do not need convincing. We are currently in Ula Province on the floating mountain halfway between Ker'an and Chy'kyn. We will be here until half Full-Light tomorrow. If you can get her here today, it would give us time to spend with her."

"I'll try my best. She believes we're supposed to stay here at the Speaker Archive until tomorrow. Do you have any suggestions about how I could get her out of here?"

"Do you have Speaker Kelda's journals?"

"Yes. I found them this morning. Other than being all-knowing, how do you know I'd need those?"

She meant it as a joke. But neither Dragon smiled nor laughed.

"My sires were involved with the negotiations," Lady Lita said. "Vidarr, Drás, and Dragons have always worked together to protect Aras' borders. Any plans regarding them would have included us."

"Do you have their collected memories like the Drás do?"

"No. But I know much about what happened."

An idea sprang to Cassandra's mind, and she laughed. "I can tell Lady Achima that I found a Dragon source that can give me information about the Dragon's side of Speaker Kelda's talks, and they're on the mountain. Hopefully, that will convince her to go."

"Tell her the skeevals are plentiful on the mountain. She cannot resist skeeval. It is one of her favorite foods," Lord Lysander said.

"I will," Cassandra said. "Thank you for speaking with me and for your help."

"You are welcome," the Dragons said together. "We will see you soon."

Both faces finished, and she shut the talking disk.

"Okay. Now, how in the world do I get her there?"

"Get her where?" Lady Achima said, approaching from behind her.

Cassandra jumped, whirled around, and shot a ball of lightning at the Dragon. Lady Achima countered with a blast of ice that locked the energy in an ice sphere.

"Sorry," Cassandra said. "You startled me."

"This is why Eímai does not let his power be at your command. You do not have control."

*True. Why did he let me shoot at her?*

"What were you saying before about getting someone somewhere?"

*Eímai, please help me not blow this.*

"I found a Dragon source on the floating mountain halfway between Ker'an and Chy'kyn who has information about the Vidarr negotiations about the Southern Forest," she said. "They will be there until mid-Full-Light tomorrow. Can we go?"

Achima moved to block her way and brought her head down to Cassandra's level

"That is not good enough," Lady Achima said in a no-nonsense tone. "Who are they?"

The sudden change made Cassandra's stomach lurch. Ice crystals swirled between her teacher's jaws. Cold fear raked its talons down her back.

*She's mad. But why? Will she attack me? I wanted it to be a surprise. But I don't think she's going to let that happen.*

"Why are you mad?" she asked.

"I am not mad. The Legion is in Aras, and we have already seen where they have disguised themselves to bring destruction. You are young and naive. You do not yet know who to trust. I have seen too many good… too many fall to Ba'rel's influence. It will not happen again if I can prevent it."

*She's talking about her brother. She hasn't talked about him since that one time over Rün, and she doesn't talk about Lusare at all. But I have a feeling she knows her from before the War. She's afraid I'll end up like them. I'm not going to end up in black armor with a red sword, choking people for a lack of faith. And I'm definitely not going to be eating people. Maybe if I tell her about the skeevals, she'll change her mind.*

"I know for a fact that this source is legitimate. They also told me the skeevals are plentiful on the mountain."

"I do not care if they are," Lady Achima said, dripping saliva, replacing the ice storm. She licked her lips and swallowed. "We are not going anywhere until you tell me their name."

*If I tell her, it'll ruin the surprise. She's got that same look Mom has when she won't budge until I do what she wants.*

"I want the name now," the Dragon snarled in Cassandra's face, fangs bared and eyes flashing.

Cassandra scrambled back, putting her hands up to defend herself.

"Tell her," Eímai said.

"It's your parents," Cassandra said in a small voice.

All hostility vanished. Lady Achima's eyes shot wide, and her mouth dropped open.

"My sires? How?"

"I called them."

"You what?"

"You're missing them so much, and I couldn't stand you hurting like that. So I called them, and they said they'd be at the floating mountain until half Full-Light tomorrow. They'd love to see you, if I could get you there. It was supposed to be a surprise."

"I am not fond of surprises."

"Really? I didn't notice."

"We will go. However, you must promise to stay close to me and follow my instructions exactly. Enemies are everywhere, and not just from the Legion. Go pack. We  leave in an hour."

An hour later, Cassandra stood by the entrance to the archive in her green and brown outfit from earlier in the day. She wore a green cloak with a gold brooch at the neck. She had a satchel hanging from each shoulder, their straps forming an X across her chest. Lady Achima strode to the entrance with two large packs hanging from her back spikes.

"Did you remember the journals?"

"Yep. They're in my satchel."

"Good. Climb onto my back."

Before Cassandra could protest, Lady Achima said, "It will be faster if you ride. You will have plenty of time to practice flying later in the journey. But for now, we need to get away from the mountain as quickly as possible. We do not want to give the King's Scelto an opportunity to seize you. They will see us leave, but hopefully, they will allow us to pass. Frankly, I am surprised they allowed us to enter the archive last night."

"I think Eímai blinded them so they couldn't see us. There are stories of that kind of thing happening in my world."

"Touch the entrance to open the wall."

She pressed her palm to the stone, and she heard a faint click. The wall parted as it had done the previous night. She flew to Lady Achima's back, and her wings faded as soon as she sat between the back spikes. Panic sprang up in her.

*Can I get them back when I need them?*

"Do not be afraid. They are not gone forever," Eímai said.

"Let us petition Eímai's protection," Lady Achima said. "Great Eímai, we thank you for this day and the opportunity to see my sires. I am grateful. We ask your protection and grace as we travel. Get us to our destination safely and without incident. Thank you."

The Dragon spread her wings and launched herself out of the mountain. Cassandra braced herself, half expecting a net thrown down on them from above. But no net came. The wall of soldiers around the mountain parted for them to pass, and when Cassandra looked back, the soldiers drifted back into their original positions.

"Thank you, Eímai," Cassandra said.

"Yes," Lady Achima said.

They followed the Miwa River south, and Cassandra took in the panoramic view. The Armorer's Forest, with its pink leaves, covered the landscape to her left, and the wide-open plains of Ula Province spanned out before her to her right. In the far distance, she caught sight of dark shapes moving about on the land and in the sky.

"Lady Achima, what's that to the right?"

"A battle."

"Do you think they'll see us?"

"It is hard to say. If we can see them, they may be able to see us. Hopefully, our forces will be victorious."

Lady Achima flapped her wings harder and put on extra speed.

"Whoa," Cassandra called.

"We must get as far from here as we can. The more distance between them and us, the less likely they are to reach us if they are the enemy."

The battle faded from view as the miles rolled by. Cassandra pulled one of the journals from her satchel, but the wind blowing over her nearly yanked the book from her hand and sent it into the river. She quickly shoved it back in the satchel.

"Since you will be meeting the Dragon Lords for the first time," Lady Achima said over her shoulder, "tell me all you know about Dragons."

"The Dragons have thirteen families spread throughout Aras. Color, wings, horns, and a bunch of other things I can't remember, tell you which Dragon belongs to which family. Some of the families don't get along, but they've never gone to war with each other. There have been only five hundred times in Aras's 80,000 years where the Speaker had to intervene in a spat between the houses."

"The last large feud ended when my sires mated," Lady Achima said. "They were from opposite sides of the feud."

"Romeo and Juliet," Cassandra said.

"Who?"

"A guy and girl from feuding families who fell in love. It ended with both of them dying."

"Depressing."

"That's for sure."

"What else can you tell me about the Dragons?"

"They're split into West and East. Each has its own council of elders with thirteen members, one from each of the dragon families. The Dragon Lords are two chosen from their number by secret ballot. They are always members of two different families and a mated pair. Every family gets to be Lord. Before the Dragon/Drás War, there was a Council of Councils where both sets of Dragon Lords would meet to discuss things that impacted both groups of Dragons. But after the Council was betrayed and the Lords killed, there hasn't been another meeting. Did your parents become Lords after the murders?"

"Yes. But their time as Lords is coming to an end." Sadness coated the Dragon's words.

"Why's that?"

"Dragons usually do not live past nine to ten thousand years. The oldest of us was King Vasileios, who lived 13,942 years. Many believed he would live forever because he consumed only Eímai's fruit and water. My sires approach their ten thousandth year."

*So that's why she's missed them so much. They're going to die soon. I'm so glad I contacted them.*

"If I may ask, how old are you?"

"4,644."

"Wow. And I thought it was great to get to eighteen."

"How old are you, young Speaker?"

"Well, I had three Earth days until I turned eighteen. It's been longer than that here, so I guess I'm eighteen now."

"You are barely a hatchling."

Cassandra laughed. "It's when we humans become adults. But I guess to someone who's lived for thousands of years it's nothing."

"You should have told us. We would have celebrated your hatching day."

"We had a party planned and everything. We were going to celebrate my high school graduation, and Mike graduated too. But I guess that won't happen now."

"When we arrive at the floating mountain, I will treat you to a skeeval. It is the perfect celebration meal."

"Thanks."

*I hope it's not some gross creature.*

"There is Xjin to our left," the Dragon said. "We will soon be passing the Mushroom Forest."

More armored cats than she could count surrounded the portal outside of the Mushroom Forest. Red streaks and splotches covered its surface. Another group stood in the river and hacked at a black bridge spanning it. Pieces flew into the water, sending up tendrils of black smoke.

She searched for Maja and Frida and could not find them. *I wonder where they are. Maybe they're fighting in that battle I saw. I hope they're safe.*

"The portal to Ula Province is to our right," Lady Achima said.

Another group of Vidarr guarded a portal at the top of a high hill, surrounded by other hills. It reminded Cassandra of the hills north of Theitai. At least fifty Hikaru hovered above the portal, arrows on bow strings.

"It's good to see at least two of the portals are guarded," she said.

"Yes. But I wonder what those red streaks across the portals are."

Cassandra squinted and her eyes zoomed in to see an odd assortment of red streaks and splotches covering the portal's surface. "I don't know. But that same pattern is on the one by the mushrooms. They normally don't look that way?"

"No. I wonder what happened. Perhaps my sires know. Speaking of which, if you look ahead of us, you will see the mountain."

A mountain similar to the one she had seen in Citali Province hung suspended in the air over the southern edge of the hills. Rich forests covered the mountain, and splashes of color decorated it from top to bottom. But this one did not have ornate buildings carved into it. Instead, holes dotted the entire rocky structure. Dragons of every color combination flew in and out of the holes. Along the outside edge of the mountain's base stood a line of dragons in silver armor.

Each had a helmet wrapped around their head, with their horns protruding from it. Their breastplates bore a tongue of fire, and armor covered the fronts of their legs. Their presence, in no uncertain terms, declared that the mountain was well protected.

"Wow!" Cassandra said.

"That is what most outsiders say when they see so many Dragons in one place. But we used to number in the hundreds of thousands and could blot out the suns if we all took to the sky at once."

"I'm sorry you lost so many." Cassandra rested her hand against the side of Lady Achima's neck for a moment.

"That was a long time ago, young Speaker. My statement was to inform where we came from."

"Who are the armored Dragons?"

"Kerato, the knights of the Dragon race."

"Mike would love to see this."

"He must not be told about this place," Lady Achima said firmly.

"Why?"

"The El'esh is not to be told anything that has to do with the Dragons. Do I make myself clear?"

Cassandra frowned. "Yes, ma'am. But I don't understand."

"You are to unify the races, not equip those who would destroy."

"But he wouldn't destroy the Dragons. He loves Dragons. He always has. Even in our make-believe games, he was always a knight riding a dragon who fought monsters."

"Age brings about change. In this you must not disobey me. Do I make myself clear?"

"Okay, I won't."

*What in the world is that about?*

Lady Achima flew past the Kerato, and the knights sent up a roar that vibrated Cassandra's chest. She leaned to the left and flew past conversing Dragons walking along paved paths among flowering trees. She descended to a large, paved area circled by trees. Her claws clicked on the stones as she landed.

*I'm too sore to climb down. I'll fly.*

"No," Eímai said. "Climb down."

Cassandra groaned and made her way down. She stretched her back as soon as her feet touched the stones, and it gave a satisfying pop. "Much better," she said.

A silver dragon with a white belly, four horns protruding straight up from the top of his head, and wings tipped with three claws appeared between the trees. Next to him walked a smaller dragon with purple scales, two horns aiming forward from the top of the head, and a beak instead of jaws. A single claw tipped each wing.

"At last, you are here," Lady Lita said.

"Sires!" Lady Achima cried as she charged forward to embrace her parents, knocking Cassandra over in the process.

# Chapter 29: Michael

***Melania Desert, Emer Province, Aras: Spring, Day 16, Year 1, 5th Age***

Michael's team materialized at the base of a giant dune. It was one of five forming a wall around the Legion's sacrificial site. The sandstone statue and altar added to the camouflage so that anyone passing by or flying over would miss it. The only thing that did not blend in was the giant black swirling mass a hundred yards in front of the altar and the nine Matu and their seven Akzari guards.

The Matu stepped away from the altar while Akzari pulled the statue in the form of an Ichtaca from the altar and tossed it on a pile of other statues.

*No, it's not a statue. Ichtaca turn to stone when they die and bleed sand when they get cut. It looks like there are at least 30 Ichtaca in that pile. I wonder how much of this sand is actually Ichtaca blood.*

Michael cast a glance at Qualoc to see his reaction. He could not read any emotion on his face, but the Ichtaca gripped his shields and swords tighter.

The Matu and Akzari separated and chatted with their own kind.

"This is the last one," Michael said. "First things first. Eímai, please give us wisdom and help us to be victorious in this battle as you did with the others."

"So be it," they all intoned.

Michael scanned their surroundings. Pieces began to put themselves together in his mind. He pointed as he spoke.

"They've got to know we're coming. If it were me, I'd have troops all over these dunes, camouflaged to look like the sand. It'd also have Dragons, Umoni, and at least a battalion hiding on the other side of these dunes. This whole area is a giant bowl with no easy way out or good place to hide. They'd be able to fry us or fill us full of holes without a problem. Even if the idol and altar were destroyed, the corrupted ground would be safe. They could throw up new ones and be back in business in a day."

"You have a very disturbed mind," Ry'lek said. "Where do you come up with these dark ideas?"

"My race has perfected the art of warfare and killing. I also spent the last ten years studying history that was filled with warfare."

"You boast," Hákon said, standing straighter and pulling his gladiuses.

*Is he offended that my race might be better at killing than his?*

"Hardly. It's a mark of shame, not honor. We've fallen far from where we originally were. Instead of attacking the statue right away, three of us will attack the Matu and Akzari. Hit them from three sides. In the process, we may draw out any hidden forces. The rest of us will attack when they show themselves. Chegar can fly up to see what might be hidden that we don't see. He can tell us using the talking disk."

"That is a good plan. But they will not strike until they see you," Hákon said. "Vold will stop at nothing to have you. Word has spread that he will give great honors to whoever delivers you to him."

"It's nice to be wanted," Michael said, resting his hand on his stomach.

"How do you know this?"

"I say you purify the ground first. That way, if we are overwhelmed, it will take them a long time to re-corrupt it," Gweldig said.

"Good idea. What about the rest of you? Do you want to try the new plan, or stick with the tried and true?"

"I'm willing to try the new plan," Ry'lek said. "You haven't steered us wrong so far."

"Thanks, I think."

The rest agreed to try the new plan. After petitioning Chegar took to the sky while Baldoin, Qualoc, and Ry'lek took up positions on the outskirts of the depression. Gweldig moved to engage Matu while Hákon moved to the Akzari. Michael knelt next to the altar and raised his sword, ready to plunge it into the sandy soil. Chegar's face appeared above his vambrace.

"We have a serious problem," he said. "Hundreds are waiting on the other side of the dunes. I count ten Dragons and one Umoni. I don't see Vold anywhere."

"That's a small comfort," Michael muttered.

"You were right. As soon as we attack, they'll pour down on us."

"Unfortunately, we don't have a choice. Ry'lek, have those boxes ready. We'll take out as many of them as we can."

"I have three," Ry'lek said.

"It'll have to do."

"But be careful," Qualoc said. "We don't want to bring the dunes down on us. Each dune holds at least 18,000 tons of sand. Even I would be crushed under its weight."

"All right, let's start the party. By Eímai's grace, we'll get out of this alive."

He drove his sword into the sand and commanded the ground to be purified. Blue fire rippled outward from his sword to the surrounding area, disintegrating all the sand covering the bowl and revealing bare ground. At the same time, Hákon and Gweldig attacked. From his kneeling position, Michael could not see the fight. But the echoing screams and incantations cut short told him the two were doing a good job of eliminating the enemy.

"Here they come," Baldoin said, appearing next to him. "You'd better destroy the statue and altar before we're overrun."

Michael looked where he pointed. The Legion poured over the edge of the dunes like a tidal wave. They ran, slid, slithered, and crawled toward their prey faster than Michael expected. In a matter of moments, they would pack the bowl, and Michael and his team would have no room to move. Dragons rose to encircle the sacrificial site. The Umoni also ascended and drifted in Michael's direction, not appearing to be in a hurry. The agent of evil had a slender build. Their wings, armor, and the kite shield on their left arm were made of red flame. Unlike Vold's helmet, this fallen El'esh's helmet was made of sharp angles. A blade-like ridge ran from the forehead down the back of the head. The Umoni drew a slender sword with a blade made of crimson flame.

Michael placed the dragon statue between himself and the descending Umoni and hacked at the statue. Decapitated heads shattered upon impact with the ground. Michael's line of sight became clearer with every head that dropped. The Umoni drew closer. He hacked faster, reducing the statue to rubble. He checked on the portal. It's swirling form collapsed in on itself and ceased to be. Unfortunately, its disappearance revealed huge white bears with black streaked fur and forward-pointing horns on their backs and sides.

"What are those?" he asked.

"Dubu," Eímai said. "They were Ajabu from the Northern Isles of Parrésia and are the last Parrésian race to be corrupted by Ba'rel."

"Lovely. And how do we kill these things?"

"Do not worry about them. The altar and Umoni are your concern."

"Who and what am I facing?" he asked as he hacked the altar to pieces.

"Her name was Nicette, and she is King Tarin's daughter."

"What? Did he hand his daughter over to Ba'rel? If so, I'm so glad he's going down."

"No, he didn't hand her over. He did something far worse. As for King Tarin, do not rejoice when your enemy falls, and do not let your heart be glad when he stumbles. I have no pleasure in the death of the wicked. Rather, I desire that they turn from their evil and live."

"Why didn't you tell me her evil name?"

"She did not change her name when she submitted to Ba'rel's corruption. She wants everyone to know the king's daughter is the one slaughtering Arasians."

The last pieces of the altar thumped in the sand, and Michael looked for his teammates. Smoke filled the far end of the bowl, and without his helmet, he never would have found them. They stood in a circle, protecting each other's backs and fighting for their lives. Ry'lek threw his boxes into the swarm and sang a song Michael could not understand. The boxes exploded, and long darts dripping Eímai's water flew in every direction. They burned holes in every evil thing they touched, piercing five rows of enemies. Three columns of black smoke billowed into the air.

Michael flew over the rubble and made for his comrades. But Umoni Nicette appeared before him, red blade arching toward his head.

"They will die, and you will die," she said, her voice deepened by her helmet.

Michael deflected the blow with his shield the way Captain Ragnar had taught him, and stepped forward, stabbing toward her chest. She batted away his attack and delivered one of her own. They moved about the bowl, exchanging attacks.

*She fights like me. She's agile and doesn't depend on overpowering the way Vold does. She's really good. Eímai, what's the best way to beat her?*

"She is unskilled in grappling. Step within her guard and subdue her," Eímai said.

*Why? Isn't she completely evil with no chance of salvation?*

"You need to hear her story."

The sides of the dunes erupted, and the triangular heads of vipers large enough to swallow a Vidarr rose from the sand behind them. Their tan diamond-shaped scales glittered in the sunlight and blended with the dunes. They devoured everything in their path as they descended toward the bowl. More vipers followed, and the area became oppressively crowded.

Faced with a new threat, the Legion abandoned their attack on Michael's team and engaged the vipers. Sundered Dragons unleashed their inferno on the snakes with little effect. Two vipers launched themselves into the air and grabbed a Dragon each. Their white fangs pierced scales, and the impaled Dragons released a gargled scream. Their wings slowed, and they dropped to the sand, crushing the vipers. They rolled down the dunes, viper and Dragon corpses crushing fleeing Legion warriors and dissolving into smoke.

"Sand vipers," Umoni Nicette screamed, lowering her sword and shield.

Michael released his sword and made his shield extinguish as he dove toward her. He grabbed her wrist and twisted, throwing her to the ground. He pinned her to the sand. Michael's team encircled him, weapons pointed at Umoni Nicette.

"We need to get out of here before we're lunch too," Michael said.

"I have just the thing," Qualoc said.

He bent and touched the ground with his large hands.

"Roast them," Umoni Nicette screamed.

But the Dragons were busy and ignored her.

The ground around them sank as though it were an elevator. They descended into a cavern lit by trillions of tiny white stones embedded in the ceiling, walls, floor, and stone pillars.

Umoni Nicette's armor vanished, exposing the long-sleeved black tunic with a jewel-encrusted belt underneath. She released a feral scream and struggled to throw him off. But he kept her pinned. The ground above them closed and sealed them into the subterranean world.

"No," his captive screamed and fought harder to break his hold.

"I'm not going to let you go, Nicette, so you might as well be still," Michael said.

"Nicette?" Chegar said, bending down to look her in the face.

"Yes, it's me," she spat as she looked up at him.

"Why'd you betray Eímai?" Michael asked.

"Phah," said Umoni Nicette. "I didn't betray Eímai. He betrayed me."

Chegar reached out a hand to touch her face, and she snapped at him. He yanked his hand back and retreated from her. His expression became a mix of tenderness, horror, and anger.

*I didn't know a person could show so many emotions at the same time.*

"How did he betray you?" said Michael.

"Release me, and I'll tell you," she said, sneering at Chegar.

"Don't do it," Qualoc said as the platform came to rest at the bottom of the cavern. "Her words mean nothing. She is filled with lies, and the truth is not in her. The moment you release her, she will flee or attack us."

An idea came to Michael, and he released her. He stepped back and crossed his arms. The Umoni jumped to her feet with a wolfish grin.

"Fools. Now you will die, and I will devour you."

She grabbed onto something he could not see and pulled. Nothing happened. She pulled harder. Still nothing. She made a sound like a wounded animal, grabbed the object with both hands, and yanked as if her life depended on releasing the invisible object.

"You will not be able to draw your sword until you answer my question," Michael said, crossing his arms.

"What have you done to me? Why can't I use my armor? My wings?"

Michael's gaze moved to the space above her shoulders. She had no wings.

"What happened to your wings?"

She growled at him and pulled harder. She tossed her hands up in frustration and tried to catch her breath. Chegar stood behind her, and again his hand extended toward her. Pain twisted his expression.

"Don't touch me," she snarled at him, fixing him with blazing eyes. "Save your sentiments for someone who cares."

He lowered his hand and tightened his grip on his sword.

"What happened, Chegar?" Michael asked. "You know, don't you?"

"Yes," the Hikaru said, his eyes locked on the seething Umoni. "King Tarin summoned Lady Nicette to take the oath. He said she'd be the perfect tool to solidify his power. She'd wipe out the Savelins and other malcontents. When she refused, declaring her loyalty to Eímai, he had her wings cut off."

"You tried to stop it," Michael said. "You tried to protect her."

"Yes. I was his Captain of Captains. I thought he would listen to me. But he refused. I fought. But there were too many. They beat me until I blacked out. When I woke, he had me stripped of rank and cast me out. He said the only reason I wasn't dead was my years of faithful service. I tried to find her, but she had disappeared."

"Poor Chegar," mocked Umoni Nicette. "Fought so hard to fail so magnificently. My *father* had me cast out of Ker'an." She locked eyes with Chegar. "They literally threw me from the mountain."

Chegar's horror became a mask of rage. The Umoni gave a bitter laugh and turned from him to lock eyes with Michael.

"I landed several yards from the Miwa River. I crawled, bleeding and half dead, to it and pulled myself in. I begged and pleaded for

Eímai to heal me. He said he had. The wounds had healed, but not my wings. He claimed to love me, yet he let this happen to me. He refused to heal me. So I went to Ba'rel. He gave me wings and made it so I would never be hurt again."

"Didn't you still have Eímai's fiery wings?" Michael asked.

"Yes. But what good are they when my feathered wings are gone? I would never again feel the exhilaration of floating on the wind. Of soaring."

"But Ba'rel didn't give you feathered wings either."

"Yes, he did," she said, her hands rising before her to caress something only she could see. She looked like she stroked a cat. "Aren't their feathers gorgeous? His wings are far better than Eímai's."

"She's crazy," Ry'lek said.

Umoni Nicette snarled at him, and the Talah retreated a step.

*She might be crazy. But she's also deceived. It's too bad her story ends like this, and she'll never come back to the light.*

He drew his sword, and the world around him blurred. When it returned to normal, he stood in Eímai's Inner Sanctuary. A Gwenfrewi Sage with a clown fish head and body coloring approached him.

"Come. Eat and sleep. You've had a busy day."

Michael looked around him for the rest of his team.

"Did anyone else suddenly appear?"

"No, El'esh Michael. You are the only one."

*They're alone with Nicette. Eímai, please protect them.*

# Chapter 30: Cassandra

***Floating Mountain, Ula Province, Aras: Spring, Day 16, Year 1, 5th Age***

"It is good to see you, little one," Lord Lysander said.

"It is good to see you as well," Lady Achima said.

"I am glad you decided to come," Lady Lita said.

"I as well," Lady Achima said.

The sounds of their conversation and scales and wings rubbing against each other reached Cassandra, who lay face down on the paving stones. Her knees and palms complained at the sudden impact.

"She's not excited at all," Cassandra muttered, looking at her hands. Droplets of blood dotted the long red scratches covering her fingers and palms. "I wonder what my knees look like. Be healed in the name of Eímai."

Lightning danced around her hands, tickling the wounds and closing them. The droplets of blood turned to ash and blew away. She rolled over, and the golden energy arched to her knees, diving into the holes in her leggings. When it finished healing her torn flesh, it mended her leggings and faded.

"Much better."

A colossal shadow shrouded her. She looked up into Lord Lysander's serious face. She felt tiny in comparison. He reached out a foreleg, claws open.

"He is offering to help you up," Eímai said.

She took the proffered foot, and he gently raised her to her feet.

"Speaker, thank you for bringing our broodling to us," he said.

"You're welcome."

"Were you seriously injured?" Lady Lita asked.

*Leave it to the female to care about whether or not I'm hurt.*

"Not too badly. Scraped hands and knees. I'm better now. Thank you."

"I apologize, young Speaker. I did not mean to knock you over," Lady Achima said.

"It's okay. I did the same a few years ago when I ran to my mom. Plowed a little kid over and sent him to the hospital with a concussion. I don't think I apologized so much in my life. His mom was cool, though. She wasn't mad."

"She is strange for a Talah," Lord Lysander said to his daughter.

"She is not Talah. She is from another world."

"Another world?" Lady Lita asked, looking Cassandra over from head to toe.

"Yes. I'm human. That's why I bleed red."

"The crimson river," Lady Lita said.

Cassandra nodded. "Is there a place where I can go while you catch up with Lady Achima?"

"You have access to anywhere, but what is guarded by the Kerato," Lord Lysander said. "Follow their instructions and no harm will come to you."

"Thank you," Cassandra said, giving them the Dragon greeting, and walked toward the nearest grove of trees.

"Where did you find her?" Lord Lysander said.

"I caught her when she fell into the hole she blasted in Rün."

"She what?" Lady Lita said, her voice rising in surprise.

Cassandra stepped among the flowering trees. Large clumps of light purple lilac blossoms hung from the orange, oak-shaped leaves. The scent of lilacs washed over her.

"Mmm, lilac. My favorite. I wonder if it's okay for me to pick some of these."

"By all means, Speaker," a voice said above her.

A white, hornless Dragon the size of her dog Oreo, stood in the branches of the tree next to her. The Dragon smiled at her, and to Cassandra it looked like a hungry smile. She kept her eyes on the Dragon and backed away, heading in the direction she had come.

"Is something wrong?" a rumbling voice said behind her.

She whirled and found herself face to chest with a red Kerato. He looked down at her with purple eyes.

"What is wrong, Speaker?" the red Dragon asked.

"I am trying to return to Lord Lysander," Cassandra said, feeling the white Dragon's eyes on her. Everything in her screamed to run. But something held her in place.

"There is no need for that," the red Dragon said. "You are perfectly safe here."

"I will return anyway," she said, moving to step around the Kerato.

The white Dragon dropped from the tree and landed behind her. He let out a low hiss.

Terror stabbed her heart and stopped her mid-stride.

"You are not going anywhere, morsel," the red Dragon said, giving her a broader grin.

It was the same grin Lusare had given her.

*Sundered!*

"Achima," she screamed at the top of her voice as she yanked her staff from her back.

The Sundered Dragons laughed.

"She cannot hear your little voice," the white Dragon said.

"Your time as Speaker is at an end. But we will have the privilege of stealing Lusare's prize from under her," the red Dragon said.

"Achima," she screamed again.

A flash of red flew at her from the left. She dropped and rolled as the red Dragon's claws flew over her, and the white Dragon pounced on where she had lain seconds before. She rolled to her feet. Gripping her staff like a bat, she cracked the white Dragon across the head. The impact sent vibrations through her arms. She dropped it and rubbed her hands on her legs to remove the tingling. The white Dragon hissed, and the two stalked toward her.

She backed up, hoping she would not run into any more Dragons. She dared not look behind her. Her taekwondo teacher, Master Soh's voice rose from the depths of her mind.

"Never turn your back on an opponent, especially one that wants to kill you. But use their strength against them. If you face more than one, position yourself so one is between you and the others. Take that one down and repeat the process. When able, flee. Avoidance is the first step to safety."

Cassandra stepped to her right, and the Dragons moved to follow. She continued to circle until the white Dragon stood between her and the red.

*Okay. I have one between me. Now what? No one taught me what to do when facing a Dragon. I wish Mike were here. Huh. All that time I spent being mad at him for acting like a knight, and now I want him to be one. Eímai, what do I do now?*

"Retrieve your staff," Eímai said.

She held out her hand, and it leapt toward her. The red Dragon snatched it from the air.

"No, no. You won't be getting this back."

"How'd you do that? It's invisible."

"I'm Kerato. We are taught to detect a Speaker's invisible weapon in case another Speaker tried to slaughter us as Savelis had."

She held out her hand again and willed the staff to come to her. But the Dragon held it in a crushing grip.

The white Dragon opened his mouth, and blue fire leaped at her. She turned and ran, zigzagging between the trees. She flipped off stumps, boulders, and rock ledges in an attempt to avoid the fiery onslaught following her. Flames shriveled flowers and leaves, igniting trees and sending columns of acrid smoke into the air.

The forest ended, and a green Dragon and a blue Dragon, both in Kerato armor, landed before her with such force that they cracked the stone. Cassandra slipped and slid between the two knights. The fire from the white and red Dragons slammed into their chests. Cassandra continued to slide over the smooth stones. She tried to grab onto them, but her fingers could not get a grip. She slid off the edge of the mountain and tumbled toward the ground a mile below.

She screamed.

"Wings," Eímai said.

They appeared at her frantic call, and her body jerked as they righted her.

"Thank you," she breathed.

She rose over the edge of the mountain and found a battle raging. Ten more dragons had joined the white and red. Six more had joined the green and blue, and a host more not wearing armor approached from behind the Sundered Dragons. Seven Kerato lay in pools of silver blood. Black smoke rose from the dissolving corpses of the white and red Dragons that had attacked her. The remaining Sundered took to the sky at the sight of the reinforcements. Cassandra willed her wings to vanish and ducked behind a scorched boulder.

*I hope they don't see me.*

They flew by with the host of Dragons in hot pursuit.

Cassandra emerged from hiding and gasped. Dragons lay in unnatural positions, pools of silver blood under their torn bodies. She ran to the blue Dragon and put a hand on the shuddering chest. He wheezed. Claws had rent his breastplate and chest.

"Be healed in the name of Eímai," she said, placing her hands over the wound.

Hot blood scalded her hands. She hissed, but kept them on the wound as lightning poured from her hands. The flesh closed, and the Dragon released a shuddering sigh. When the power ceased to flow, she ran to the next Dragon. Two of the Dragons were already dead, and Eímai told her not to try to resurrect them.

When the last rose to their feet, Cassandra collapsed. She struggled to keep her head up as she lay on the bloody stone. Dragon claws wrapped around her and lifted her limp form. Lady Achima's face appeared before her.

"Are you hurt?" she asked.

"Tired," Cassandra said, "and messy. I need a bath."

"I will carry you to the Miwa River. You can bathe in its healing waters. I told you to stay close to me, but I did not back up my words. I was so focused on gorging on skeeval I forgot about you. I apologize. Please forgive me."

"Of course, I forgive you. I'm glad you got your skeevals. I'm also glad those Sundered were discovered. I hope we stopped them from doing whatever they were here for."

"As do I."

After the river cleaned and strengthened Cassandra, the Dragon carried her to the mountain. Kerato blew fire into the air and slapped their tails in a drumming rhythm.

"What are they doing?" Cassandra asked.

"They are honoring you. You proved to be a friend of the Dragons. Well done."

"Why didn't those Dragons look Sundered? They looked like any other Dragon."

"I do not know. The enemy has discovered a way to hide his Legion among us. This is a disturbing development. Matu disguised as Ridarri. Sundered disguised as Kerato. The Legion hiding in the hills north of Theitai. What else has Ba'rel devised?"

"Is it wrong to wish I were back home in the safety of my own house?"

"No. I too long for the days when I lived in safety. But until evil is forever destroyed, there is no true safety to be had. That is, except in the arms of Eímai."

Cassandra's stomach rumbled.

"It is time for you to eat. I still have to get you a skeeval to celebrate your hatching."

"What is a skeeval?"

"The most scrumptious rodent you have ever tasted."

*I had a feeling it was something like that.* "I'm going to pass on the skeeval. Go ahead and eat mine."

"Nonsense. You must have one."

*Is this an eat it or risk insulting them kind of thing? Eímai, please help me.*

Lady Achima entered the bottom of the mountain and flew through a series of tunnels until she came to the mountain's heart. Luminescent stones dotted the walls and ceiling, casting a warm glow similar to what Eímai's water had done in the archive. Thousands of Dragons sat in groups, roasting giant chunks of meat with their fire and devouring them. Conversations rolled through the cavern like thunder from an approaching storm. At the center of the activity sat Lord Lysander, Lady Lita, and eleven dragons of varying sizes and colors.

"Is that the Dragon Council of Elders?" she asked.

"Yes. They have gathered for the choosing of the next Dragon Lords."

"But your parents aren't gone yet. Why choose now?"

"My sires believe that in this dark time, there must be stable leadership for the Western Dragons. It will take too long to mourn and choose after they have gone to Eímai's Rest. If new Lords are chosen now, leadership can transition without delay."

"Did they want this or is it being forced on them?"

"As I said, they believe this is the best course of action. They do not mind stepping down. It will give them a chance to spend time with me before they leave."

"I'm glad you'll get to spend time with them. I'll head to the Southern Forest tomorrow, and you can stay with your parents."

"No," Lady Achima said forcefully. "I am not leaving you. Eímai called me to teach and protect you. I will not abandon his call now."

"But what about your parents? How are you supposed to spend time with them if you're going to Aras with me?"

"They are coming."

"Really?"

"Why not? As you said, they know about what happened when the Vidarr divided. What could be better than having the direct source of the information you need traveling with you?"

"I hope the Vidarr don't mind."

"From what I remember, the southern Vidarr have always been against the strife that has filled Aras. They even refused to build a racial capital or acknowledge Sigvarrd as the racial capital of the Vidarr."

Cassandra flew from Lady Achima's back and sat on a stone bench offered to her by a slender green Dragon with a chocolate brown belly.

"Speaker Cassandra," Lord Lysander said, quenching his fiery breath. His meal sizzled and released an odor similar to grilling hamburgers. "You have done a great service to the Western Dragons. We are in your debt."

"You don't owe me anything," Cassandra said. "I'm just glad it didn't end up worse than it did."

"Spoken like a true Speaker," the silver Dragon said. "I was wrong about you. I apologize."

The eyes of the cluster of Dragons widened as the Dragon Lord lowered his head until his nose rested on the floor.

*He must not do this often. What do I do?*

"Accept his apology and express your gratitude to me for the safety of the dragons on the mountain," Eímai said.

"I accept your apology. I am grateful to Eímai that everyone here is safe. My biggest desire is for Aras' races to be unified and dwell in peace and security, no longer threatened by Ba'rel."

Lord Lysander raised his head, a small smile revealing his flashing fangs.

"There is no need to attempt to convince us. We agree with you. We were about to vote. As Speaker, it is right for you to witness this occasion."

"I would be honored."

Lady Achima walked the circle of elders with a stone bowl. Each elder dropped a flat stone with cuneiform carved onto one side into the bowl. When she returned to her place, she handed the bowl to a yellow elder with an iridescent pink belly.

"Thank you," the elder said in a quavering female voice.

She poured Eímai's water into the bowl.

"What's going on?" Cassandra whispered to Lady Achima.

"Each stone has the name of an elder. Eímai's water is poured over them, and whichever stone rises to the surface is the one Eímai has chosen. This way, no one can be accused of cheating or bending the results to their will."

A stone rose to the surface, and the yellow elder plucked it from the water with two claws.

"Noe is chosen," she said.

An iridescent black dragon rose and bowed to the others. They, in turn, bowed and roared, spewing fire into the air.

"Hail, Noe and Zephyra, Dragon Lords of the western Dragons."

Cassandra repeated the words, giving the Dragon greeting. Noe stood tall and soaked in the accolades.

"What happens now?"

"We eat. Afterward, we will go to my sires' quarters and continue to converse. While we speak, you search the journals for what you need for your meeting with the southern Vidarr."

# Chapter 31: Michael

***Ker'an, Aras: Spring, Day 17, Year 1, 5th Age***

Armored hands grabbed the front of Michael's tunic and yanked him out of bed, throwing him to the hard floor. His head slammed against the side of the bed against the side of the bed and the pain rocketed through his skull. The disorientation of being yanked from a deep sleep vanished as metal boots kicked him in the side and stomach. A fist sliced three long gashes in his cheek. He glanced up to see the King's Scelto he had encountered in the passage standing over him. The brown-winged knight's gauntlet dripped crimson.

"You made fools of us," the knight snarled.

*You didn't need me to look like a fool.*

"Provoking him further is not wise," Eímai said.

"I saved Aras," Michael said, the throbbing in his cheek making it hard to talk.

"You have no right to commit violence in Eímai's Sanctuary," a quavering voice said behind the knights.

*It's that old Drás. Please may she not get hurt or killed.*

"Be silent. You have no right to hinder the king's business," a white-winged knight said.

"My king is Eímai, and his law states no one is to be harmed in his Sanctuary."

"You speak treason," the brown-winged knight said.

"The king over all kings is Eímai, young one. Now, if you wish to take this man who has done you or the king no wrong, then do so. But there will be no more violence in this sacred place."

"If Eímai is so sovereign, then let him stop me himself."

The brown-winged knight's foot flew toward Michael's face.

Michael's armor ignited, and the boot buckled upon impact with the fire. The man screamed. He stumbled backward and crashed into his comrades. They fell in a heap.

*See what I mean?*

The aged Drás shuffled to Michael as he pulled himself onto the bed. She crushed dry leaves into a goblet and picked up the pitcher sitting on the table next to the bed. She filled it with Eímai's water and held it out to him.

His wounds healed as he drank.

"Thank you."

She smiled at him. "I rejoice that I have lived long enough to see how my king will save his people. I go to his Rest in peace."

Michael heard a blade entering flesh, and the Sage crumpled. The injured knight stood over her with a bloody sword in his hand. Michael leaped up and smashed his fist into the man's face. The knight plowed over his comrades a second time and slid across the stone floor into a table holding food and drink. A pitcher fell over onto him, soaking him with Eímai's water. The man screamed and dissolved into black smoke. Michael knelt beside the stricken Drás. She smiled at him and motioned for him to draw close.

"Forgive," she said and breathed her last.

He draped the blanket over her.

"Thank you, Eímai, for this awesome lady. Thank you for the blessing she was to you and others. May she have a rich reward."

He turned to the battered knights who stood at a distance.

"Take me to the king."

One pulled shackles from his belt and nervously walked toward him.

"Let's get one thing straight right now. You came in here, assaulted me while I slept, and murdered an ancient Drás. There's no way I'm going to let you put me in chains. So, let's skip the illusions of control and get this over with."

"Hey, we didn't murder her," one protested.

"You stood by and watched it happen. You're as guilty as the one who did the killing. If I had my way, I'd take you into Eímai's throne room and let him deal with you. But since he hasn't told me to do that, I'm going with you. But I'm not going to have you murderers behind me where I can't see you. Now go or I'm going to throw you out."

They still didn't move. Michael grabbed the Hikaru who had pulled the shackles by the front of his breastplate and lifted him off the ground. The knight repeatedly punched Michael in the helmet but only managed to hurt his hand. Michael carried him to the curtain and threw him through it. The loud clang of armor and surprised shouts followed. He went to grab another, and they stepped around him, hurrying through the curtain. He burst through the curtain, and three of the knights jumped on him. He grabbed each and threw them to the floor. They groaned and made no move to rise. The other two drew their swords and attacked. Michael sidestepped their cuts and shattered their swords with a punch to the blade. They stumbled back, dropping their broken weapons.

"What is the meaning of this outrage? There is to be no violence in this sacred place," a Hikaru in a white robe with a silver and gold sash around his waist said as he stalked toward them. His silver hair, beard, wings, and gold staff reflected the light emanating from the floor.

"These men assaulted me while I slept and murdered one of your Sages in the Inner Sanctuary," Michael said, pointing at the defeated knights. Whispers rippled through the assembled worshipers. "The one who shed her blood died by Eímai's water. I'm getting them out of here before they blaspheme Eímai further. My deepest condolences for your loss."

Michael pointed to the two standing King's Scelto.

"Pick them up and get out of here."

They helped their comrades to their feet and led the way out of the Sanctuary. Michael kept his eyes open for any ambushes as they reached a platform overlooking the hollowed-out interior of the mountain. Hundreds of levels lined the walls and beings of all the races except Ichtaca and Dragons flew across the gulf or traveled along walkways connected by stairs or ramps.

The knights took to the air and descended ten levels. Michael followed close behind. King's Scelto and regular Scelto watched their descent, but none moved to intercept them. They landed before two giant stone doors decorated with gold and gems the size of Michael's fist. In front of them stood fifty King's Scelto with weapons drawn. They quickly surrounded Michael, and his armor was quenched. But his wings remained.

*Eímai, please give me the strength for whatever's coming next.*

"I am with you always, even to the end of this age," Eímai said.

*Is that Drás enjoying herself?*

"Immensely. She is particularly glad to be able to move without shuffling."

Michael chuckled, and the surrounding knights glared at him. "What? Are we going or not?" he asked.

"You will speak only when spoken to," a knight in gold armor said.

*Obviously, the one who took Chegar's place.*

"Do not think you can escape or that the power you wield will save you. Without your armor, you are nothing, and we are skilled in killing El'esh."

Fear tried to rise in him, but Michael smashed it with passages from Eímai's Writings.

*Fear has no place in me, for I have been given power, love, and a sound mind. I am strong and courageous. I am not frozen with fear, and I am not dismayed for Eímai is with me. His perfect love casts out all fear, for fear has to do with torment and punishment. Those who fear are not mature and complete in love.*

The doors opened to reveal a vast room. Millions of orbs of light floated near the sixty-foot-high ceiling. The room had a main floor and balconies on either side. The balconies had seats that could accommodate every Arasian body type, including Dragons. A row of ten pillars supported the balconies with tapestries bearing the crests of each of the races.

*It looks like each race has its own section. Did the Hikaru split everyone up or was that around before the Hikaru took over?*

Down the center of the aisle was a red carpet with pictures in gold thread of planets and stars being born, the formation of trees and plants, and animals and winged people rising from the ground. At the other end sat a throne in front of a tapestry bearing the rotating crest of Aras. The floor around the throne radiated light, but the Hikaru on the throne rested his feet on a footstool.

The king had green hair, a beard, and wings. He wore a circlet made of braided gold and set with seven star sapphires. Over his broad form hung a green robe trimmed with gold thread. He had a ring on each finger, including his thumbs. A gold chain hung around his neck, and six large diamonds hung on pendants from the chain.

The entourage stopped twenty feet from the throne, and the knight in gold armor moved to stand at the king's right hand. The knights in front of Michael turned to face him, weapons leveled at him. A flash of color to Michael's right caught his eye, and he saw the floor-to-ceiling tapestry depicting King Tarin. He stood under Khane, Ache, and Chay and wore white, gold, and green armor. He held a large spear in his right hand, and a sword sat on his left hip.

*This guy's all ego. He'd need a throne room this big to contain it.*

The tapestry slid aside to reveal a portal.

*It's dangerous having a portal in the throne room. Or does the king use it if he has to escape and attack?*

"It's a talking disk," Eímai said. "When he uses it, every Arasian has his face appear on their talking disc."

*How does he get to talk to everyone? Obviously, he doesn't say all their names.*

"He says, 'All Aras' and it activates. But it must be uncovered first."

"El'esh," King Tarin said, his voice filled with authority, "I am King Tarin, absolute ruler of all Aras."

*So that's what Eímai meant when he said all of Aras would see what the king and I did.*

He kept his eyes on the king, not wanting to draw attention to the activated disk.

"You defied my command to come before me," King Tarin continued. "You wandered my kingdom, sowing seeds of chaos and rebellion. You destroyed the portal in southern Emer Province and the land where it stood. Lastly, you assaulted my knights and murdered one of them in Eímai's Sanctuary. What do you say to these charges?"

An obsidian pedestal with a round top rose from the floor in front of Michael. He placed his hand on the top. His captors pressed their weapons against his body. One false move and he would be filled with holes from his neck to his rear end.

"Witness the truth," he said.

The pedestal blazed with white light. Above, Michael appeared in a replay of the main events of his time in Aras, from his fight to save Lady Jovena to his team shutting down the portals. But it did not reveal anything about Cassandra as his sister, his training, or his time with Eímai in the holy river.

King Tarin's face remained expressionless until he saw the unveiling of his daughter and their conversation. At that point, it reddened, his nostrils flared, and he gripped the armrests of his throne, knuckles turning white. His lips parted to reveal clenched teeth.

The replay ended with the murder in the Inner Sanctuary. The pedestal sank into the floor, and Michael returned his hand to his side. His heartbeat thundered against his ribs. All of Aras had seen what had been done. Now came the moment that would strip the king of his position.

Again, fear tried to swallow him, and he struggled to fight it off. The tips of the weapons pressed against his body fed the anxiety.

*No, I will not give in to fear. Eímai said I wouldn't die. I choose to believe his words.*

King Tarin pointed at Michael.

"You proved yourself a threat to me and my kingdom," King Tarin said, pointing at Michael. "I do not tolerate threats. I cannot simply imprison you. I must use a more drastic method."

He waved a finger to Michael's left, and the Hikaru in gold armor walked with a blue and white tapestry bearing the Hikaru crest. He pulled a hidden cord, and the tapestry slid aside to reveal one of

Ba'rel's portals. Michael's chest constricted, and he gasped. He searched everywhere for Ba'rel's statue but found none.

*How did they get a portal in here without an idol?*

"Much innocent blood was spilled here," Eímai said, "and not just El'esh."

The portal's surface bulged out and a Dubu lumbered into the throne room. Three more entered, and then came sixteen Akzari, and ten Isoni, their crimson armor seeming to absorb the light in the room.

Michael reached for the handle of his sword, but the edge of the sword against his neck stopped him.

"You're powerless here, El'esh," the king said. "Eímai is powerless against me. I am the supreme ruler of Aras, and I eliminate all who challenge me. You will vanish like those before you, and no one will be the wiser. I hope they make you suffer long before they kill you. Maybe they'll eat you alive."

The King's Scelto backed away as Ba'rel's slaves moved to surround Michael. An Isoni clapped heavy shackles on his wrists and ankles and a thick collar with a chain hanging from it around his neck. The Isoni connected the chain hanging from the collar to the shackles on his wrists and ankles. An additional chain ran from the connecting chain to the Isoni's hand. The warrior yanked on the chain, and he lurched forward. He followed his captor to the portal. Writing on the wall to the left of the portal caught his eye.

Eímai shall judge the worker of good and the worker of evil.
His justice is a delight to those who do good.
But destruction is the fate of those who choose evil.

*The writing is on the wall, and he doesn't even see it. Writing on the wall declares judgment. Huh. That fits.*

He stopped before the portal and turned, locking eyes with the king.

"Mene, Mene, Tekel, Eímai," he said. Then he turned and walked into the swirling darkness.

# Chapter 32: Cassandra

***Floating Mountain, Ula Province: Spring, Day 17, Year 1, 5th Age***

The smell of lilac and something narrow and wet licking her cheek welcomed her into consciousness. Her eyes drifted open, and she found herself face-to-face with a stubby snout belonging to a Chihuahua-sized rodent with puffy pink fur, octagonal ears, and tiny black eyes. It licked her cheek with its long pink tongue."Hello," she said, scratching the creature behind the ears.

It emitted a cooing sound and hopped to her left. That was when she realized giant clusters of lilac blossoms covered most of the colossal cushion she lay on. More of the rodents hopped around her, licking the pollen from the flowers. She sat up. They scurried away from her, but when she stayed still, they returned to their meal.

"Not exactly what I expected to wake up to. But you guys are cute. I hope you don't morph into bloodthirsty monsters."

She looked around the room and found herself alone. On one wall sat a giant bronze disk that reflected the sunlight against the opposite wall. The cushions where the Dragons had slept still carried the indentation of their massive bodies.

*I bet I could fit my whole family on one of those and there'd still be room for more. I feel so tiny on this thing. Oreo would have a ball lying on this thing. She'd roll and wiggle on her back. I wonder how she's doing. How is everybody doing? Do they know I'm gone? Or will I return the moment I left, like in Lewis' books? I hope they're not worried and searching everywhere for me. If they are, maybe Uncle Xander will tell them about what Prof. B said about going on an adventure.*

"Good morning," Lady Achima's cheerful voice said from the doorway.

The rodents' cooing changed to panicked squeaking as they scrambled up the wall and out the window. They looked like a fluffy pink caterpillar.

"Oh, no. There goes your present," Lady Achima said.

"Present?"

"Skeevals. I told you I would bring you some. They feed off the pollen from the flowers. I filled your bed so they would be drawn to you. Now I will have to track some down for you the hard way."

"It's okay. You don't have to. The flowers are better than the skeevals. I love this flower. We have lilac bushes in our backyard, and I can sit back there for hours reading and smelling them."

The Dragon shot her a concerned look and shook her head. "I mean no offense when I say you are a strange one, Speaker. Choosing flowers over skeevals? That is not natural."

Cassandra laughed and picked up a bunch of flowers. The skeeval that had been crouching behind the flowers squeaked and bolted for the window. In a flash of purple bend silver Lady Achima launched herself at the fleeing rodent. It disappeared into her mouth. Cassandra looked away as the Dragon ate her meal.

*Ugh. Gross. I think it's time to get up before she finds any more in the flowers.*

She gathered her journals as quickly as possible, grabbed her satchel, and left. From the shuffling sound behind her, she assumed the Dragon was looking for more hiding rodents. Cassandra didn't feel bad about hoping the rest got away.

She spent the walk from the room to the main dining chamber talking to Eímai. Passing Dragons greeted her with smiles and "Greetings, Speaker." It made her feel special to have the giant reptiles acknowledge her so warmly. But she still longed for a friend to talk to and have fun with.

*I don't think I'm going to be allowed to have fun here. There's too much work to do. And with the Legion trying to kill me all the time, it's like I can't let my guard down. I wonder if this is how Mike felt after the bus bombing.*

Her heart went out to her brother, and she wished he were there to talk to.

*It's funny that I want to just talk to him and not try to prove I'm just as good as he is.*

She found Lady Achima's parents sitting off to the side, roasting meat and enjoying the company of the yellow-scaled elder.

*I never got her name. I need to ask.*

"Greetings, Lord Lysander, Lady Lita," she said when she reached them.

"I am Lord no longer. Call me Lysander," Lady Achima's father said.

"You may call me Lita as well. To us, you are a friend."

"I am grateful you think of me that way. You can call me Cass. The whole Speaker thing is way too formal."

"I know what you mean," Lysander said. "I was content with being an elder and living a quiet life before I was made Dragon Lord. But things do not always go the way we plan."

"That's for sure. I had planned on having a quiet summer before heading off to school. But BAM, here I am hanging out with Dragons."

"Yes, Eímai's ways are not our own. Yet we are better when we take his path," the elder Dragon said.

"I'm sorry, I didn't introduce myself yesterday," Cassandra said to the yellow Dragon.

"I am Sophia. You may call me Sophia. I have little use for titles at my age."

"If I may ask, how old are you?"

"Eímai has graced me with 11,089 years. It will be ninety on the fifth day of winter."

"Wow. I hope I look as good as you when I turn eleven hundred years."

Her words brought laughter from the three Dragons and those seated around them.

"I hope so, too," Sophia said. "Commune with Eímai always, drink his water, eat his fruit, and follow His Writings, and he will grant you long life."

"Actually, my race is only allowed to live for 120 years at most. At least, in our current physical form. One day, we will get immortal bodies and live forever. But that's a while away."

"It may be closer than you think," Sophia said. "Three hours before First-Rise Eímai woke me and told me great change is coming. Some good and some bad. But he will make sure the bad works for the good of those who love him and are called according to his purpose. He also said we must gather in Lysander and Lita's chambers in one hour from this moment. He did not elaborate. I have learned to obey whether I understand or not."

While other Dragons laughed and enjoyed their meals, the small group sat in serious silence. Lysander used his claw to cut a section of meat for Cassandra and handed it to her, pinched between two claws.

"Is it skeeval?" she asked.

"No, skeevals do not grow this large. It is rugi," Lysandre said with a chuckle. "I take it you did not appreciate our broodling's gift?"

"I don't mind the furballs. But I'm not going to eat them."

"It is an acquired taste," Lita said. "I do not much care for it. But little Achima cannot get enough of them."

"I noticed," Cassandra said, making a face as she recalled the Dragon chomping on the fleeing creature.

She looked for something to put it on and found a nearby stone slab that would make a decent plate.

"May I use this as a plate?"

"Of course," Lita said. "We are not used to eating with those who do not have tough scales as we do."

After the delicious meal, they gathered in Lysander's family quarters. They all sat on cushions, looking at each other, and silently waiting. Sophia sat next to Cassandra since the elder was smaller than the others. Sitting there, Cassandra realized the cushions were in the perfect position to see the bronze disk.

"What's that disk for?" she asked.

"It is a talking disk," Lita said. "It is primarily used to receive messages from the capital. When the king has something that he wants all of Aras to hear, he uses it. He is also able to project his face on every smaller talking disk."

As if on cue, a giant sphere showing a throne room appeared before the bronze disk. A Hikaru with dark brown wings, hair, and beard, and wearing a jewel-encrusted crown, stood before Michael. A King's Scelto stood on either side of him, gripping his upper arm. Shackles bound Michael's wrists.

"What's going on?" Cassandra shouted, jumping to her feet.

"Be seated, and we will find out," Sophia said.

Cassandra lowered herself to the edge of the cushion. Every muscle tensed, and her heart drummed rapidly in her chest. Her palms started to sweat.

*Is this what Chief Jovena warned us about? Is the king going to make him swear the oath or kill him? Why would he make everyone watch it? Is it to make everyone obey him?*

"Calm your mind, young Speaker," Sophia whispered to her. "In time, all your questions will be answered."

*It is so freaky how they know what I'm thinking. Eímai, please protect Mike.*

As the scene played out before her, Cassandra's sweaty hands started to curl into fists. Heat rose to her face, and her teeth started to clench. After what seemed like hours, the image vanished, leaving the room as silent as a tomb.

Cassandra exploded off the couch and bolted for the door, tears blurring her vision. Her body shook with her rage. King Tarin, smugly watching Michael step into the evil portal, repeated over and over in her mind.

*He's going to pay for this. He's going to wish he'd never been born by the time I'm done with him.*

"Cassandra Eloise Jenkins, you stop this instant," Sophia roared.

The use of her full name and the authority in the elder's voice caused her to skid to a stop before she fully exited the room. She turned and met Sophia's stern gaze. The Dragon motioned for her to come to her with a bent claw. Cassandra walked quickly to the Dragon; years in the Jenkins household had taught her that walking slowly when an adult summoned her led to unpleasant consequences.

"He killed my brother. My brood-mate. He can't get away with this," Cassandra said, her anger making her voice shake.

"Eímai has told us that revenge and justice belong to him. He will repay evildoers for what they have done."

"He's killed so many people already, and nothing's happened. How's this going to be any different?"

"That is a valid question. But is the power to deliver justice in your hands? Is that what a Speaker does? One tried such a path, and it caused his destruction. The same will happen to you if you do the same. I am not telling you not to be angry. Anger over evil is a good thing. We should be angry. But you must remember not to let that anger consume you to the point that it leads to hate and uncontrolled actions. That is wrath, and we are not to let wrath control us. Do you understand?"

Cassandra silently nodded, keeping her raging thoughts to herself.

"I know how you feel more than anyone here. I watched my broodlings being murdered during the War. Barely out of their shells and yet slaughtered without mercy or care. Years later, I had the opportunity to slaughter the murderer's family. I looked upon them as they walked through the field, unaware that I watched. I drew in a breath to unleash my fury upon them. At that moment Eímai spoke to me and said, 'You take matters into your own claws because you believe I will not give you justice. You see him seemingly unpunished, and you believe I have done nothing. But I have declared judgment. Do you see that female? She urged her mate not to take part in the slaughter. She tried to prevent what happened to you. Would you destroy her and her cubs because she could not overcome the free will of another?' I knew he was right. I could not destroy them. I quenched my fire and flew away. It was not easy to release my wrath. But with Eímai's help, I did. Do you know who the murderer became?"

"Captain Ragnar," Cassandra said in a small voice, tears pouring down her cheeks.

"Yes, young one. He who had bathed in the blood of the innocent now fights with every bit of his being to defend the innocent who remain. Had I slaughtered his family, he never would have come back to the light."

Sophia wrapped her in a rough, warm embrace, and Cassandra wept. When she calmed, Lady Achima handed her a handkerchief. She thanked the Dragon, wiped her face, and blew her nose.

"Do you remember the expression on El'esh Michael's face?" Sophia asked. "There was no anger or fear. Only calm. As though he knew this would happen and what would follow. Did you notice he did not fight? He walked into the portal as though he had chosen that fate, and it was not forced upon him."

"Are you saying he knew the king would do this to him?" Cassandra asked.

"It looks that way," Lady Achima said. "Another odd thing is that El'esh Michael said something before he stepped into the portal. They were strange words, like an incantation. But incantations are for the servants of Ba'rel."

"I don't remember what he said," Cassandra said.

"Mene, Mene, Tekel, Eímai."

*Why does that sound familiar? Eímai, why does that sound so familiar?*

She looked around her, and her eyes settled on cuneiform carved into the wall. She had not noticed the writing before. Inspiration dawned.

"I know what it means. Thousands of years ago in my world, a hand without an arm or a person attached appeared and wrote a message on a wall. It was the words Mike said. Well, he put Eímai's name at the end instead of the last word in the original message. If he meant it to apply to King Tarin, then he spoke judgment on him as well. *Mene* must mean Eímai has numbered King Tarin's kingdom and finished it. It's over for him. *Tekel* means King Tarin was weighed in the balances and found wanting. Whatever he was supposed to measure up to, he failed miserably. *Eímai* means Eímai has removed Tarin as king and replaced him with a king of his own choosing. He's going to find a king that is after his own heart."

"Then we wait to see how events play out," Lysander said, rising from the cushion. "For what it is worth, young Cass, I do not believe your brood-mate is dead. El'esh Michael entered the portal with the confidence of one who knows he is not going to his death."

"I hope so."

"I know this seems like hardly the time," Lita said. "But we must leave for the Southern Forest if we are to arrive in time."

Cassandra cast a glance out the window. Part of her wanted to search for her brother. But deep down, she knew she had more important things to do.

"Okay. Let's go," she said with a sigh.

# Chapter 33: Michael

***Crith Prison, Kabas: Spring, Day 17, Year 1, 5th Age***

The Dubu guards shoved Michael down the dimly lit corridor. His boots clacked on the stone floor while the long claws of the Dubu rasped out a counter rhythm.

*How is it that Ba'rel was able to corrupt these bears? I thought they were immune to every form of corruption.*

"The only being immune to evil is me. Everyone else has the potential to fall," Eímai said.

The group entered a vast room with pillars and walls dotted with hanging chains. Matu chanted as they tortured a majestic-looking polar bear.

"Ajabu," Eímai said.

Pink blood stained its once white coat. The beast begged for the torture to stop, and the Matu increased the pain. To Michael's horror, Ajabu transformed into a Dubu with crimson claws and fangs. Long, forward-facing horns grew out of its body, bringing fresh blood. The pink stains turned black. Its tears still stained its face.

*Oh, Eímai. Such evil.*

This led to an epiphany. Every single member of Ba'rel's Legion was once a being Eímai created, and Ba'rel twisted them. He thought of all those he had slain defending Aras. They had been someone's father, mother, brother, sister, wife, or husband. They had had a future and so much potential to do great things. Tears poured down his cheeks when he thought of the suicide bombers who had blown up the buses that had given him his scars. He had mourned the innocent lives they had taken. But he had never mourned the bombers. He had only seen them as pure evil. But now he saw them as beings twisted by evil, the same as those before in this torture chamber. He fell to his knees and wept.

"Father," he whispered, "please open the eyes of all those in every world who are twisted by evil. Bring people into their lives to bring them into your light, so you can heal their spirit, soul, and body. In Jesus' name, Amen."

The Dobu's raucous laughter grated in his ears. "See how he breaks. We heard he was a powerful El'esh, and yet when facing pain, he weeps like a newborn cub."

*They mock me when I pray for them. Before now, that would have made me mad. But now I pity them. This is all Ba'rel's fault. He is the real enemy.*

"For we do not wrestle against flesh and blood, but against principalities, against powers, against the rulers of the darkness of this age, against spiritual hosts of wickedness in the heavenly places," popped into his mind, and he nodded.

*Please help me to keep my mind in the right place and see my captors through your eyes.*

He wiped his face with his hands and stood. He smiled at his captors. "Shall we continue? No doubt you have an unpleasant cell for me."

The Dubu looked at each other, their confusion evident on their scarred muzzles.

"We will take you to your cell soon enough," hissed a Matu with crimson robes and a black staff capped with a crimson orb. "First, we have to give you a proper Kabas welcome. String him up."

They chained him to the walls and ripped off his shirt.

"Master," called an Akzari with a whip covered in barbs from handle to tip. He pointed the coiled whip at Michael's chest. "'e's been 'ere before."

The Matu sauntered over and scanned the burn and knife scars. He spent longer looking at the scars caused by Vold's talons.

"Captain Vold will be glad to hear you are here. He has something special planned for you."

The Matu turned to three Akzari. "Lock him up with the cripple. That way, he can see what awaits those who injure Vold."

*Injure? I didn't injure him. Did he get hurt when the pits exploded?*

Akzari guards dragged him to a cell, oblivious to the bloody trail he left behind. They chained him to the wall with shackles and a heavy collar. Silver blood covered both. A guard laughed when he saw Michael staring at the silver.

"She screamed for hours before dying. She tasted delicious."

The heavy metal door clanged shut, and the bolt snapped into place.

"It's been a long time since I have seen another El'esh," a male voice said from the darkness at the back of the cell.

A bright green glow illuminated a man sitting with his back against the wall. He had a thick collar around his neck, and a heavy chain ran from the collar to a ring in the wall. Swirls of green fire burned under skin covered in scars in the shape of arcane symbols. His grimy kilt bore hints of yellow and purple. Someone had chopped off his fingers, thumbs, and half of his feet. The right side of his head had been horribly burned. His right ear and eye were missing. A green flame burned in the empty socket.

Despite the carnage done to him, the man smiled.

"Greetings. I am Miklos, El'esh of Eímai. Who are you?"

"Michael Jenkins, also El'esh of Eímai. I've heard a lot about you. I'm glad to finally meet you. The Matu said you'd show me what happens to someone who injured Vold."

Miklos chuckled. "He is a vindictive scum. He harms you the way you harmed him."

"You're the reason he looks horrible," Michael said.

"Yes. He didn't like getting a face full of Eímai's water. Too bad it didn't burn his head off. But he got hold of me and burned me." He raised his arms and legs. "He went above and beyond to make sure I'd never do anything like that again. What did you do to him?"

"I don't know. As far as I know, I never hurt him. He almost killed me, though. Stabbed me in the gut with his claws and ripped open my shoulder. The only thing I can think of is the skepna pits blew up, and he might have been caught in the explosion. Captain Ragnar was also caught in the explosion."

"Ragnar? Hah! That furball isn't dead. I've seen him cut in two and still come back to life. He's fine."

"I hope you're right. How'd you end up here?"

"That's a long story."

"We're not going anywhere at the moment," Michael quipped.

Miklos laughed. "Indeed. It was 18475 of the 4th Age, and I returned home from the market with my arms full of parchment, ink, quills, and other supplies."

Miklos will return in *The Saga of Miklos*, releasing in 2027

# Timeline of Aras as Recorded by Michael Jenkins

## 1ST AGE

Unknown Time - Eímai creates Parrésia, establishes Aras with its Seven Races and Sages. Age ends when the crystal dragon Teleiotes leads a rebellion and is expelled with his followers. Eímai renames him Ba'rel. Fallen members of the races are renamed Sundered.

## 2ND AGE

1 – Eímai establishes the Speaker to support unity among the races and the El'esh and seven knightly orders to protect Aras.

3 – Ba'rel and his Legion conquer the country west of the Rogue Mountains, corrupt its people and rename them Akzari, mutate its beasts into abominations, and change the country's name to Kabas.

1,481–1,487 – First invasion of Aras by Ba'rel's Legion.

1,581 – Ba'rel invades Selucia to the east of Aras and does not conquer it. He corrupts his captives and turns them into sorcerers named Matu.

1,588 – Aras allies with Selucia.

3,688 – Ba'rel sends Matu into Aras to corrupt members of the races and undermines Aras' alliance with Selucia. Expands conquests to other lands of Parrésia.

16,015–16,048 – Second invasion of Aras by Ba'rel's Legion.

18,022 – Vidarr race divides, one-third moving to the Southern Forest.

## 3RD AGE

8,914–8,939 – Third invasion of Aras by Ba'rel's Legion.

9,022 – El'esh begin to fall to Ba'rel's corruption and are renamed Umoni.

11,111 – Two hundred El'esh leave Aras to set up outposts on the Northern Isles to stop Ba'rel's continued conquests.

13,441–13,486 – Fourth invasion of Aras by Ba'rel's Legion causes the "Great Fall", Emer Province turned into a wasteland, and Ichtaca Race severs contact with the surface.

13,613 – One hundred of the two hundred El'esh return from the Islands. The other one hundred had died mysteriously.

## 4TH AGE

15 – Delegates from the surface fail to restore good relations between the Ichtaca and the surface races.

18–78 – Aras' surface races decide to build racial capitals as a way to better care for their racial needs. The Vidarr in the Southern Forest refuse, stating this act defies Eímai's will for a unified Aras.

17,430–17,436 – Dragon/Drás War; last of El'esh loyal to Eímai killed; the Hikaru seize the throne.

17,437 – Savelis, the last of the Speakers, fails in "Talah Insurrection" and declares the Prophesy of Restoration before his execution; the Talah race is made subservient to the Hikaru race.

## 5TH AGE

1 – Fifth invasion by Ba'rel; arrival of Michael and Cassandra Jenkins.

# Telling Time on Parrésia

Hour 0: First-Rise: Debash Rises

Hours 0-8: Half-Dark

Hour 8: First-Zenith: Debash At Zenith and Chalab Rises

Hours 8-16: Full-Light

Hour 16: Second-Zenith: Chalab At Zenith and Debash Sets

Hours 16-24: Second Half-Dark

Hour 24: Second-Set: Chalab Sets

Hours 24-0: Full-Dark

Since Parrésia has 32 hours in its day and two suns, it doesn't use a normal clock like people on Earth do. They had to create a time-keeping system that fits their chronological uniqueness. Therefore, after a Main Time Event occurs, the time is calculated using an eight-hour system for each In Between Times Category.

For example, Debash breaks the horizon, and that is First-Rise. Two hours after First-Rise would be called "The second hour of Half-Dark", seven hours after First-Zenith would be called "The seventh hour of Full-Light," and so on.

# Number of Days in a Parrésian Year

| Season | Comparison: 365 Days In An Earth Year | |
|---|---|---|
| | Total Days In Standard Parrésian Year | Total Days In Extended Parrésian Year |
| Spring | 112 | 113 |
| Summer | 145 | 146 |
| Fall | 113 | 114 |
| Winter | 145 | 147 |
| **Total** | **515 Days** | **520 Days** |

# Glossary

## Astronomy

Khane (Kahn-ay): Purple and orange gas giant planet

Parrésia (Par-ay-see-a): habitable moon orbiting Khane

Chay(ch-ay): pink moon orbiting Khane

Achi(ah-key): green moon orbiting Khane

Chalab (khaw-lawb): one of the two suns Khane orbits

Debash (deb-ash): one of the two suns Khane orbits

## Parrésia

Aras (ahr-ah-ss): Central country on the southern continent and where this story takes place

Kabas (kah-baas): Country ruled by Ba'rel on Aras' western border; formerly called Nadej (Nah-day)

Northern Isles: The Arctic islands above the central continent on which Aras is located.

Selucia (cell-oo-sha): Country on Aras' eastern border

Zlatar (Zlah-tar): Island country between Kabas' western border and Selucia's eastern border

## Aras

### Holy Rivers

Brenus (bray-nus): River flowing East from Ker'an

Jes (j-ez): River flowing West from Ker'an

Miwa (mee-wah): River flowing South from Ker'an

Tirta (teer-tah): River flowing North from Ker'an

# Geography

Ker'an (kay-ron): Mountain in the center of Aras from which flow
the sacred rivers

Melania Desert (mel-a-nee-a): Desert in Emer Province

Sea of Siana (see-anna): An inland sea in Siana Province

Ozias Sea (oh-z-i-ah-ss): Aras' northern border

Rogue Mountains (Roe-g): Aras' western border between Aras and
Kabas

Srol Mountains (seer-ole): Aras' eastern border between Aras and
Selucia

Southern Forest: Dense forest on Aras' southern border


# Provinces

Citali (sit-a-lee): Southeast Province of Aras

Emer (ay-mare): Northeast Province of Aras

Siana (see-ah-nnah): Northwest Province of Aras

Ula (oo-la): Southwest Province of Aras


# Races

Dragon (dra-gon): Dragon race

Drás (drah-ss): Reptiloid race

Gwenfrewi (gwen-vreh-wee): Aquatic race

Hikaru (hee-kah-roo): Winged race

Ichtaca (itch-ah-ka): Underground race

Talah (tah-lah): Human-like race

Vidarr (vih-dah-r): Feline race

<h1 style="text-align:center">Capitals</h1>

Ker'an (kay-ron): Capital of Aras

Xipil (Zip-ill): Ichtaca racial capital

Perrin (Pear-in): Eastern Dragons and Drás racial capital

Rün (roon): Talah racial capital

Sigvarrd (Sig-vard): Vidarr racial capital in the Great Forest

Ceridwyn (Ker-id-wen): Gwenfrewi racial capital

Shoichi (Shoh-ee-chee): Hikaru racial capital

Efrosyni (Ef-ro-SY-nee): Western Dragons and Drás racial capital

<h2 style="text-align:center"><u>Names</u></h2>

**A**

Achima (ah-key-mah): Dragon female; daughter of Lysander and
  Lita

Ademir Braga (add-eh-meer brah-gah): Brazilian jujitsu teacher

Amoxtli (ah-maw-sh-lee): Ichtaca male; chief adviser of Ichtaca king
  Tonauac

**B**

Baldoin (ball-dwa-n): Drás soldier

Braith (br-ay-th): Gwenfrewi female; Sage

Broodling: Name used by Dragons and Drás for their children

Brood-mate: Name used by dragons and Drás for their siblings

## C

Chata (kaw-ta): Invisible holy steel

Cynyr (kie-ner): Talah male; Hod'ji

Chegar (chay-ga): Hikaru male

Cuneiform (cue-may-i-form): Wedge-shaped writing used in the ancient Middle East.


## D

Djavan (dyah-vahn): Talah male; son of Chieftain Ewan and Ilka

Duwalt (doo-wah-lt): Vidarr male; leopard elder; Mushroom Forest


## E

Eímai (ay-my): Lord of Life and Light; Creator of Aras; High King over all kings in Aras

El'esh (el-esh): Fiery knights of Eímai

Ewan (ay-von): Talah male; chieftain of the Talah; husband of Ilka and father of Lady Jovena and Djavan


## F

Frida (free-dah): Vidarr Female; Cub of Captain Ragnar and Maja; Litter-mate of Kari and Hákon; Outcast Clan


## G

Gratien (grah-tee-en): Drás male

Gwyneira (gwin-ay-ra): Gwenfrewi female; Outcast Clan

Gweldig (gw-ayl-dig): Gwenfrewi male

**H**

Hagia (ha-gee-a): Dragon female; Outcast Clan

Hákon (hah-cone): Vidarr male; Cub of Captain Ragnar and Maja; Litter-mate of Frida and Kari; Outcast Clan

Havard (hah-vard): Vidarr male; clouded leopard elder; Mushroom Forest

Hod'ji (hoe-j-eye): Talah knightly order


**I**

Ilka (ih-l-k-ah): Talah female; wife of Ewan


**J**

Jattir (ya-teer): Hikaru male; Grand Sage

Jovena (yo-way-nah): Talah female; daughter of Ewan and Ilka, sister of Djavan, and fiancée of Todor


**K**

Kaj (kah-j): Vidarr male; lynx elder; Mushroom Forest

Kari (kah-ree): Vidarr female; Cub of Captain Ragnar and Maja; Litter-mate of Frida and Hákon; Outcast Clan

Kardeiz (car-deez): Talah male; Master Scholar of Arasian History, Outcast Clan

Kelda (kell-dah): Vidarr female; Speaker


**L**

Lennart (l-eh-n-ert): Vidarr male; lion elder; Mushroom Forest

Lita (lee-tah): Dragon female; Lord of the Dragons; Achima's mother

Litter-mate: Name used by the Vidarr to describe a sibling

Lysander (lie-sand-er): Dragon male; Lord of the Dragons; Achima's
    father


**M**

Maja (mah-ja): Vidarr female; Outcast Clan, Mate of Captain Ragnar

Markos (mar-koh-ss): Dragon male; Outcast Clan

Miklos - (mick-loss): - Talah male, El'esh who lived toward the end
    of the 4th age


**N**

Neric (n-air-ick): Osulf male

Noe (no-ay): Dragon male; Western Dragons


**O**

Ohtli (oh-t-lee): Ichtaca female; Qualoc's mate

Osulf (oh-z-ulf): Wolves living in the southern region of Aras.


**P**

Peithoi (pay-thoy): Hikaru male; baron of Citali Province

Phontina (fon-tee-nah): Dragon female; owns The Snoring Traveler
    inn located in Theitai; Dragon/Drás Confederation

Pugal (pew-gahl): 4-foot-tall, gray-skinned animal with long trunks
    and small pointed ears that looked like a cross between cats and
    elephants

**Q**

Qualoc (koo-lock): Ichtaca male; heir apparent of Ichtaca King Ueman; Outcast Clan

**R**

Rabblefizz (rah-bble-fizz): carbonated strawberry juice drink

Ragnar (r-aw-ng-ah-r): Vidarr male; Tiger Captain, formerly called Bergr and Fléau

Rugi (roo-gee): Gentle six-foot-tall lizards covered with light brown fur

Rün (r-oo-n): Talah racial capital located in eastern Citali Province

**S**

Saara (sah-ah-ra): Vidarr female; Elite in the Outcast Clan

Savelis (sah-way-liss): Talah male; last of the Dragon Sages

Sire (sy-er): The name used by most of the races when referring to their parents

Soh (so): Taekwondo teacher

Skeeval (ski-vahl): Rodent with shaggy blue fur that dwell on the floating mountains

Suri (s-oo-r-ee): Vidarr female; cheetah elder; Mushroom Forest

**T**

Tarin (tar-in): Hikaru male; king of Aras

Teodr (tay-oe-dr): Vidarr male; lynx counselor; Mushroom Forest

Theitai (thay-tie): Town in southern Citali Province

Todor (toe-door): Talah male; fiancé of Jovena; Hod'ji

Toula (two-la): Dragon female; works at the Snorting Traveler Inn; Dragon/Drás Confederation

Tryggyr (try-guy-er): Vidarr male; lion cub of Elder Lennart, Ridarri; Mushroom Forest

**U**

Ueman (oo-eh-man): Ichtaca male; King of Ichtaca and sire of Qualoc

**V**

Vigdis (way-g-diss): Vidarr female; tiger elder; Mushroom Forest

**X**

Xesa (z-e-ssa): Osulf female, mate of Neric

**Z**

Zephyra (Zef-aye-rah): Dragon Female; Mate of Noe

## <u>The Legion</u>

Akzari (ahk-zah-ree): Main fighters of Ba'rel's Legions; originally from Nadej

Ba'rel (baa-rel): Dragon, Lord of Darkness and ruler of Kabas; original name Teleiotes (te-lay-oh-tays)

Crith (krith): Prison in Kabas

Dubu (doo-boo): The corrupted form of Ajabu, a white polar bear-looking race from the northern islands

Fenrir (fen-reer): Osulves mutated by Ba'rel

Isoni (eye-son-ee): Red armored fighters; formerly of Velox

Lusare (lu-zar-ay): Sundered Drás female; former Sage

Matu (mah-tu): Sorcerers; formerly of Selucia

Miseó (mis-eh-o): Sundered Dragon; formerly Kephas (kay-fahss): broodling of Achima; brood of Lysander and Lita

Pemakin (pem-a-kin): Clipper beetles corrupted by Ba'rel to be flesh eaters

Sundered (sih-bye): Corrupted members of the seven races of Aras

Umoni (oo-mon-ee): Corrupted El'esh

Vold (v-old): Umoni Vidarr; formerly El'esh Rasmus (Ra-smus); Ragnar's great-grandsire

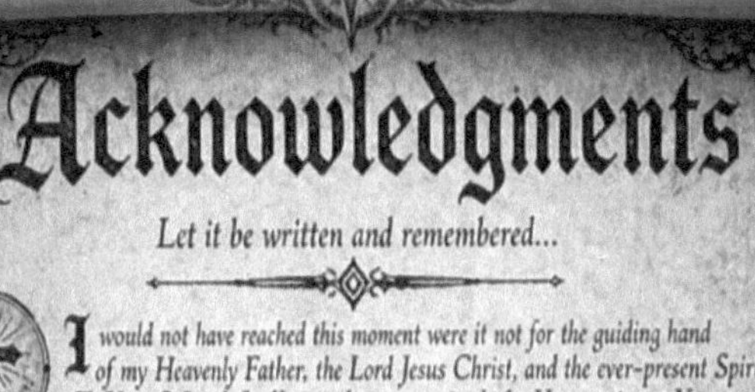

# Acknowledgments

Let it be written and remembered...

I would not have reached this moment were it not for the guiding hand of my Heavenly Father, the Lord Jesus Christ, and the ever-present Spirit. To You, O Lord, I offer my deepest gratitude for Your patience, Your mercy, Your grace, and the inspiration You have so freely given.
May this work be pleasing in Your sight and bring honor to Your name above all else.
For this alone matters.

I give thanks to my mother, my steadfast encourager, who has long awaited the day she might see this story brought to life upon the screen.
Your faith in me has never wavered.

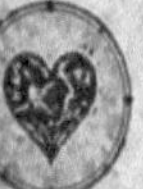

To my beloved wife, Shauna, whose voice urged me onward when the path seemed long, I am forever grateful.
Your encouragement gave strength to weary hands and resolve to a wandering mind.

To Russell, whose words came like a steady drumbeat through the years, reminding me, "You are farther now than you were before,"
your wisdom carried me forward when I could not see my own progress.

My gratitude extends to Katherine Hutchinson–Hayes and to the fellowship of writers who stood beside me.
Your counsel, your insight, and your willingness to labor through scenes with me have left their mark upon these pages.

And to Amy Bright, whose guidance sharpened both blade and mind, you revealed that the art of the sword is more than the thrust of steel, but the discipline, rhythm, and understanding behind it.

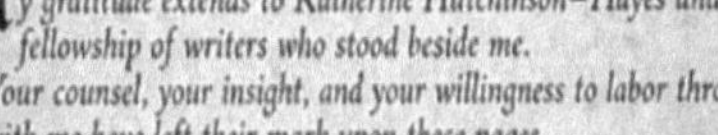

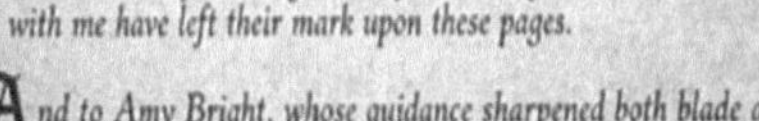

May this record stand as a testament of gratitude,
and may all who read it know that no journey is ever walked alone.

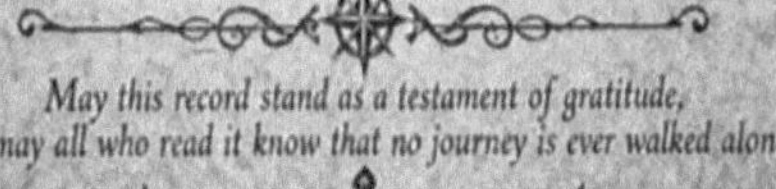

Terrance Niedziela Jr. grew up in Wisconsin, immersed in shows, movies, and books that celebrated the timeless theme of good triumphing over evil. He began writing stories in the fourth grade, and what started as a childhood passion grew into a lifelong calling to craft meaningful, imaginative fiction.

Terrance's goal as a writer is to create speculative fiction filled with the noble themes found in the Word of God. Through immersive storytelling and compelling characters, he desires to draw readers toward the God who loves them so deeply that He willingly sacrificed His Son, Jesus, to restore a relationship with humanity.

He earned a Bachelor of Science degree in Ancient Middle East History with a minor in Creative Fiction from University of Wisconsin–La Crosse and later completed a Master of Arts in English and Creative Fiction Writing from Southern New Hampshire University. His writing has been recognized with several honors, including a First-Place Foundation Award at the Blue Ridge

Mountain Christian Writers Conference, a Fiction Carolina Christian Writers Award, and a Second-Place Florida Tapestry Award.

In addition to writing fiction, Terrance contributes devotional writings to The Man Cave blog on the website of Dr. Katherine Hutchinson-Hayes. His devotionals were included in published devotional collections in both 2024 and 2025, further reflecting his passion for sharing biblical encouragement through the written word.

Terrance enjoys spending time with his wife, watching cartoons, reading, exploring nature, and witnessing the moment when his students' "light bulbs" turn on. He currently lives in South Carolina with his beautiful wife, Shauna, and their dogs. When he is not writing, he teaches English to middle school students and continues building imaginative worlds that inspire courage, faith, and hope.

www.ingramcontent.com/pod-product-compliance
Lightning Source LLC
Chambersburg PA
CBHW032145050726
47591CB00001B/87